THIRD WHEEL

Richard R. Becker

Copywrite, Ink.

Hardcover ISBN 979-8-9853811-5-3
Spark Trade Paperback ISBN 979-8-9853811-6-0
Ebook ISBN 979-8-9888816-0-5

Library of Congress Control Number: 2023907368

Cover design by Richard R. Becker
Published by Copywrite, Ink.
Produced in the United States of America

copywriteink.com

First Edition

For Jim
Can't dance. Might as well laugh.

CHAPTER 1

BLOOD BROTHERS

Mick and I jumped into the pool to cool off. We were hot, having just cut the twenty-foot oleanders that framed his family's backyard to eight feet, about a foot higher than the dull gray cinderblock walls that cemented boundaries between families.

They called them privacy walls in Las Vegas, making the backyard barbecue subculture of this desert suburbia feel all the more exclusive. It took more effort to be a nosy neighbor than it had at my childhood home in the Midwest, where kids ran barefoot across open backyards with toy machine guns and water pistols.

Nobody did anything like that in the desert. Unless you owned a pool, people hid away from the heat inside with central air or outside under big trees that were as foreign to the area as the people who called it home. We had one of those big trees in our unusable backyard, which is why I considered myself lucky to have Mick as a best friend. His family owned a pool.

Helping cut down oleanders was a small price to pay for having what amounted to a second home. Sure, the work was hard but bearable. It had taken us the better part of the morning, attacking the bushes with machetes and trying to make the job go faster by pretending to be the living incarnations of our Dungeons & Dragons characters. We imagined hacking away a path through the Amedio Jungle on an adventure.

Like our characters, Mick did most of the muscle work, while my approach was more akin to a ranger or woodsman. It suited us. We had custom modeled his character after an overman out of a Lawrence Watt-Evans novel because he was a big kid, already standing six foot three at the end of ninth grade. I was a year behind and not exactly short, about five ten, but my frame was growing faster than I could fill it. So he hacked, and I trimmed.

Looking up at it out of the pool confirmed we had done a good job. We deserved to take the rest of the day off. We might have too, had the two brothers who lived in the cul-de-sac behind our houses not taken the shortened privacy wall as an invitation. They hopped right up on the bricks and looked down at the tangle of branches, leaves, and pink and white flowers that we would clean up tomorrow.

"Man, you're both nuts." Travis whistled, surveying our work. "You should have used a hedge trimmer."

"Didn't have one." Mick shrugged from the water.

"Yeah, who does?" Travis laughed.

"What's your point?" Mick said, putting his arms up around the side of the pool.

Travis was the more annoying of the two brothers. They were another year behind me and already had a reputation as being punks. My younger sister was friends with a girl who lived next door to them, and I always told her to steer clear. We mostly did the same, except when it came to business.

"Hey, Mick," Trevor said, swinging his legs over the back wall and perching himself between two of the haggard oleanders. "Give us a dime?"

"No way, unless you got cash," Mick said, grabbing a towel off the yellow and green plastic tubing of the lawn chair. "Your credit isn't good with me anymore."

"You're kidding me, right?" he said. "I'm not good for a dime?"

"You already owe me twenty, and I was coming over to collect today."

"So, what's stopping you?" Travis said, crossing his arms.

"I'm waiting for Alex. He's the one floating you."

They didn't like hearing it. And truth be told, I didn't like hearing it much either. Alex was the most troubled kid I had ever met, but Mick added him to our group anyway. Alex always had a sour milk sort of look about him and a permanent smirk that suggested he knew an inside joke about you. Some people thought it was because he felt superior. I knew better.

His gray-tinted aviators and long-sleeved concert T-shirts hid the marks his mom's boyfriends made on a regular basis. Somewhere along the way, long before we knew him, he stopped caring about anything — black eyes, cigarette burns, schoolwork, life. You might even feel sorry for him if he wasn't such a jerk.

"Yeah, you'll get your money tomorrow," Trevor said. "Thanks for nothing."

Trevor flung his legs around his side of the wall, ready to follow his brother until Mick stopped him.

"Hold on," Mick said. "I can give you a pinner. It's all I got."

"Yeah, what is it?" Trevor asked.

"Skunk," Mick said, climbing out of the pool before registering Trevor's disappointment. "I was saving it for later."

"All right." Trevor smiled and shrugged. "Beggars can't be choosers."

Mick walked over to a side table where he had left his Velcro wallet. Tucked inside was a skinny joint. Had we smoked it, Mick would have crushed it into a pipe.

"It's cool," Mick said. "Alex's filling the store today anyway. Tell your friends."

"I'll do that," he said, reaching down to take the joint before jumping down.

I shook my head. Their friends were degenerates.

"Why'd you do that?" I asked.

"It's good for business," Mick said.

"As long as you deal with them," I said. "I don't like dealing with them. Besides, now we'll have to listen to Alex gripe all afternoon about the money they owe us."

Mick gave me a funny look. He was always pulling stunts like this without thinking it through. He wanted to be a nice guy in a bad business. I didn't have any delusions about it. We were running a modest criminal operation out of his house, which wouldn't have been such a big deal if his dad wasn't a cop.

"I'll handle Alex," he said. "He's more my friend anyway."

He was right about that. When Mick struggled to keep his place on the high school basketball team, one of his teammates slipped him some speed. It gave his game a lift, but not a passion for the sport. He decided to quit but not before getting the name of the dude who supplied it. It was Alex.

The first time he came over, I didn't know he was a pusher. He sat down at the dining room table with us, filling our friend Brett's chair to play Dungeons & Dragons. Brett had moved away to West Virginia at the start of summer, leaving us in a lurch for a third player.

Alex gave the game about twenty minutes before declaring it dumb, and then we spent the rest of the night siphoning more booze out of the liquor cabinet. Mick and me weren't novices. The first time we raided this liquid treasure chest, we split a bottle of Triple Sec with Brett. We drank it all, microwaved a dozen monster chocolate chip cookies, had our characters sack the Steading of the Hill Giant Chief, and then retched most of it up before the night was over.

When Alex spent the night, everything took on a much more sinister tone. We turned down the lights, turned up Ozzy Osbourne's *Blizzard of Oz* album, and listened to Alex tout the merits of Anton LaVey, founder of the Church of Satan in California. None of it, Alex stressed, should be confused with a meandering game for nerds like I played. After a few more drinks, who could argue? While Mick and I would still play on our own from time to time, the game became a smokescreen for a real-life adventure, no characters needed.

"Hey, Brady," Mick said, extending his hand to help pull me out of the pool. "He's here."

"Cool," I said, feeling vulnerable in swim trunks as Alex rounded the side of the house dressed in a trucker's hat, Iron Maiden concert shirt, and bell bottoms.

"Hey, man," he said to Mick, giving him a high five and a laugh. "What's the skinny tonight?"

"The man's working graveyard, so we're down," Mick said. "You got the stuff?"

Alex smiled, showing off his retainer and the pockets of tiny bubbles that would sometimes build up on the corners of his mouth. He pulled a black canvas fanny pack around to his front and unzipped it, yanking the flap forward to show us the merch. Most of the pouch was packed with weed, but I could see a cigarette box, a few smaller bags of rainbow-colored content, and another with the all-too-recognizable white of cocaine.

I started to say he had a haul, but Alex made a face and held a finger to his lips. He was hushing me, and it wasn't in jest. It was a warning. I shook my head and turned away to towel off and grab a shirt. Mick was already dry. It didn't take long in the heat.

"Did Trevor and Travis pay up?" Alex ignored me.

"Nah, I gave them till tomorrow," Mick said.

"That won't do," Alex said, taking the pack off and stuffing it under Mick's towel. "This isn't all a party pack, so we'll need some beer or something."

"Right," Mick said, putting on his shirt. "I don't think they have it, but sure, we can walk over."

"No, but their mom will have it," Alex said. "She always has a stash of money somewhere around the house. How do you think they pay for anything?"

"Good point," Mick said. "They just smoked some too. Shouldn't be a problem."

"So let's go," I said.

"Not you," Alex said, pushing the towel at me. "You can watch the store."

"What?" I said. "Why not?"

"You're not needed," Alex said. "And I'm not carrying all over the neighborhood."

"Then I'm going home," I countered.

"Brady," Mick tried to appease me, always the peacemaker.

"What?" I said, pushing the towel toward him. "I'm not going to babysit his girly purse."

I was looking at Mick when I said it. That's why I never saw Alex's fist bending around my peripheral vision until he hit me square in the sternum. It was like a small cherry bomb had exploded in my chest, and I couldn't breathe, my lungs forgetting how to draw in air. Alex didn't stop there.

His other hand followed around and grabbed my Adam's apple, guiding me straight to the ground, and he cocked his punching hand behind him to give me another blow. It didn't come because I never had a chance. All I could do is lie there with his weight on my chest and croak out that I couldn't breathe. I said it three times before he released me.

"I'm tired of your smart mouth," Alex said. "You said you wanted in, and you're in, but this isn't a democracy. Do as you're told."

It would be a few minutes before I could talk, so I didn't try. I held up a hand in surrender and watched them leave. Mick had left the towel-wrapped pack on one of the lawn chairs. What stood out was that I was lying on my back in my best friend's yard, and he wasn't offering me a hand up as he did from the pool. He looked at me with a strange expression, somewhere between disappointment and pity.

We had been friends a long time. Mick was already living here when my family moved in next door. We would have become friends sooner, but Las Vegas had this weird rule about busing middle-class kids to poor neighborhoods for sixth grade. It somehow made up for poor kids being bused to middle-class neighborhoods for eleven years. With Mick in seventh grade and me in sixth, we had different schedules back then.

We met when his parents had invited mine over for a get-to-know-you barbecue at the start of summer after that first year. It was important for them to get to know us because Mick's parents both worked the graveyard shift. If either of their kids ever needed help, they needed to know they could count on my parents. I would have laughed at that had they asked me, but they didn't.

Mick and I hit it off, and the first set of friends that I had made on bus rides to what we called the Beirut Sixth Grade Center fell by the wayside. Who needed them? My best friend lived next door.

We had been best friends for closing in on three years, and it never occurred to me that this might change. But something had changed. Maybe Alex wasn't a third wheel as much as I was anymore. Or maybe that's the way Alex wanted me to feel by leaving me out on the collection visit. It was hard to know.

I eventually got up off the lawn and made myself comfortable in the chair, clutching the pack on my lap. For a while, all I did was sit there and look at the walls that framed

Mick's backyard. That's what it was all about in Las Vegas. You were on the inside or the outside, and I was always on the inside with a gram of confidence and an ounce of doubt.

CHAPTER 2

BORN WILD

You could always find a party on the west end of town, but Mick's house was the best. We had cultivated the sweet spot between those boring stand-around jock keggers and the rowdier hardcore crowds that bought from Alex but didn't hang with us.

Everybody knew to keep it cool because we had a good thing going. Both of Mick's parents worked twelve-hour graveyard shifts. They ate early dinners, packed up his sister to spend the night with grandparents, and didn't come home until sometime between six and eight in the morning. So the house was ours as long as we kept things low key.

If the neighbors ever called the cops, his dad would be the first officer dispatched. He was a bear of a man, barrel-chested and towering over everyone and everything at six foot eight. And while he came across as an oversized teddy bear, there wasn't anybody who wanted to test his jovial, good-natured disposition. He worked vice before returning to the dusty tan, green, and gold worn by the Las Vegas Metropolitan Police Department.

There was no question he was formidable, subtly proving it by playing the part of a Nordic jokester. One of his favorite pranks was demonstrating any number of passive restraints he learned as a police officer — anything and everything from twisting a wrist to tucking Kubotan between his thumb and your earlobe.

"Hey, Brady? Do you want to see a neat trick?" His eyes lit up with excitement.

"I don't know," I would say. "On Mick or me?"

That made him laugh. He thought my answer was pretty clever. So he called his son over instead. Mick feigned protest but ultimately gave in just like I did when it was my turn. The pain was hot and instantaneous — the kind that makes you laugh to mask the fiery intensity of it. Then it dissipates as quick as it came on, never injuring anything except our pride.

He played it off like a parlor trick, and we knew it would feel very different in a live-fire event. That was the main reason we always came around for more. He wasn't a sadist, and we weren't masochists. He was teaching. We were learning. If someone messed with us, we became better equipped with his bag of tricks.

Mick's mother was a spirited Irish woman. She wasn't tall like his dad but still stood out in the crowd as a loud, stout ginger. She worked as an emergency room nurse, taking the graveyard shift so they could sync their lives together and preserve what seemed to be a stable marriage.

She always used to joke that she would be the second person we would see if we got into trouble. Big Al would be the first. She would be the second, right after we woke up in a hospital bed.

If that wasn't incentive enough, my parents were right next door with only a cinderblock wall and partition of oleanders dividing the two houses. My folks were the reason for all the house party rules. No more than two people in the backyard at any one time. Nothing louder than a three on the stereo dial. No group activities outside designated areas.

With a dozen or so people congregating there every weekend and some weeknights in the summer, friends and acquaintances would assemble for drinking games in the dining room, self-medication in the kitchen, and chilling in the family room where the television, stereo, and dart board resided.

The living room shielded us from the front of the house. The backyard isolated us from behind. Partygoers always parked on the backside of our horseshoe-shaped street. From the outside, Mick's home looked as sleepy as the retiree's house across from it. As long as my mother kept her nose in a book and my stepfather was set up with a whiskey sour, we were confident no one would come knocking. Until somebody did.

Nobody knew what to do except Alex. He calmly started cleaning the kitchen counter, sweeping the pot pile into one bag and lines of cocaine into another.

As the knocking persisted, the group in the dining room caught on. Empty beer bottles clinked as they swept them into trash bags. Partials were tucked under the table. Someone flew upstairs to hide. It was Mick of all people.

"Who's going to get the door now?" Tom asked.

Tom was the oldest person in the house and had the most to lose. He was eighteen years old, one year older than his girlfriend, Denise. She lived in the inverted corner house across the street. Denise still had another year of school while Tom graduated a few months ago.

Tom always looked so confident under a mane of mousy brown hair that landed at his shoulders. But with his usual bravado shaken, his mustachioed smile was replaced by a frown.

"What if it's the cops?" Will asked.

Will lived next door to Mick and opposite Denise in the corner house. He was also a high school senior who hustled most nights at Farm Basket to pay for car parts. He was always the last to get a joke, but we kept him around because his dad owned a gun store.

"It's not the cops," Alex said. "If it was the cops, it would be Mick's dad."

"Well, where is Mick?" Tom asked.

I shrugged.

"Get the door, Brady," Alex said.

"Me?"

"You practically live here."

I took a deep breath. I was the youngest in the house, except for Denise's younger brother, Donny. He was passed out on the couch in the family room.

"Get the door," he said again.

"Chill out," I said, feeling some of the buzz I picked up playing quarters slip away. "I need a minute."

There are right ways and wrong ways to open a front door. When you're not expecting any trouble, one right way is to open it about four or five inches with your body blocking as much of the opening as possible.

"Hello?"

I had never seen this guy before. He was a stocky Black man with a caramel complexion and a large Afro. One golden earring dangled from his left ear. He looked at me and gave me a knowing smile.

"Are you all having a party?"

I had to think about what to say. Lying came easy enough but not when the evidence was a few inches away.

"Ah, just a couple friends hanging out," I said. "Were we too loud or something?"

He smiled, squinting his eyes and asking me to let him in on the joke. We both knew I was drunk and high. Not much, but enough. I wanted to slam the door in his face.

"Is this your house?" he asked before adding his own assessment. "It's not your house, is it?"

"Yeah, sure it is," I said.

"Look, it's cool. I don't really care what you all are doing. I was a kid once, too," he said. "I just want to know if Jamie is here. I'm his dad."

"I dunno," I said. "Let me check."

I shut the door. I didn't know what else to do. We were busted.

"Where's the new kid?" I said. "What's his name? Jamie."

Everyone in the dining room looked at me like we were playing red light, green light, and I had just called out "red light." They were frozen in place, too busy wondering if it was too late to sneak out the back to be of any help. A couple of them looked to their right and left as if the one Black kid at the party was somehow standing right next to them but avoiding detection.

"Man, it's his dad." I pleaded. "We've got to find him."

"You shouldn't have opened the door," said Trish One, coming out of the family room with glassy, bloodshot eyes. "Never open the door."

We called her Trish One because there were two Trishes. She was the harder looking of the two, passing as a sister to Keith Richards if he had one. She always looked elegantly wasted, with disheveled long dark hair, framing sunken cheeks, and sleepy eyes — tired with big circles and too much mascara. She was laughing at me.

"He knew someone was home," I told her and then called out to Tom from the back of the dining room pack. "Can you get her out of here?"

"Brady," she laughed, drawing out my name before kissing a long slender finger and holding it out to me. "You're such a cutie."

She didn't mean it. She only showed interest in me when I was holding the last joint, but that was about it.

"What do you want me to do with her?" Tom wanted a pass, using his girlfriend as a shield.

"I dunno. Take her back to the family room or something. Anywhere, just not here," I said. "The rest of you can help me find this Jamie kid."

There were six rooms downstairs, and he wasn't in any of them. Mick's parents always locked their room, so that left three upstairs. Two were empty, and the one person in Mick's room was Mick.

"Who's at the door?" Mick asked.

"That Jamie kid's dad," I said. "Did you see him?"

As soon as I said it, I could see him shrug off some of the paranoia that hit him before he flew up the stairs. I don't know what Alex had given him, but it wasn't any of the same things the rest of us hit, except Trish One. Alex was always trying to loosen her up.

"No," he said. "So, his dad. Do you think everything's cool?"

"I don't know, Mick," I sighed. "It is unless he tells your parents. Do you want to help look?"

"Okay," he said. "You go first."

It always bugged me how Mick acted when he was stoned. He was a fun drunk and not so fun stoned, swinging from acting like everything was funny to acting like everything was threatening. Most people don't expect a kid as big as Mick to be afraid of anything, but he always was after a few bowls. I almost told him to hit a line of blow just to get his nerve back.

By the time we went downstairs again, most of the party had shuffled away from the front door and dining room. They were all standing around in the family room and kitchen. Two dozen high school kids were standing around, and none of them were looking anymore.

"The guy was knocking again," said Alex. "You got to get rid of him, Mick."

Mick knew what he meant. Being caught with a few beers or baggies wouldn't ruffle many feathers, but the package Alex had brought was something else altogether.

"I'll do it," I said. "He's already seen me."

Mick came along anyway, for better or worse. I slowly opened the door. Jamie's dad was still standing there, somewhere between bemused and losing patience.

"Um, we can't find him," I said. "Maybe he went home."

"Look, is he messed up? It's okay if he's messed up," he said. "I'll take him home."

"No, he's not here," said Mick, standing taller to show off his size. "He must have left."

"Well, he didn't come home, so maybe I can take a look," he said. "Do you mind?"

"Sure," Mick said, opening the door. "We've got nothing to hide."

We had everything to hide. Jamie's dad stepped inside.

They looked nothing alike. Jamie was almost as tall as me and lean, with dark skin and short-cropped hair. He almost came across as serious. His dad was the opposite. He was a player, with a Kings Road disco shirt unbuttoned below the break of his chest, showing off a river of gold chains that matched the rings dancing on every finger.

"Cool, cool," he said, bemused by the looks as he passed from one room to the other.

I led him around. First upstairs to every room except the locked master and then back into the small crowd. It gave everyone more time to hide anything harder than a Budweiser or a Marlboro.

"You all look pretty well lit," he said, smirking at an open beer behind a family room lamp. "How old is he?"

He waved a hand at Donny, who was still passed out on the couch, one arm draped over his eyes to ward off any light. The pose showcased his T-shirt, an X-wing rising up from his tan corduroy shorts into a rainbow-colored sun. He looked twelve.

"I dunno, sixteen maybe?"

"Sixteen," he whistled. "And how old are you?"

"He's old enough," Alex cut me off.

"Oh yeah? You the boss man?"

"Something like that," he said.

"I figured," he said. "What, with you answering other people's questions and all."

"This isn't *Match Game* either," Alex said. "You've had your look. Jamie ain't here."

"Alex, it's cool," I said. "I got this."

I could feel the heat from his eyes. Laser beams of rage cut my head off. I had to avert my eyes, unable to look at him or watch the foam rise up in the corners of his mouth. It was an early warning signal before he boiled over.

"What's down there?" asked Jamie's dad, gesturing down the hall leading to the laundry, downstairs bathroom, and garage access.

"The last bathroom," I said. "Come on, I'll show you."

We were walking down the hall when one of the accordion closet doors rattled. Jamie's dad and I looked at each other and then at the door again. Someone was in there.

It was Jamie. He had wedged himself between the lowest shelf and floor, looking up at us like he had gone one too many rounds in a boxing ring. The first thought that flew into my head was that we were all dead. I tried to play it like a joke.

"Jamie!" I said. "What are you doing in there?"

He looked at me and shook his head.

"Hey, man," I tried again. "Are you all right?"

Jamie didn't answer. He put two fingers to his lips instead, eyes growing wide as his cheeks expanded like he was blowing up a balloon. Then he was up in a flash from a crawl to a run, pushing past his dad and me and dashing toward the bathroom — cheered on by an ensemble of hoots and jeers from the kitchen. But the loudest of them was right next to me. His old man found the humor that failed me.

"Man, that kid is messed up," he laughed, putting a hand on my shoulder.

"So, it's cool?"

"Yeah, relax. I was a kid once, too," he said. "I'll get him home when he's done."

He followed Jamie into the bathroom and stayed with him for the next twenty minutes. I cut back to the kitchen and immediately regretted it. Alex gave me another death stare.

"You think you're so smart, don't you?" he hissed.

I shrugged, which was the wrong answer.

He moved around the breakfast bar to face me. I knew he wouldn't do anything while Jamie's dad was in the house, but who knew what would happen once they left.

"What?" I managed.

"Why did you let him in?"

"It wasn't me. It was Mick."

"Don't be smart," he said. "You answered the door."

"You told me to."

"To keep him out, string bean," he said.

"Yeah, well, I'm surprised you don't like D&D," I said. "You'd make a good lich."

He smirked and gave me a shove. My heart was thumping, but I tried to stand my ground by leaning forward with my chest out, arms back, and fists clenched.

"What you going to do about it?"

"Guys, chill," Mick said, stepping between us. "Wait until they're gone."

I threw up my hands like I was disappointed, but Mick saved my life. I might have a chance in a fair fight, but Alex never fought fair. The laid back look and a rolling slouch were a ruse. He may not have grown up in a tough inner city like I had, but he had picked up some karate somewhere. So I took Mick's cue and backed off. I was defeated twice in the same day. Alex knew it too. It was a big joke to him.

I slid out the back door and into the backyard to cool off, but the deep red glow of a cigarette told me I wasn't alone. You can be lonely but never alone at Mick's house.

"Well, aren't you a fish of another color," she said before taking another drag. "What's your name?"

"Brady," I said, retreating to the door. "Didn't mean to bother you."

"Don't run away," she said. "Maybe we came out here for the same reason."

I didn't say anything.

"My name's Cheryl."

"Nice to meet you."

"Such manners," she said with a laugh. "So what's a nice kid like you running with a pack like that?"

I stiffened. "I belong. Mick's like a brother to me."

"I didn't mean...," she said. "Hey, I'm sorry. Want a drag?"

"Nah, I don't smoke." It was a lie. I did smoke, but not cigarettes.

"Come on," she said. "Keep me company anyway."

I pulled another lawn chair over and sat next to her. There was just enough light from the moon to make out her features. She was pretty, but not in a girlish high school way.

"You go to Bonanza High School?" I asked her.

"Just graduated with Tom," she said. "I'm trying to figure out what's next."

"I get it," I said. "I'll be doing that too, soon enough."

It was another lie of sorts, but I didn't want her to know the truth. At the end of the summer, I'd be a sophomore at the school she was leaving behind.

"Tom's friend?"

"Yes, well, I should say more a friend of Denise," she said. "So, why did you come out here?"

"I had a disagreement with Alex," I said. "I didn't want it to get rough."

"Oh, you're a tough guy then?" She laughed.

"I wouldn't say that," I said. "I can hold my own in a fight. It doesn't matter what kind. Fists, pool cues, knives, whatever."

"Are you trying to impress me?" She laughed again. "Keep going. I'm a sucker for a bad boy."

I don't know what possessed me, but I rattled off all the trouble we caused a couple nights ago. We were already high when Alex had produced a Sherm Stick — a dark brown Moore cigarette dipped in PCP — and started passing it around. First to Mick and then Jamie. When it was my turn, he said it was too strong for an amateur like me and grabbed it back. I left that part out while talking with Cheryl.

It hit everybody fast and hard, with Mick and Jamie saying they felt like supermen. So we started roaming the neighborhood, trying to walk off the pent-up adrenaline that was overtaking everyone. The walk only agitated them all the more.

Alex was the first to do something stupid, taking out his switchblade and sticking it into the front driver's side tire of a car we knew all too well. In my retelling, I made it sound more like dark justice and retribution. The guy who owned the car deserved it, some guy who bullied Jamie for being Black.

"See that," Alex laughed. "That's a bad day."

Jamie was the one who pulled it out, giving it a twist as he did. I could see a gleam in his eye as an inside joke came over him. He took the knife and stuck it in the back tire.

"Now that's a very bad day," he howled. "Even a redneck don't got two spares."

"Nobody's got two spares," Mick echoed, hooting and running down the street with his arms outstretched like an eagle.

We chased him, eventually stopping in front of a house with a thick log fence, something that would look more at home on a ranch. We all knew the place well enough. A football player who stiffed Mick for fifty on a bet lived there. So Mick gave the fence a kick and declared he was invincible.

"I hate forty-eight, his house, and his stupid fence," he roared. "This ain't no rodeo town. I'm bringing it down. It's all coming down."

He gave it another stomp, growing frustrated with its resistance. Alex egged him on, telling him how embarrassing it would be to lose to a fence. Mick jumped into the air and body slammed it, not once but three times, until the top log started to snap. He was about to go again when the porch light turned on, and the four of us ran off.

"I don't know that I like your friends that much," Cheryl said.

"No?" I doubled down. "They had it coming. Everyone who had something we wrecked. They all had it coming."

"Maybe," she said. "But I don't think you believe that."

"Why do you say that?"

"I listened to your story, Brady. You didn't do these things," she said. "You just went along for the ride."

She said it like a pardon, so I folded my arms across my chest. If she didn't get it, we didn't have much more to discuss. I was just as bad as the rest of them.

"Believe what you want," I said.

The back door slid open, and Denise stuck her head out. "Hey, Cheryl, we're headed out."

"I'll be right there," she said, dropping her butt in an empty beer bottle before turning back to me. "Hey, I need some help washing my car tomorrow. Why don't you come by and give me a hand."

"Maybe," I said, mimicking her earlier assessment.

"I hope so," she said, handing me a folded piece of paper. "There's something about you, Brady, even if you don't think so."

I stuffed the paper into the front pocket of my shorts. Maybe it was because I was still coming down from my earlier high and the rush from almost tangling with Alex, but I couldn't make sense of it. I met some girl, spouted off some nonsense, and she gave me her address. I didn't get it.

She wasn't like the usual suspects who circled Mick's house, hoping to get high for the favor of their company. There was something about her too. So I picked up her empty and headed back into the house. I would help Mick clean up before his parents came home, even if everyone else had cleared out.

CHAPTER 3

SCHOOL'S OUT

I woke up early and left the house before anyone else was up. It was the easiest way to avoid the constant barrage of harassment. How late were you out last night? When are you going to mow the lawn? Why is your room a mess? Where do you think you're going? How long are you going to primp in front of the mirror?

I wasn't primping. I was trying to tame the tangle of hair that hadn't seen a barber since I lived with my grandparents. If I wanted a cut in this household, I had to sit under some shears wielded by my mother. The scissors were too dull for a proper cut but sharp enough to draw blood. She didn't slip often, just enough that I let it grow longer.

My hair was one of a hundred reasons I didn't understand the invite from Cheryl. I wasn't an ugly kid, but most girls didn't take an interest in me outside of those who gravitated to our group for drugs. It was sometimes like being in a band without having to play an instrument. All that mattered was what you had stashed in your pocket.

Cheryl didn't strike me as that type, which made her a mystery. She didn't live too far away, maybe two miles. It would take less than thirty minutes to find out if she had made a mistake about me in the dark, under the haze of smoke and yellow streetlights that had bled into the backyard. There was nowhere to hide under a crystal blue summer sky.

The route was easy enough, winding through a few neighborhoods that made up what everyone else called the boonies and then west up Charleston Boulevard past a checkerboard of small subdivisions and empty desert lots. She lived in a newer neighborhood, closest to the edge of town.

The sawtooth path I cut to Charleston followed the same way I used to walk to a school bus stop in the sixth grade. The houses weren't anything like those I knew in Cleveland. They were all the same here — four or five models with a different coat of paint on lap siding and brick accents to create the illusion they were different. They weren't. They all had air conditioners humming on low-slung roofs. They all had two-car garages facing the street. They all had curtains drawn, owners trying to protect their possessions from fading in the summer sun.

The people who lived in these cookie-cutter homes were mostly the same. There were only four or five kinds of families who lived this far out. First responders, nurses, and mailmen. Mechanics, salespeople, and service workers. Small shop owners and retail managers. Retired military and test site workers. A handful of mobsters who didn't want to draw attention to themselves by living close to The Strip.

We all lived the same way, a large eclectic swatch of lower-to-middle class families cobbled together on the west end. It was far enough away from The Strip that we could pretend what the tourists knew as Las Vegas was a mirage on one horizon. On the other, we imagined the vast and deadly desert in our backyard could be tamed into submission. The illusion was convincing to anyone who took a walk past the endless rows of freshly minted houses with dark green lawns fed by underground sprinkler systems and the vacant desert lots that neighbored them in varied stages of excavation.

One of the few breaks in this sea of desert suburbia were two small corner retail plazas along Charleston, making it the last chance to stop for something before driving out into the wilderness of Red Rock Canyon. The west corner was anchored by a semi-popular Shakey's Pizza Parlor and a neighborhood bar best known for its young waitresses and two bowling lanes. The east corner catered more to my crowd.

It was a little past eight in the morning when I walked by and there was already trouble in the parking lot between the arcade and corner convenience store. Two punks were passing a clutch purse back and forth like a football. There was a blonde girl in the middle of them, trying to make an interception.

One of the punks had on a white shirt and jean jacket, which didn't fit the weather. It was already warm and expected to hit ninety degrees, if not triple digits, by noon. The other wore a generic striped T-shirt, horizontal earth tones that were popular a few years back but losing ground to pastels. I didn't recognize them, but the girl looked familiar.

I tried to shield my face as I walked by because it wasn't any of my business, but the girl recognized me. Andrea Bigelow was a crush of mine in middle school before she shared the poem I wrote for her with that steady boyfriend.

"Brady Wilks? Is that you?"

"Andrea?" I said, squinting like I couldn't see her from the sidewalk. "Hey, I didn't know you lived up here."

"Yeah, it's me," she said before sprinting to the point. "Give a girl a hand?"

"What's the problem?" I said, cutting into the parking lot.

"I was going to get some donuts and these two clowns jacked my purse," she rattled on. "They won't give it back."

I turned my attention to the two guys. They were my age, maybe a year younger, which is why I didn't recognize them from school. Neither one looked bothered by the fact I was taking an interest. Nobody ever does.

"Hey, you guys had your fun," I said. "Just give it back."

"For a few quarters, no problem," said the jacket, the taller of the two kids. "A couple bucks."

"Why? Does she you owe you or something?"

"No, but she can afford a few," said the shorter one. "What's it to you?"

"Oh, I see," I said. "So you're merry men or something."

"What?"

"You know, like Robin Hood," I said, closing in on the jacket. "Take from the rich and give to the poor. Except, I think you'd steal from just about anyone who can't fight back. Am I right?"

He didn't know what I was talking about and neither did his friend, but it didn't matter. I could've said anything while closing the distance between me and the bigger of the two threats.

"Want to know what else?" I asked.

"What?"

I jabbed and hit him square in the nose. I could feel the cartilage give a bit before breaking. A fresh stream of blood followed the crunch. As he brought his hands to his face and backed away, I grabbed the purse as he dropped it and tossed it to Andrea.

"I'll take care of this," I said. "Get out of here."

She didn't wait around.

"You broke my nose!" He wailed as I moved in again to give him another shove.

The other kid, late to the party but not out of the fight, grabbed my shoulder to stop my advance. I turned with a roundhouse punch to his temple. He stumbled back on his heels and fell, holding his head.

The taller kid was trying to recover, coming at me but in no shape to finish the fight. I caught his left hand as he threw a weak punch and put him down next to his friend. I had one hand on each of them, holding them down.

"Stay down," I told them. "I'll let you up, but you have to give it up."

They were still resisting but understood. They were in the wrong, and I had called them out. Besides, there wasn't anything left to fight over. Andrea had already taken off. And it would have been over right there if a third kid hadn't gotten involved.

I hadn't seen anybody come out of the arcade, but several other kids had poured out with the promise of a fight. One of them was the shorter punk's older brother. He blindsided me by putting the heel of a hiking boot to the side of my head. I rolled with it and away, seeing nothing but stars and his silhouette against a cloudless sky.

"Maybe you should pick on someone your own size," he said, waiting for me to get up and take some more.

"Maybe you should ask them what started it," I said, not bothering to get up.

He relaxed and looked back at his brother and the taller kid, whose white shirt was ruined with blood. He was busy wrecking the rest of it, pulling it up over his belly to stem the slowing flow.

"What's he talking about?"

"Nothing, Del," he said. "It's cool ... it was a misunderstanding."

"You could say that, "I said. "Or you could say they stole some girl's purse."

The older kid eased off. He looked at his brother and the taller kid, shaking his head. Then he turned back to me.

"Take a hike," he spat at me and then gave his brother a shove.

"Yeah, sure," I said, getting up. "Next time, let's try a fair fight. You all bring a few more guys, maybe."

I flipped them off before making a beeline into the 7-Eleven. They charged me a dime for a cup of ice after making me promise not to cause trouble. It felt like another robbery, but I gave it up anyway. I wanted to get the swelling down before Cheryl saw me.

I didn't know what it looked like, but I assumed it wasn't too bad. The throbbing stopped about a block after I pressed the cup to my temple. My ego had the bigger bruise. I was on a losing streak.

When I reached Cheryl's street, I almost cut my losses and headed home. I stood there for what felt like an hour replaying the night before, searching for some inexplicable magnetism that had occurred between us. I couldn't remember any feeling like that, but my emotions were running pretty high at the time. We were flying, almost busted, and then Alex had come at me hard for being the only one who did anything.

I tipped the cup back and let some ice fall into my mouth. I was an idiot. Girls don't give you their address if they aren't interested. They don't even give you their address if they are interested. I took out the piece of paper and rechecked the address. She was a few houses in, which meant the orange Pinto in the driveway was probably her car.

I took a breath and started walking toward it, trying to keep my head up. She was already outside, pulling a hose over from the house and filling a couple of buckets with soapy water.

In the crispness of late morning, she was more attractive than I remembered — white canvas shoes but no socks, denim cutoffs framing bronze legs, a red university tee without sleeves, brown hair with amber highlights landing on her shoulders. She was slender but not skinny, toned, and a few inches shorter than me.

My pace slowed as I closed the distance between us, partly so I could drink her in for a minute and partly to postpone the inevitable. She wouldn't have the same reaction when she saw me.

I was wearing cutoffs too, but my legs were skinny, and one knee was scraped from the fight on the way over. My plain Henley tee hung loose around a narrow frame. I had some muscles because when Mick's friend Brett still lived in Vegas, the three of us used to walk to a community center to lift weights. Even so, everybody considered me the skinny kid still trying to grow into oversized feet that looked larger in cheap white Pumas. My heart was racing with anticipation while I tried to decide what to do if she pretended not to know who I was or why I was there.

"You made it," she said, lifting her head with a smile.

And then I watched her smile fade as she took me in.

"Hey," I said, putting my hands up in surrender. "Something wrong?"

"Yeah, you're hurt," she said, putting a hand to her temple to mirror to where I had been blindsided. "The skin's broken too. Let me get you something for it."

I was going to tell her not to bother, but she made it clear I didn't have an option. She didn't have to make a case. The peroxide fizzed around the wound, a tender scuff wreathed by a brown and yellow bruise.

"What happened?" she asked, dabbing a wet cotton ball to the abrasion.

"You should see the other guy," I mused, trying to brush it off.

The frown said it all. She wasn't having it.

"A couple of guys jumped me for some quarters outside the arcade," I said. "They were disappointed. I don't go down easy."

"Did they steal anything?"

"Nah," I said. "Guys like that are looking for easy prey. So they backed off when I proved to be something of a problem."

"You're like a magnet for trouble," she said, referencing my run-in with Alex.

"Funny you should say that," I said. "My very first fight was less than a block from the arcade at a school bus stop."

"Back in sixth grade?"

"Yeah, my family had just moved to town from the mistake on the lake, that's Cleveland, and it took a while before I found my crowd, meaning Mick and everybody," I said. "So, you know, like a lot of times, the first ones to make friends with the new kid are usually geeks and whatnot. You fall in with them, and everybody assumes you're an easy mark. Except I'm from Cleveland, the toughest city in the country."

"I didn't know that," she said. "What happened?"

I told her about that fight so I wouldn't have to talk more about the one that happened in the morning. I don't know why, but I didn't want her to know I got into the scrape because those punks took some girl's purse. I didn't want there to be some other girl who knew me well enough that I would help her like that.

The pre-fight initially started on a bus ride home from school. I was kicked back in the corner of the bus seat against the window with my arm over the back of it. A couple of the popular kids wanted to make a big joke about it because, from their perspective, they said I was putting my arm around this geeky kid I knew.

The geeky kid wanted me to let it go, but I couldn't. I kept on pushing back and pushing back until one kid, Eddy, told me to expect to throw a few blows the next morning.

The following day, we squared up like boxers. I let him throw a few, slapping his hands away while measuring his reach. I knew I had him by a few inches because my wingspan has always been long for my body. I took a couple on the chin to test his mettle. He was a weak fighter, so I returned his stabs with a series of roundhouses, coming in on the sides of his head instead of his face, which he was protecting.

"Everybody protects where they think you're going to hit them," I said. "It's a mistake. I mean, of course you're going to fend off a punch, but you leave too much open against a fighter who is looking for any opening."

"So you won the fight?"

"Nobody wins a fight," I said.

I didn't tell her that I have anger issues and don't always know when to stop. So when Eddy started to wilt but wouldn't give up, I took him in a headlock and drove his head into the side of the house. I kept screaming at him to stay down, but the dummy kept getting back up and putting his hands up in front of him.

A couple of his friends eventually intervened and sat him down. They were as stunned as he was, though he was the only one with a face that was red and bloody. The only thing I had hurt were my hands, landing every punch until it was over.

"You think you're a tough guy," one of his friends said to me. "We'll see about that."

I don't know why, but I started crying about how I didn't want any of it. I wasn't looking for a fight, but I wasn't afraid to get rough either. I told them to expect more of the same if they came at me, using my bravado to calm myself down. I don't know if they understood where I was coming from or not. I wasn't scared of them as much as myself and what I might do if nobody was around to keep me in check.

"Did they leave you alone after that?"

"Everybody left me alone," I said. "Even the geeky kid. He didn't want anything to do with me after that. He said it put too much of a target on his back."

"What a jerk," she said, trying to lighten the mood. "So where did you learn how to fight anyway? I mean, I get it, Cleveland, home of the tough guys."

I was the kid who had to fight because a handicap had confined me to these weird corrective shoes that everybody thought were a joke. What do they say? When people are backed into a corner, they either fight or flee. God forgot to give me a flee switch.

"Hey, let's talk about something else," I said and gestured to her shirt. "You going there or something?"

"I was admitted to Cal State Northridge, but I won't be going there," she said. "We can't afford it. So I'm going to take a few classes at the community college."

"Oh, sorry," I said.

"Don't be," she said. "I don't really know what I want to do anyway. So I'll take the core classes at the community college, and maybe I'll enroll somewhere else once I figure it out. You?"

"I dunno," I said. "I was going to be an artist, but my mom said I wasn't good enough and would end up starving. So maybe something else. Psychology or something."

She laughed, little creases forming around the corners of her eyes. She liked to laugh.

"What's so funny?"

"I can see you sitting across someone laid out on the couch," she said. "Yo, Adrian. Toughen up already and learn to throw a punch."

I put my hands up like a boxer because she expected it. I smiled, trying a little too hard to praise her punchline. She pushed my hands away with a laugh and dabbed at the cut one last time. It didn't sting anymore.

"So are we going to wash your car or what?" I asked. "It's only going to get hotter."

She pressed a small Band-Aid against my injury. I flinched but it didn't hurt. It was more of an act to score extra sympathy points.

"Let's do it," she said.

We spent the rest of the time washing one of the least understood cars on the road. She drove a 1974 hatchback model with chrome bumpers and trim — not all that different from the newer one driven by Kate Jackson as Sabrina Duncan in *Charlie's Angels*. I teased her a few times, asking her if her car might grow up to be a Mustang like Farrah Fawcett sported on the show.

She rebutted by turning the hose on me, a few flirtatious splashes followed by her thumb creeping over the nose to increase the pressure. I dodged the stream and threw my soapy sponge on her. My willingness to fight back only encouraged her.

She came at me with the hose, only rethinking her advance when I came toward her with one of the buckets. She was laughing. We were both laughing, dodging ribbons of water like two kids at one of the splash pools back home. Then I telegraphed my intent to empty whatever remained in the bucket on her head.

"Don't you dare," she said, backing up into the grass. "Brady!"

I dumped the water off to the side while knocking her off balance, laughing as we fell back and landed on the lawn together. I was on top of her for a brief moment, eye to eye, until she tossed the hose to the side and rolled me over, so she was on top. It was the first time I noticed she wasn't wearing a bra.

She could see the realization written all over my face because she gave me a mischievous wink and smile. Then she grabbed my hands, pressed them to her hips, and leaned over to kiss me. When her lips touched mine, it shocked me — not in the electrical current sort of way but in a stupefied daze of disbelief.

She must have felt my stupefaction because she stopped and moved my hands off her hips and above my head. She adjusted her position. Instead of getting tangled up with a new boyfriend, she took on the role of being the big sister pinning her kid brother down. She never stopped smiling, but she looked at me sideways.

"How old did you say you were again?"

"Sixteen, seventeen this year," I lied.

"I don't think so," she said, shaking her head with a laugh.

She got up and held out a hand to help me up. I didn't need her help, but I let her pull me up all the same, waiting for the hammer to drop because there was no question it was going to fall. I was too young for her, and she also caught me in a lie. I kept expecting the worst, thinking there was no way this would end well. She surprised me again.

"Come on," she said, warmly but with reservation. "We still have to wax it."

That's what we did. We shared a few stories about growing up while applying white wax over the car. When we were done, we rubbed all the wax off. The Pinto almost looked new compared to how it looked when we started.

Cheryl never did ask me my age again, but something had changed. It wasn't a definitive "I can't believe how stupid I am" kind of change, but more of a "what am I going to do" kind of change. Strangely, I felt the same way. Here was a girl so out of my league but somehow into me anyway, and I blew our first and probably last kiss.

After we finished, she gave me a ride. The whole way home, I could tell that the boundaries hadn't settled yet. They kept rolling in and out like the tide of an ocean. She liked me. She couldn't like me. I liked her. I didn't have a prayer.

CHAPTER 4

OLD FRIENDS

I breezed in through the front door and straight to the kitchen, foraging for some hard salami and sharp cheddar. Calories weren't a problem as much as my metabolism.

I never ate breakfast, so I was always famished by lunchtime. I didn't want to skip the first meal of the day. I just didn't live in a breakfast household. There were no breakfast foods. My folks didn't buy cereal. Bacon and eggs were a hassle. Waffles and pancakes were saved for special occasions like my sister's sleepovers. French toast was food from a foreign land and best left forgotten.

It was very different from the three square meals my grandmother served up when I lived with her. Breakfast was one of the most important meals of the day. Every morning, there would always be something in front of the television: pigs in a blanket on the best days, Cream of Wheat with a fruit smile when she couldn't manage her malignancy.

In this house, nobody else wanted breakfast, so there was none to be had. During the summer, everybody slept in except my stepdad on workdays. He left the house well before sunrise and wouldn't be seen again until late afternoon. His breakfast was coffee. My mother and sister slept until it was too close to lunchtime to bother with it. So it was every person for themselves until dinner.

My head was still in the refrigerator when I felt her presence. She was upset. I didn't have to look to see the pose. It was burned into my memory. She was standing there, arms crossed, and weight shifted to one side.

"Where have you been?"

"I had an errand," I said, acting casual as I moved the meat and cheese to the cutting board.

"You could have left a note."

"Didn't even think about it," I smiled and grabbed a knife from a drawer, avoiding the scowl. "Sorry?"

"Damn right, you're sorry," she said. "What if I had something to do this morning?"

"Did you?"

"That's not the point," she said. "Where are your glasses?"

I tried to measure my words as I cut off a few chunks. There was no way to win with her. Deflection seemed like the best option.

"I didn't need them this morning."

"They cost too much money to be a paperweight," she snapped.

"I know," I said. "Sorry?"

She didn't say anything, and it took me a minute to figure out what else was bothering her. Then I knew. She might not have noticed if I had been smart enough to grab my glasses before hitting the kitchen.

"What happened to your eye?"

"Oh, this, it's nothing," I said, trying to force a chuckle. "I was helping Mick lift something and dropped one end. Pow, right in the kisser."

"Good story, but you might want to get it straight before you tell it next time," she said without missing a beat. "If you were with Mick this morning, he wouldn't have been looking for you."

I swept what I wasn't going to eat back into their packages and opened the refrigerator, trying to act like she didn't catch me cold. There wasn't anything I could do about it except ride it out.

"Yeah? What did he want?"

"He came over to say Brett's back in town," she said, her lips disappearing into a tight line.

"Brett's back from West Virginia? Booyah!" I said. "What? He's next door?"

"Yes, but..."

"Awesome. Bye, mom!"

I scooped up my deconstructed sandwich in a napkin and attempted to move to past her like a running back, hoping my enthusiasm would fuel my escape. My mother always liked Brett, so maybe she liked him enough to give me a pass. No such luck.

"Not so fast, mister."

I stopped and turned around, putting on a sad puppy expression that I outgrew four years ago when I moved in with them.

"I've had enough of your lies, Brady," she said. "And if I find out you're getting in fights again or drinking or doing drugs ... we're all going to be sorry."

She meant that I was going to be sorry. This was the same woman who locked me in a room for a month because the knife I put away had a water spot.

"Mom, come on," I stammered. "I fell. It was a dumb thing, and I didn't want to admit it."

"Fine, but I want you back in twenty minutes because I do have an errand, and someone has to watch your sister."

"Seriously?"

"Twenty minutes or ten," she said. "Your choice."

"Twenty minutes," I said and tried to leave.

"Forgetting something?"

I turned around again, searching her face for a clue. She pointed to her own pair.

"Your glasses," she said. "Take them with you."

It's always best to shut up when you're ahead. I gave her a theatrical bow and stopped by my room to pick up the glasses on the way out. She didn't say anything on my second pass, and neither did I. One wrong word and she might rethink my departure. I held on to the screen door as I left, ensuring it latched shut without the slam.

Of all the friends I had met through Mick, Brett was my favorite. The last time the three of us were together was at a spontaneous wake we held for Brett's idol John Belushi, about a month after the comedian died of a cocaine and heroin overdose. What we didn't know was the wake wasn't just for Belushi. It was for everything we had come to know.

When we played Dungeons & Dragons, Brett's primary character was Gimli, named after the notably famous dwarf in J. R. R. Tolkien's *The Lord of the Rings*. He played the dwarf like a cross between its namesake and Belushi, giving our fictitious crew a comical complainer who always did the right thing despite reserving the right to grumble about it.

His character fit him and he fit his character. Brett was short and stocky and could impersonate his idol on command, effortlessly raising an inquisitive eyebrow at the most inappropriate times. It had gotten us in trouble on more than one occasion. It always played out the same.

"What do you boys think we should do about this?"

Cue Brett's inquisitive eyebrow lift, followed by a snort or a laugh from one of us.

"You think this is all a big joke?"

Cue the slow stroke of his chin, followed by our near hysteria. Yes, we thought it was all a big joke — thinking that sometimes cost one of us house restriction for a day, days, or a week. I spent most of those days developing the adventure or breathing life into the story by making sketches of characters, castles, or campaigns.

Aside from the time we spent sitting around Mick's dining room table, we shared plenty of real-life experiences too. We met up at the community center twice a week to play a game of nine-ball and lift weights. We climbed onto the pergola and jumped into Mick's pool as a precursor to diving off cliffs at

Lake Mead. We hiked and climbed every trail inside Red Rock Canyon, cutting our own paths from time to time.

We were doing our best in a town that wasn't made for kids. It was a world we left behind when Brett left and Alex entered with an assortment of adventures that didn't require imagination. All we had to do now was pass the bowl, pop the pill, or cut the line.

"Brady!" Brett said as I crashed through the front door. I never knocked anymore.

I smiled and met him with a fist bump.

"Wow," he said. "You look the same."

"It's been a couple of months, maybe three?"

"Feels a lot longer," he said.

He didn't look the same. His flyaway hair had been tamed with a perm. He looked heavier, but some weight came from wearing an open flannel over a white T-shirt. He was wearing glasses, new aviators held together with a plastic wire instead of a frame. One of his ears was pierced.

The only thing that looked the same was a small scar under his right eye. He earned it after we had turned some of the empty land around our neighborhood into a war zone, shooting at each other using BB and pellet guns.

He and Mick had traded guns after Brett became frustrated using a pump pellet rifle against a CO_2-powered Luger with an endless clip. The only problem with the trade was Mick decided to pump the gun up to the velocity of a .22-caliber to cover more distance. The ricochet almost took Brett's eye out before we called it a day.

"How's West Virginia?"

"Country roads, take me home," he sang with a laugh. "It's cool. There's more to do if you don't mind everything shutting down in the early evening."

"Crazy. Kind of like Ohio."

"So what are we doing tonight? Any chance our characters are still navigating the demon web pits?"

"We can't play tonight," Mick said, coming in from the kitchen with two drinks, one for himself and one for Brett. "Alex is coming over. He's got something he wants to talk to us about."

"I'm only here for twenty minutes. Babysitting."

Mick frowned like it wasn't an acceptable answer. He was thinking of something to say.

"Who's Alex?" Brett asked.

"You remember him at school, always trolling the smoking area," I said. "Dirty blond, braces, glasses, trucker hat, slouched shoulders."

"The stoner dude?"

There was a tinge of disgust in his voice. I was happy to hear it.

"He's cool," said Mick. "A few things have changed since you left."

"A lot of things if you're hanging around a drug dealer," Brett said. "Wait, what? You guys are doing drugs now?"

Brett looked disappointed. His reaction surprised me because I wasn't disappointed when I found out Mick was doing drugs. He confided in me about a week after Brett left. I was spending the night like most weekends when Mick announced he wanted to smoke a bowl in the backyard. He told me not to come if I wasn't interested. There was no peer pressure at all. He even said it might be better if I didn't join him.

I did, of course. He was my best friend, and it wasn't like we were saints. We drank like fishes — so much so that his parents started marking the bottles in their liquor cabinet. We topped a few off with water and then made our own marks to know which ones were too watered down to risk. But most of the time, we would hang out at 7-Eleven and hustle someone to buy us a case of beer for a six-pack.

Mick started doing drugs during basketball season. Speed made him more alert and improved his reaction time. He played the best game of his life. Smoking pot came later because he said it helped him relax and take the edge off the speed.

"There's more to it than that," said Mick.

Brett shook his head. He knew what it meant. In the three months since he had left, we had transformed from casual users to part-time dealers, Alex cutting us in to expand his territory.

"Pot?"

"And other stuff," Mick said. "Mostly pot, but not that much of the other stuff."

"And you went along with this?" Brett asked, looking at me.

I shrugged, feeling guilty. The three of us were drinkers but never drug users. Stoners were considered the lowest rung of the social ladder at school. Except, Mick and I discovered this was only partly true. Outside of school, the stoner social circle was huge. They didn't stick to class years, clubs, schools, or sports teams.

Stoners melded together to create what felt like a world behind the world. They didn't play at being adults. They made adult choices. They didn't break the rules. They made their own. They didn't answer to anyone. They understood you only lived once.

"The money's good," I finally said.

"Yeah, sure," Brett said. "But that's the stuff that killed Belushi."

"Don't get the wrong idea, Brett," Mick said. "Most of the stuff we sell is pretty mild. The best weed, rush, and a little cocaine. Nothing crazy like all that other stuff. We're not speedballing or selling heroin. That's what killed Belushi."

I could name a dozen things Mick wouldn't mention, but I held my tongue. I was the one who stuck to mostly weed and cocaine. Alex, Mick, and Jamie would try anything, anytime. It made me wonder what Brett would think if he knew Mick was taking speed and smoking after school long before he left.

"Hey, I get it," Mick added. "If you don't want to be around when Alex gets here, it's cool. I can call him off if it makes you feel better."

"You don't have to do that," Brett said. "I'm surprised is all."

Looking back, me too. The past few months were a blur, a rollercoaster ride of people who had made our game place into party central.

"I'm not doing drugs, though," Brett added. "You know that, right?"

"There's no peer pressure here, Brett," Mick said. "It's chill. Everybody gets what they want."

For a minute, I wondered what might have happened if I hadn't stepped outside that first night after he showed me his pipe. We smoked what he had and then kicked back the rest of the night, finding everything funny. He was my best friend, but that experience made us closer, like brothers. Had I passed or headed home, we would have parted ways, and I would have had no one.

"The girls are good too," I said. "There weren't many of those coming around to hear about Garth the overman, Gimli the dwarf, Argon the ranger, and Spinner the wizard."

"Not even with a natural twenty?"

The three of us laughed together, the first time since we were reunited. Rolling a natural twenty on a twenty-sided die during the game was treated like a miracle roll. It saved you from any spell, negated any trap, and won any battle by severing your opponent's head clean off.

I could have used one right then because Mick urged me to make the meet with Alex. I understood his reasoning. Alex never liked me, so every misstep on my part was another excuse to cut me loose altogether. Lately, I wondered if Mick wouldn't mind it.

I envied Brett in the moment. He had a choice. I had already made mine when I stepped outside for a few fake laughs. That was the thing about pot. A good high made everything funny, even when there was nothing funny.

"I'll see what I can do," I said. "I should probably head back over there anyway."

"Man, I never got that," Brett said.

"Got what?"

"Your parents are the coolest people I know," he said. "But that's not how you see it."

"No, you're right. They're cool," I said. "It's different when you live there."

I heard it before, all the time. My super mom made sure everyone knew what a great mother she was, taking me in when my grandmother became too sick to care for me. Back in Ohio, she had given up her job to spend more time with my sister and me. Although, all that meant was more time sunbathing at the apartment complex pool. My sister and her water wings went right along with her.

I did my own thing, which she always said was part of her grand plan. Her mother had spoiled me, she said, and I had to learn how to become independent, responsible, and a contributing member of the household. It wasn't always that way. At first, I thought it was a dream come true, living with a mother and stepfather for the first time in my life. I would never have to explain why I lived with my grandparents again.

"See you guys later," I said.

She was waiting for me when I returned, standing in almost the same pose as when I left. The only difference was she didn't hang her head in disgust as much as on the minute hand of her watch.

"Wonders never cease," she said.

"What?"

"That's a compliment. You made it home on time. Wonders never cease."

I sucked in a breath to say something, and nothing came out. It happened to me sometimes. She would say something, and I would just shut down, thinking it was for the best. Never poke a bear with a stick except in self-defense. Except, doing nothing was dangerous too.

"Hello, did you hear me?"

"What?"

"I gave you a compliment," she said.

"Thank you," I said, and it came out flat.

"You can't go through life like a blob," she said. "You have to learn to emote. Stand up for yourself. Express your emotions. Be a real person. It's for your own good. Everything I do for you is for your own good."

Then she huffed that she didn't have time for this and left. I didn't have time for this, whatever this was, either. Her tone had already convinced me of what I needed to do.

I would wait fifteen minutes. Then I would drop by my sister's room and suggest she go to her friend's house. Dina lived around the corner in the cul-de-sac behind us, one place over from Trevor and Travis. She went over there on her own all the time.

"If you need me, I'll be next door," I told her. "Come back in about an hour. And don't tell mom."

"I won't tell," she said.

And that was that. Babysitting made easy. I headed back to Mick's house, locking my bedroom door but leaving the front door open just in case. If she beat me back, the house being open and my door being closed might cause just enough confusion to keep me safe.

All I had to do was check the driveway first. Then, if her car was there, I would sneak back and climb through my bedroom window. If her car wasn't there, I'd be home free and waltz through the front door. A perfect plan.

CHAPTER 5

BROWN SUGAR

When he smiled, Alex reminded me of a bullfrog catching crickets with a fat sticky tongue and pulling its prey into a gaping black mouth. Small pools of bubbles accumulated on the corners of his mouth as it turned upward. His eyes were made bulbous by his glasses as he looked from Mick to me to Brett. He relished the attention.

It had taken us a few minutes to get to this moment, Mick finally convincing Alex that Brett was cool. He wouldn't say a word to anyone, Mick had promised. Besides, Brett added, he was headed back home in a couple of weeks. So who cared in West Virginia?

The back and forth between the three of them was almost too much to watch. It was all an act anyway. There was no way Alex could keep his dirty little secret. He was too keyed up. The feigned resistance was a ploy to build anticipation — Alex playing Mick like Eddie played the devil on Alex's Iron Maiden T-shirt.

"Blessed are the strong, for they shall inherit the earth," Alex said as he pulled a small bag from his front pocket and tossed it on the dining room table. It looked like cocaine, except the fine powder was brown.

"What is it?"

"It looks like cocaine," I said.

"It's better than cocaine," Alex said. "It's brown sugar. Heroin."

"So that's the stuff," Brett said. "That's what killed Belushi?"

"Nah," said Alex. "Belushi was speedballing, mixing heroin with cocaine. That's like telling your head to push and pull at the same time. I won't judge, but don't recommend it."

"Why is it brown?" I asked.

"You asked the stupidest questions, Brady," Alex said. "Whatever they cut it with is brown. We can cut it even more, with brown sugar, maybe."

"You guys do that? Snort sugar?"

"It's no big deal," Alex said, rolling his eyes. "The sugar makes it smell sweet."

"So, we're going to cut it," said Mick. "That means you want to sell it."

"Yep," said Alex, beaming now. "A lot of it."

"What's a lot?"

"I know a guy who knows some guys who want to sell us two bricks," Alex said. "A half-pound each. If it works out, there'll be more."

I did the math in my head, one of several perks that came with playing Dungeons & Dragons. The game asks players to sharpen life skills: reading, writing, arithmetic, and imagination. This bit of trivia is something the evening news always leaves out when it does a special report on the game, warning parents to protect today's youth from demonic possession by dice games. They want to ban it outright.

Adding up drug money wasn't much different from calculating character experience points. The bag he tossed on the table was a single hit. We could make about twenty of those out of every gram. There are twenty-eight grams in an ounce and sixteen ounces in a pound. So Alex was talking about nine thousand bags, give or take.

"We've never done anything like that before," said Mick. "The biggest was an ounce of coke."

"Yeah," Alex laughed. "Awesome, isn't it?"

"How much will that go for?" Mick asked, pointing to the bag on the table.

"We can sell it for fifteen or twenty."

"Fifteen or twenty? That's triple what people pay for dope."

Alex made a wheezy laugh. He was giddy with excitement. He had every right to be. He was talking about selling about one hundred and fifty thousand dollars worth of drugs or maybe two hundred thousand if we cut it right and it sold for the higher amount.

The numbers gave me a head rush. We made about a hundred per ounce for weed, and our biggest coke score netted about twenty-five hundred after taking some off the table for personal use. This was a different level altogether. What Alex was talking about was eight or ten times more than Mick's dad or my stepdad could make in a year. Brett couldn't believe it.

"Who's paying that for a little baggie?" Brett asked. "I could buy two cases of beer for that much."

"Everybody," Alex said, his lips drawing back to show yellow teeth caged behind strands and bands of braces. "Want a bump?"

"I'll pass," Brett said. "Who knows what's in it."

"I'll tell you," Alex said. "A little bit of magic. A little bit of love."

"I'll try it," Mick said, getting up to go into the kitchen. I'd seen him do it before. He was getting a toothpick.

"How much do they want for it?" I had to ask.

"It doesn't matter," Alex said.

"Of course, it matters."

"Look," Alex said. Losing his patience with me came easy. "You're only along for the ride, so what do you care?"

"What is that supposed to mean?"

"I've never asked you to put anything up," Alex said. "You do a few things and sell a little weed now and again. You don't get a vote."

I could feel my face growing flush. Brett was sitting next to me, and he could see it too. He didn't understand what was happening because he assumed the three of us did everything together like we used to do when he lived here. Now he knew that this arrangement was different. These new friendships were volatile, maybe dangerous.

"Give that kid a sucker!" Brett said with an unexpected hoot.

"What?"

"It's nothing, just something we say in West Virginia," he said. "It means the kid's a winner. He asked a good question, because I want to know too."

"I thought you just moved there," Alex said.

"I did just move back there," he said. "But I was born there. We moved to Vegas ten years ago."

I didn't know this about Brett. I always assumed he had been born here like Mick. But this new revelation made sense. Most people in Las Vegas were from somewhere else, just like I was. If America was a melting pot, Las Vegas was the double boiler. It smoothed out all the cultural differences that people hung on to in other regions. This town didn't have an identity.

"It will only cost us a few thousand," Alex finally told Brett.

He was lying and I intended to press him on it, but then Mick came back in and reached for the bag. He scooped out a healthy pile on the flat side of a toothpick and looked at Alex.

"What's this going to do to me?"

"You're not going to have a care in the world, my friend," Alex said.

Mick snorted up what was on the toothpick and then dipped it in again to get another hit for his other nostril. He had a look about him, like he was expecting an immediate rush that didn't come.

"It might take a few minutes," Alex said. "It's quicker if you smoke it or shoot it."

Mick held the bag. "Brady?"

"No," I said. "I think I could really get into a lot of trouble with something like that."

"Suit yourself."

He tossed it back to Alex, who didn't waste any time stuffing it into his pocket. I thought it was odd that he had taken a pass too. But what did I know? Maybe he had tried some earlier.

The three of us sat there and looked at Mick like expectant idiots. It never occurred to me before, maybe because I was usually wasted, but watching someone take a hit borders on voyeurism. Mick didn't have to say anything. We could see it happening. He looked more relaxed, moving in slow motion to the family room. He stretched out on the sofa, kicking his long legs up over one end. We followed him, each finding seats while the drug took hold.

"Whoa," he said. "This is something special."

His eyelids looked heavy, but he looked happy — as if a gratifying dream had come to him. He laid there for a few minutes, opening himself up to whatever he felt. His eyes closed, almost like he was nodding off, and then they would fly open again.

"Yeah," he said, sitting up and blinking. "Yeah, what do we have to do?"

Alex laughed, a hiss of satisfaction like a crossroads demon signing a contract for someone's soul. Brett took notice of it, squinting his eyes in suspicion. My expression must have betrayed my feelings, too, because Mick gave me a big self-confident smile.

"You're going to love this, Brady," he said. "This is a game changer, man."

How he said it, relaxed and self-assured, made my skin crawl. It made me wonder if people on heroin were more susceptible to suggestions because Mick was ready to hang on Alex's every word.

"Tell me everything, Alex," said Mick. "We good with the source on this? Because if we are, we'll sell the crap out of it."

Alex reassured him that the source was safe. It was the same guy who sold us some pot with little purple hairs in it a few weeks ago. The weed, called Indigo, sold faster than anything we had taken on, aside from coke. The only thing that would be different this time is that Alex's guy would introduce us to someone higher up on the chain, traffickers who had come up from Mexico.

The rub was that Alex didn't know these men. He only knew Felix, some kid who worked as a middleman. So Alex wanted some insurance, the presence of others, to show this connection that it wasn't amateur hour.

"I'm thinking two people, me and someone else, meet them in the desert as we planned," he said. "But long before the meet time, we plant three shooters around the site. Brady, Jamie, and maybe you, Mick, can do it."

"What about Will?" Mick asked.

"He'll get us what we need from his dad's shop," Alex said. "But I don't want him in on the deal outside of driving his truck up there if we need to get out. You know he doesn't have the head for it."

"Who's going to be down there with you?"

"Not you." Alex laughed. "You're too memorable, carrot top."

We all laughed. Mick wasn't someone anyone forgot, a jolly lean giant crowned with wavy red hair.

"I know someone who might be interested in making a few grand," Alex said. "But I wanted to know your thoughts before I started asking around. Have any ideas?"

"What about me?" Brett asked. "Nobody will remember me. And even if they did, I'll be gone."

"No," I said. "You don't want to do this."

"He's got a good point, Brady," Alex said and then looked at Brett. "Can you shoot?"

"I was born in West Virginia," he said. "Shooting is a class we take in grade school."

I appealed to Mick. "He doesn't need to get wrapped up in this."

"Shut up, Brady," Brett said. "I can speak for myself."

Mick shrugged as if it was decided. I should have known better than to bother Mick about it. The only thing he could feel right now was what the drug told his brain to handle. I wasn't sure what that might be, but it was something that I couldn't compete with.

"Brett, man," I tried again. "Can I talk to you a minute? Alone?"

"You're not going to change my mind," Brett said.

"Come on," I said. "Do me the favor."

We walked over to the hallway between the kitchen and the back bathroom, where I had found Jamie hiding from his dad the night before. Mick and Alex could still see us from the family room, but they couldn't hear us.

"You don't need to do this, Brett," I said. "Take a pass."

"Give me one good reason."

"Remember when Mick wanted to play football on the freshly staked church lawn?"

"Sure," he said. "He caught his ear on one of the metal stakes and ripped it open."

Mick did more than rip it open. He almost lost the entire earlobe.

"This is like that, or the time he almost shot your eye out, or the time he broke his toe jumping off the roof into the pool because the patio wasn't high enough," I said. "Mick likes to dive into everything like that — with both feet. You just saw it with the heroin."

"I don't know, Brady," he said. "It sounds like easy money for me. You guys are the ones that have to sell it after the buy."

"Right," I said. "One of the many reasons I don't even know if I want to do it."

"Now you're saying you want out too?" He considered. "What do you know that I don't?"

"Alex is what I know," I said. "I don't trust him, and neither should you. Heck, I would trust that Felix before I'd trust Alex, and I don't even know that guy. Alex is bad news."

"Why do you hang out with him then?"

"I don't," I said. "I'm stuck with him because he's Mick's friend."

"You could say the same thing about me."

"It never felt that way with you."

Brett shook me off again. "It didn't? I suppose not. But even if Alex isn't your friend, he sure the hell is your ice cream man. Nobody twisted your arm to smoke his weed, snort his coke, or take a taste of the good life he's pushing onto other kids, Brady. Nobody's twisting mine either. I could use the cash so it's none of your business."

"But it is my business," I said. "It's a business that I'm in and you're out of."

"Look, dude," Brett said. "I could use the money. My folks aren't exactly well off. A couple of grand is a down payment on a car, my ticket to a job that isn't walking distance."

"You're better off walking," I said. "Alex isn't telling us something."

"Like what?"

"I don't know yet, but I intend to find out."

"Man, I don't get you or Mick. I come back to visit because I cut out of town so quickly, and you all dump on me," he said. "Oh, we smoke a little weed now. We do a little coke. Our new best friend is a drug dealer. He cut us in on the action, but nothing too hard — except this Downtown brown mystery powder they call heroin. Give me a break. You hear me?"

"I hear you," I said. "Just say no."

"Yeah, well, I heard Alex, and he said you don't have a vote anyway," he said. "And then Mick spelled it out for you too. It's my life and my call. So stay out of it."

"I don't need a vote," I snapped. "I won't let you go down this road."

"How are you going to stop me?"

"I'll kick some sense into that head of yours," I said.

He laughed at me, so I shoved him. He pushed me back, and without knowing why, we both threw up our hands like boxers in a ring.

I turned sideways to throw an unexpected kick to his shin and Brett instinctively put both hands down to block my foot. I used the distraction to my advantage, swinging one arm around his head and putting him in a headlock. I pushed all my weight on him and wrestled him to the ground, crashing into the closet door as we fell.

"Tell them you're out." I yelled at him. "Tell them."

"Get off me!"

"Not until you tell them," I said.

He didn't have to tell them anything. Mick pulled me off him. As he did, Brett was able to throw a couple of glancing punches, knocking my glasses off. Alex was somewhere in the background laughing.

"That's enough, Brady," said Mick, holding out a hand to keep Brett back. "Freakin' hot head."

"Let go," I said. "I'm chill. I'm chill."

"Yeah? Well, maybe you need to go home and chill," said Mick. "Sometimes you're too much."

Brett was furious, pacing back and forth with his fists clenched and arms stiff. He wanted to punch something in frustration but didn't want to put a hole in the wall or break something else. I didn't blame him. I was stupid to force it. It doubled his resolve.

I fished my glasses off the floor and threw my hands up in the air. I surrendered. If Brett wanted to get mixed up in something I regretted being part of every day, then so be it.

"You know, Mick," I said. "You're not wrong."

I let the front door slam on the way out and stomped across the lawn. I didn't slow down until I cleared the oleanders that divided our front yards. My mother's car was in the driveway.

I took a breath and made a wide arch toward the house, hunching over to stay below the bushes that were meant to add an extra layer of privacy to our home. I moved around to the far side of the house, where I could access my bedroom window.

The screen popped right off because its removal was well practiced. Then I pushed against the glass and slid the window open. I always left it unlocked for this very reason. You never know when you need to get in or out of a house quick and quiet. I pulled myself in through the window, rolled onto the couch I had salvaged to use as a bed, and then reached out to pull up and put the well-worn screen back in place.

I roughed up the blanket on the couch so it looked slept on, then tousled my hair. I took in a big breath and opened the door. The lock clicked and I rushed down the short hall. My mother was sitting on the living room couch and reading a book.

"Oh, I didn't even hear you come home," I said, feigning surprise. "I must have fallen asleep."

"Yep, must have," she said.

"Where's Tab?" I asked. "She wasn't in her room when I came out."

"You don't know?"

"No, I mean, she was playing in there when you left," I said as if trying to work out a puzzle.

"Tabitha is over at Dina's house," she said before placing a bookmark in the novel she was reading. "You should know. You're the one who told her to go over there."

I felt my throat close up. She set her book down on the table.

"Is that what she told you?" I managed. "She's a funny one, that kid. She must have snuck out after I fell asleep."

"Yep, must have," she said. "Except..."

I was trying to smile like it was all a big joke but felt it wavering into a comical crooked line like comic strip characters get when they are flustered. She looked up from her seat on the couch, considering what she was going to say.

"Except what?"

"Except, I didn't have an errand to run today," she said. "No. I drove down to the corner, parked the car, unwrapped a Snickers, and waited for the show. It was a good one."

"I'm sorry," I said, sounding like a drone.

"Save it," she said. "You didn't even wait fifteen minutes before sending Tabitha over to her friend's house so you could head right on over to see Brett."

"I didn't know..."

"You didn't know what? This was a test, and you failed miserably? Yes, I'll give you that."

As the shock of being caught settled in, another emotion started to bubble up. Everything that she had done was a ruse. It was all just another trap to get me in trouble.

"But you know what, Brady?" Her lips were colorless. "I'm not even mad anymore."

Her eyes became slivers. She held her teeth together when she talked. She was enraged and doing everything she could do not to show it.

"No. I'm not mad because you gave me a great deal to think about this evening," she said. "And do you know what I think we need?"

"How many days?" The disappointment in my tone matched my expectation.

"Nothing like that, Brady," she said. "I think we need a little family time."

"What?"

"So, I hope you don't have plans tomorrow," she said, not hearing me. "We're going to take a ride up to Mount Charleston for a fresh start."

I looked at her blank faced and waiting for the catch, but she didn't say anything else. She just looked through me and at the entertainment center as if there was something other than a blank screen on the television set framed by books and knickknacks. The look told me I needed to move out of the line of fire before she changed her mind, but my feet didn't know what direction to go.

"We're going to have supper in an hour," she said. "Why don't you set the table."

Given direction, I started to move toward the kitchen. She stopped me after two steps, which was a habit of hers.

"And Brady," she said. "I don't want to talk about any of this tonight when your stepfather gets home. The games. The lies. All of it. That's in the past and I expect it to stay there."

I didn't say another word.

She picked up her book as if nothing had happened, and I walked into the kitchen. I set the table as carefully and quietly as I could and then retreated to my bedroom, where I lay on the floor and kicked my feet up on the couch.

All I could think about was Alex's concert T-shirt with Iron Maiden's Eddie pulling the strings of the devil and, when you looked closer, seeing that the devil was pulling the strings of a smaller Eddie. Except in my head at that moment, all I could think was that the smaller Eddie was me.

CHAPTER 6
MIDDAY SPECIAL

The ride was eerie, quiet and uncomfortable. My sister had stretched out across the back seat, her head propped against the door and her feet pressing into my leg. Anytime I pushed back, she would give me a little kick and then press harder.

Appealing to the adults in the front of the car was pointless. I already knew how that would play out. It was always the same on a million car rides.

"Hey, Tab is kicking me," I might say.

"So move over," my mother would say.

"Move over? I'm lucky to have one-tenth of the seat back here."

"Oh, come on, Brady. She's a little girl."

"She's hogging the whole thing!"

"Your sister is trying to sleep," George would chime in. "Quit yelling!"

The better play was to suck it up and count down the minutes. It took somewhere around ninety minutes to drive up the mountain. There were few worse things than sitting in silence and pressing myself against a car door as it rumbled across the desert and then up a mountain, sage giving way to yuccas giving way to Joshua trees giving way to bristlecone pines.

My mom would break the silence on occasion, saying something to George that was lost to me in the howl of the wind, windows cracked to let the cigarette smoke roll out down the road. They were both smokers, taking turns to crush spent butts into an overflowing console ashtray.

You learn to let it all go after a while, looking for a daydream to lose yourself. It would all be over soon enough. I've endured worse for longer.

It hadn't always been this way. My indoctrination into the family was served up as a summer vacation, except nobody told me there wasn't an end date. My grandmother was losing her battle with cancer, and presenting a permanent move as a summer vacation seemed like an easier transition for me when I was ten.

My grandmother died a little more than a year later. After fighting cancer for the better part of ten years, they said she gave up when she didn't have any more kids to raise. I was the last one, as they reminded me on occasion. When it became clear I wasn't coming home again, it broke her will to live, if not her heart. My fault.

They told me she died when I came home from school. I walked in the door, and they hit me with the news. I hadn't taken my coat off yet. I didn't want to believe them, so I turned around and headed outside to play football in the freshly fallen snow.

My friends had made plans to play during the bus ride home, but now it was just an excuse to do something physical instead of mental. So I didn't let my friends down. We won. I didn't know she would give up because she thought I had given up on her. I was lost.

It was shortly after my grandmother's death that things started to change. My mom became more critical. She didn't like the way I dusted or dried dishes. She didn't like how much time I spent watching television or drawing pictures. She didn't like the way I wore my hair or the clothes I asked her to buy. She didn't like the way I shut down when she scolded me. She didn't like how emotional I became when she broke me.

Almost everything I did or didn't do became grounds for another punishment. Sometimes I was sent to my room for days. Sometimes I would be given the silent treatment for weeks. Sometimes she would just yell, telling me that I was damaged goods. My grandmother spoiled me. My real dad gave me an ugly disposition. I looked just like him.

He was an artist too, she said. And he committed suicide. If I ever wanted to try it, there was a right and wrong way.

"Cut your wrists vertically," she told me, drawing three lines down her wrist with her opposite hand. "It's not as easy to stitch the veins back together. Anything else is for attention."

There did come the point in Cleveland when I had enough. I told her I couldn't live with them anymore — these strangers who had taken me in before my grandmother died. She said that would be a problem because nobody else in the family wanted me. I was too much trouble. I had too many issues. There was something wrong with me.

So they took me to a psychologist to figure out what it was. Three sessions in and I told the therapist what I thought the actual problem might be. I couldn't be loved because I was unlovable. She looked at me for a few minutes and then called my mother into the room.

"I think we should consider family counseling instead," the therapist said.

The revelation upset everyone — this idea that they would all have to talk to a therapist. And then, my mother wanted to know what lies I told the therapist. I wouldn't tell her. So, in a show of genuine solidarity, I declared the therapist didn't know what she was doing, and I didn't want to go back again. And just like that, I was the planet's most loved son for a few days.

From that time forward, I did my best to navigate the waters. Some days I got in trouble for what I didn't do, like not putting the garbage out for trash pickup. Some days I got in trouble for what I did do, like putting the garbage out for trash pickup but not the right way. It didn't matter. I rolled with it.

I rolled with it, just like I was doing right now until the car came to a stop. I must have been in a half-trance because I didn't realize we had reached our destination. I looked outside the window and felt disoriented. We hadn't arrived at the lodge as I expected.

"Okay, Brady," my mom said. "Let's get out."

"We're here?" Tab asked.

"No, not yet," she said. "I wanted to show something to Brady first."

"What is it?"

"Get out and talk to her," George said. "It will be all right."

I opened my door and got out. My mother motioned for me to come along. I did as I was told and joined her a few feet in front of the car.

"This is the Spring Mountain Youth Camp," she said, smiling. "They have everything here. Baseball, football, wrestling, track and field, you name it."

"That's nice," I said. I didn't know what else to say.

"Didn't you used to go to camps when you lived with your grandmother?"

"Yes, sometimes," I said. "I went to a few, day camps, week camps, and there was Boy Scouts. Oh, this one time, they took us out on a snipe hunt in the dead of night. We lit the woods with flashlights and made noises to save the snipe. The only thing you had to be careful of is these things called tinglers. They ..."

"Right, Boy Scouts," she said, cutting me off with a wave of her hand. "This camp isn't for Boy Scouts."

I frowned, not understanding.

"This is a camp for teenage boys like you with, um, problems," she said. "Some of them are here because they have drug problems."

"Oh, I don't have a drug problem," I said with a little laugh. "Don't worry about that."

"Some of them are here because they committed crimes, like robbing a store," she said, pausing for effect. "And some of them are here for raping other boys. How does that sound?"

"Not too good," I said.

"Not too good," she muttered. "I know what you're thinking, Brady. What crazy idea does this nasty old hag got into her head this time."

I wasn't thinking anything. I had no idea where she was going with it.

"Do you want to stay here?"

The tone of her voice was laced with sugar, like she was holding out for a trip to Disneyland. I studied her expression. She was smiling. There was a gleam in her eye behind the glasses.

"Do you?"

"What?" I shook my head. "No."

"No," she said, echoing my response with a hint of surprise. "The camp lasts six months with no outside contact. You will be taught independent living skills since nobody has taught you, although we both know I've tried. You will attend school and be given daily chores, with higher standards than I have, I'm sure. You'll have your own counselor to help you sort things out, since you won't believe me. And then, when you are done, you'll have a juvenile record that law enforcement can follow up on every few weeks to see how you are doing or if you need another stay up on the mountain, away from people who can live in society."

"I haven't done anything wrong," I said, looking down.

"You have if I say you have, young man," she said. "All it takes is a phone call. Wait, what? Are you crying?"

I was crying. Nobody could hear it, but my face was tight and hot. The tears were running down my cheeks. I pawed them away with one hand and tried to pull myself together.

"Oh, poor Brady," she said. "Don't you worry your little head."

I sniffled.

"We're not leaving you here today," she said. "But the next time we drive up this mountain, we will leave you here. Do you understand?"

"Yes," I said.

"I didn't hear you," she said.

"Yes, ma'am," I said.

"No more lies, Brady. I mean it," she said.

"Okay," I said.

"Now, give me a hug. You look like you could use one."

I could have used a bullet in my brain, but I knew the play. I leaned in and let her put her arms around me. She made some sort of strange cooing sound and rocked us back and forth.

"There you go," she said, pushing me away. "All better. Now let's get some lunch."

I didn't eat anything at the lodge. I couldn't. I stood outside on the deck adjacent to the dining room instead, one of the few places the German oompah band's incessant accordion-driven, tuba-laced rendition of "Roll Out The Barrel" was dampened by the lodge's thick, triangular alpine glass window.

I leaned out over the redwood rail and took in the gentle slopes of the tree-lined mountains and contrasting cliffs that framed deep, narrow canyons. The cool air and pull of freedom were as intoxicating as the droll of the band inside the packed dining room was oppressive.

What difference would it make if they abandoned me at the camp? I was a prisoner anyway, trapped in an endless series of teases, snares, and punishments because I was incapable of making any good decisions and that's where I belonged. Go figure. Bad kids go to bad places. Maybe I did deserve it.

Or maybe I just needed to get out.

Funny how your entire life can be turned upside down in a matter of days or weeks or months. When I lived with my grandmother, I used to daydream about being part of a regular family, living with and loved by my mother. Now all I could think about was escaping the pain of it, daily reminders that I was living with a regular family but didn't belong to one.

"We already had a family before you," she told me. "You have to earn a place in it."

I didn't know how to earn it. The goal line kept changing. It was so much easier to roll the dice on the outside. If Alex was right, one roll would change my life — all of our lives — forever.

I had to give the kid that. His goal lines never changed. You did the deal and got paid for it. So what if he didn't respect me. So what if it didn't feel safe. So what if I didn't trust him. There wasn't anyone I could trust anyway.

This was the part of the equation I didn't mention to Brett. It was true that I didn't want to lose Mick as a best friend, but it was also true that I played along because I could count on Alex to be Alex. I didn't like him, but I didn't have to like him.

On the ride down the mountain, I kept running the numbers in my head. How much of the total pie might be mine? If Alex scored two hundred thousand in heroin for forty or fifty thousand, then ten or twenty might be coming my way. No, not all at once. It would take a few months to move it with three of us selling it, unless he added Jamie to the equation.

I kept thinking and shrinking, disappearing in the ever-diminishing piece of back seat that Tabitha didn't claim.

"You're awfully quiet," she said when we got out of the car. "Anything wrong?"

Who was she trying to fool? We had just taken a five-hour road trip for the sole purpose of showing me her new scorched earth policy. Everything was wrong. I mean, sure, on the one hand, I deserved it because I was doing bad things. But on the other hand, I didn't because we didn't drive up the mountain after she discovered I might start dealing heroin. She asked George to drive us up because she set me up the day before and caught me leaving the house.

"No, everything's fine," I said. "I'm a bit stiff from the ride. I think I'll take a walk."

"Suit yourself," she said. "But don't forget I'm here for you if you need to talk."

"Yeah, of course," I said and started walking.

My first thought was that I would walk all the way up to Red Rock Canyon and climb around on the sandstone. I had been up there so many times with family and friends, I knew the area well enough — a few secret spots that were quiet, almost meditative.

After a couple of blocks, I knew I wouldn't make two miles, let alone the twelve it would take to make it to the overlook. I could cut the miles in half by climbing in a back way through Calico Basin, but that wouldn't work. It was hot, and I hadn't eaten lunch at the lodge. So my less ambitious quest was to pick up a personal pan pizza and Coke at Shakey's Pizza.

My plans changed again when I turned on to Charleston. Cheryl didn't live that far, and it would be nice to see someone who didn't make calling out my many deficiencies a full-time sport.

When I got there, I knocked three times to lighten my mood, conjuring up an old song by Tony Orlando from simpler times. Through the curtained glass, I could see the shadow of someone coming to the door, but they didn't open it before disappearing again. I waited a few more minutes anyway. The door opened. Cheryl was surprised but not unhappy to see me.

"Brady, what are you doing here?" She pushed her way out, pulling the door behind her.

"Bad timing?"

"No, but my dad's home," she said. "What's happening?"

She was wearing a Fleetwood Mac *Rumours* tank top and denim cutoffs. Her hair was pulled back into a loose ponytail, but I was drawn to her eyes. She was wearing a light blue eye shadow that complemented her light brown, almost amber, eyes.

"Nothing," I said. "I was going to get some pizza and dropped by to see if you wanted to go."

"You dork," she said. "You passed it coming up here."

"Guilty as charged."

"All right, I'll go with you, but not to Shakey's. Let me get my keys."

79

We drove down Charleston to Carbone's Pizza Shack. It was a family-owned place that served up the best thin crust slices on our side of town, even if its saggy, sunbaked wooden roof scared some people away in the heat of summer. The rest of us knew better. Carbone's was a local landmark of sorts, much like the Farm Basket a couple of lots over.

We didn't go in. Cheryl pulled up to a pickup window and asked if there were any mistakes.

"I used to work here," she told me.

The way the guy looked at her when he passed out a large pizza told me she did more than work here. He was twenty-something with a mustache, afternoon shadow, and dark wavy hair tied up with a red bandanna. He flexed when he leaned down to hand her the pizza, his red bandanna falling down around his neck and drawing attention to his shirt, which was unbuttoned one hole too low for the job. He gave her a wink.

"Old flame?"

"As if it's any of your business," she said and then laughed. "That obvious?"

He wasn't the only one with tells. Cheryl had pushed her chest up and opened her legs wider while taking the pie from him. Maybe it was subconscious. Maybe not. Either way, the exchange reminded me that I was still a year away from getting my driver's permit.

"You could say so," I said, laughing along with her, so I was in on the joke. "Oh, thank you, Dean. You're such a stud."

"Hey, I never said stud. I said lifesaver."

"Your body begs to differ," I said. "So who made who cry?"

"Who's driving away with a free pie?"

It was all good fun, but I couldn't help but notice that she was blushing. I had to wonder if I was embarrassing her or if she was just embarrassed.

"Yeah, about that," I said. "Why didn't we eat in?"

"It's bad manners to eat a stolen pizza in front of your former employers," she said, emphasizing an unspoken duh. "Besides, I have a better idea."

Her idea was to drive to the northwest edge of our dusty town, where we could see the entire valley from a higher elevation. Up here, the paradox was apparent. It was the ugliest city in the world during the day and one of the prettiest at night.

"I like to come here and watch the lights turn on at dusk," she said. "In a few hours, we'll forget this is a dust bowl and lose ourselves in a million twinkling lights."

Downtown, confined to a couple of blocks like most cities, would start to electrify the sky as soon as the sun touched the top edge of the mountains to the west. The legendary Strip would follow, hotel casinos blinking on in a crooked line that started somewhere near the center of town and stretched southward for miles.

Following their lead, the patchwork of suburban sprawl would light up the desert in an amber glow, bleeding out from two major highways; four trails of red and white lights that connected Salt Lake City to Los Angeles and Reno to Phoenix.

From here, it was almost hard to imagine thousands of people crammed into casinos, quarters clanking in slot machine trays, and lively hoots of excitement on the craps tables.

"There are so many lights on every street," I said. "It blots out the stars. I miss seeing them."

"I don't know; I like to think of the lights as a sea of flickering stars, and I'm standing above them all," she said. "But hey, if you miss seeing stars, maybe one day we'll drive north for an hour, and you'll see every last one of them."

I didn't say anything. I was stuck on the idea that there would be a next time while she opened the box.

"They didn't cut it!"

"So much for latent love," I said, looking down at the large pie. "Cheese and mushrooms?"

"Yeah," she said. "It's a mistake, remember?"

We somehow managed to lift the pizza up, each of us using both hands to create four corners and then biting the section between them. Every time we took a bite, there wasn't anywhere to look other than at each other, eyes locked in an awkward knowing silence until she would laugh, pulling back with a string of mozzarella trailing from the pizza and landing on her chin.

"Oh, hold on, I have to get that," she said, using her left hand to sweep the strand into her mouth while the pizza buckled.

"Whoa, don't lose it!"

She laughed again as she overcorrected, tilting the pizza toward me before putting her hand back for support.

"Don't worry, don't worry," she said. "I've handled plenty of pizzas."

"Oh right, a professional. I forgot."

"Mmmmm. It's all about balance. But the secret is in the sauce."

"So why did you quit?"

"Ha. Isn't it obvious?"

"Oh, you quit because of Dean."

"Dean ... Tommy ... Michael," she said. "Too many old flames in one place. You know."

I didn't say anything.

"Wait, am I embarrassing you?"

"No, no," I said, rolling my eyes for effect.

"The operative word is old flames," she said. "Too many guys who won't give up and try to out macho, macho man the other one. You know what I mean?"

I had no idea, but I nodded in agreement. I was too busy noticing that our faces were inching closer every time we took a bite.

"Anyway, it's not like I slept with them all. And I had other reasons to move on too."

"College?"

"Yeah," she said. "But more than that, graduation was like closing a chapter and Carbone's was part of it. If you don't get it, you will soon enough."

"Yeah, sure. I mean, I get it. It's like when my family moved here from Cleveland. We closed the chapter. A few family members came out to visit right after, the allure of Vegas and all, but then my folks seemed to break it off with everybody."

"Really? So you don't have any contact with your family anymore?"

I could see this wasn't what she meant at all. Of course she didn't.

"Not really," I said. "My mom stays in touch with her family. My stepdad stays in touch with his family. But they've always been standoffish to their parents and siblings. They're the black sheep of their families, they like to say."

"Sort of what I mean, I guess. But it's a bit extreme to close a chapter on family, I think."

She was frowning a little. I had to roll it back.

"It wasn't always that way," I said. "I lived with my grandmother for most of my life. She was the center of the family. My stepdad is a bit different. I think they're still getting used to the idea."

"Used to what idea?"

"I'm newly acquired but not adopted. I didn't want to be adopted."

"No?"

"It felt like cutting ties with my father's side."

"Oh, where's he?"

"He died when I was younger," I said, fudging the suicide. "Car accident."

"I'm sorry," she said. "And his parents?"

"I don't know. They used to send me gifts and letters, but I haven't heard from them since we moved here," I said, trying to shrug it off. "Same with everybody, I guess. They all have different reasons."

"Huh. I can see you're a real enigma, Brady."

"What's that supposed to mean?"

"Nothing, just that you have many layers," she said. "I'm a bit more straightforward."

"How's that?"

"I'm just a girl trying to figure out how to make it in this world," she said.

"I thought you had it figured out."

"I have my next step figured out, but not the rest of it. I don't know what I'm going to study in school."

"Well, what do you like?"

"I like literature," she said. "Not many reading jobs out there."

"Literature? I would never imagine it. What's your favorite book?"

"Too many," she said, trying to pick one. "*Great Expectations*."

"I haven't read that."

"It's the story about a young man who falls for a beautiful girl, but he thinks she's too good for him," she said. "But then he comes into money. He thinks his mysterious benefactor might be the girl's adopted mother, helping him elevate his social standing so he can marry her."

"Does he get her?"

"No," she said. "When he asks the mother, Miss Havisham, she tells him that he was only meant to be a boy for the girl to practice on as she became a lady."

"Who was the benefactor?"

"Hush," she said, squinting her eyes at me. "Too many spoilers. Read the book."

"Promise."

There were only two or three bites left of the pizza, but I could already imagine the last one when our lips would touch. This time, unlike our first kiss on the lawn, I was ready.

"Close your eyes," she whispered.

"All right."

This was it, my heart pounding in anticipation. I could feel her breath on my face. And then, she pushed the last three bites into my mouth, which was hungrier for her lips than extra cheese and mushrooms. She squealed as I almost choked.

"I'm so sorry," she said. "I couldn't resist."

"Yeah." I managed, my mouth too overstuffed to say more than one syllable at a time. "Fun-ny."

She apologized between laughs as I attempted to chew it, forcing the excess into my cheeks like a chipmunk. I think I was six the last time I had done anything like that, stuffing a Big Mac in my mouth so I could get a second one free after reciting the ingredients. Two all-beef patties, special sauce, lettuce, cheese, pickles, onions on a sesame seed bun.

"Oh, Brady," she laughed again. "Don't be mad at me."

"I can't be mad at you," I said, noticing some sauce on the corner of her mouth. "Hold still."

"What?"

I reached over and wiped it away with my thumb, holding it up to show her. She had stopped laughing, but she was still smiling as if she was considering something she hadn't considered before. I couldn't put my finger on it.

"Come on, it's almost time," she said, punching me in the arm and then bailing out of the car.

It was already cooler with the sun sinking down behind the mountains to the west, so we positioned ourselves on the hood. At first, we were side by side, but as the casino lights started winking on Downtown, she reached over, put her right hand in mine, and moved over, so she was leaning against me instead of the car.

Neither one of us said anything. We were locked in the moment. Two people on the fringe of nowhere, watching a city come to life while most other cities were drifting off to sleep. I could see what she meant now, daydreaming that all these little lights were flickering stars, and we were somehow standing above them all.

For the first time in a long time, I felt safe. The trauma of earlier events was drifting further and further away. I could have stayed like this with her for hours, but then she guided my hands to her breasts.

I inhaled, aroused and unsure of what to do. So I gave them a little squeeze. But as soon as I did, I knew it was the wrong thing. She pulled my hands down and pushed herself out of my embrace. I was going to apologize, but she beat me in finding the next words.

"There's a party tomorrow at the top of Ann Road," she said. "Do you want to go?"

"Yeah, sure," I said.

"Good," she said. "Let me take you home."

We didn't talk as much on the way back. Both of us were processing our last few hours together. There was no mistaking the chemistry between us. All I had to do was figure out how to keep my age in check. I was acting like some dumb kid, and it was driving me crazy.

It didn't make sense. I had been with other girls before, but this one felt so much more real for whatever reason. Cheryl wasn't a drunk or drug hookup. She was someone interested in me, and I was interested in her, which is why I was struggling to be the bad boy she had met a couple of nights before.

We said goodnight but didn't kiss when she dropped me off. We settled for a shared look that confirmed we were on the same page, even if neither of us knew what page that might be. So as I shut the door, I reinforced that I would see her tomorrow. She waved as it closed, driving off as soon as she was sure I was clear.

CHAPTER 7

DRAGGING LINE

Mick's ride was a 1967 Buick wagon. It was light tan, a color we called baby crap brown. What it lacked in style, it made up for in power and room. It had a 3-speed V8, controlled by a paddle shifter on the steering wheel that Mick could operate with his thumb. There were three rows of seats, with the third used for lying low.

I never needed to call shotgun because Alex almost always took the third-row bench seat. He didn't like being noticed and often took to rolling joints in the back unless the roads were bumpy.

Jamie sat in the second row. As the new kid on the block, it was understood he had to cede shotgun to me, even if he sensed the pecking order might change someday. He got along better with Alex than I did.

Jamie was also the one who woke me up that morning, knocking on my bedroom window. I looked over at the clock. It was a little after eight in the morning, bright and early after my binge on Saturday night.

"Come on, man," he said. "We're going down to the gun store."

"Isn't it closed on Sunday?" I asked, rubbing the sleep out of my eyes.

"That's the point," he said. "Will lifted the keys from his dad so we could do some recon."

"I'll be right there," I said, sliding the window shut and grabbing a shirt off the floor.

Most mornings I shower before heading out, but I didn't bother that day because they were in a rush. I stopped in the bathroom long enough to relieve myself and rub a dab of toothpaste across my teeth.

It took five minutes, but Alex looked at me like I had taken thirty. At least he was looking at me. Brett wouldn't look in my direction.

"Took you long enough," Alex said.

"I didn't know we were going today," I said, shrugging.

"You would have if you dropped by last night," he said. "Where were you?"

"Yeah, where were you?" Jamie asked, parroting to be a pest.

"I have one mom, and that's enough," I said. "No need to be mental in the morning. Wait until the afternoon."

"Lame," Alex spat.

"He was out somewhere with Denise's friend Cheryl," Mick said.

My mouth gaped. There was no way he could know.

"Oooh la la," Jamie sang. "Skinny got a girlfriend."

He was sitting behind Mick, which gave me a good angle to glower at him. It didn't go unnoticed. Mick saw my reaction out of the corner of his eye.

"No big deal," said Mick. "I was taking the trash to the curb when she pulled away last night."

"Out of your league, kid," Alex said, laughing through his teeth. "Does she know you're fourteen?"

"It's not like that," I said. "And I'll be fifteen soon enough."

Everybody in the back was laughing now. Jamie added hoots for effect.

"No big deal," Mick said again, dismissing it as a dead subject.

"Whatever," Alex said from the back.

The gun store was about fifteen minutes from our block, tucked into one of the dozen strip malls that lined many major streets running west to east across the city, most of them named after the casinos they passed by — Sahara, Desert Inn, Flamingo, Tropicana. They doubled as advertisements, reminding everyone who owned the town, or used to own it, given the tug o'war between the Mob and corporations.

This wasn't the first time we visited the store when it was closed. Will's dad believes in God as much as guns, putting his faith first on Sunday. I was raised the same before moving in with my mother. Now, church was optional in the new household, which meant we didn't go. She had it in her head that it was for weak people and losers who needed faith in something besides themselves. "Grow up," she used to tell me.

The first time Will lifted the keys off his dad's dresser was innocent enough. Mick and I had set up a target in his backyard, and we were taking turns shooting his pellet gun. We must have been getting pretty loud because Will poked his head over and asked if we wanted to shoot something better than a BB gun.

Twenty minutes later, we were at the store sorting through a few dozen guns that weren't on display in the front. Will said his dad wouldn't miss one or two because they weren't part of the inventory. If they weren't burners now, they might be someday.

We picked a .38 Special and antique M1 Garand rifle that Will said was used during World War II and the Korean War. We took both and drove out behind Lone Mountain, a small isolated butte in the middle of nowhere. We spent most of the afternoon shooting up an abandoned refrigerator and a few unfortunate cacti.

We did this with Will a few times, Brett joining us once before he moved. Alex changed the game when he wanted what he called a showpiece gun, something to brandish when he met up with a supplier or, more often, provoke a debtor. He never wanted a .38 Special, which he said was a narc gun if there ever was one.

He usually begged to borrow a .44 Magnum as a flashy nod to Dirty Harry, but not today. It was one of the few guns Will never let anyone borrow from the front of the store, but that was because Alex promised he would never use it. This time, Alex wanted a burner gun, a black Beretta M9. He suggested Brett go with a Walther PPK.

He told the rest of us to look at rifles. When I said I'd stick with the Garand, since that's what I shot most often, Alex argued for me to pick a gun with more capacity and without that annoying "ping" the clip made when it was spent. I told him I wasn't worried about the ping since I'd be using it like an actor with a prop.

As I passed, Jamie jumped all in. He said he wanted a Gatling gun like they used in the old mobster movies and television shows. He'd take the M16 since I wouldn't.

"Rat-ta-tat-tat," spit Jamie as much as he said it. "Aww, sookie sookie now. Hey!"

"You're not going to find a Tommy gun in here, and the M16 is too much gun for you," Will said, taking it out of his hands. "Have you ever held a gun before?"

"No," he said. "Is that a problem?"

"You'd be better off with a Remington, I think," he said. "It's newer but has a low recoil, not that you'll need to worry about that."

"All right," Jamie said. "How many shots? Fifty? A hundred?"

"Ten in the clip," Will said. "More than enough for you."

Mick said he would take an older Weatherby Mark V, deflecting Jamie's obvious disappointment. It was a curious choice, and Will picked up on it too.

"That's a downrange hunting rifle," Will said. "I thought these were for show."

"This one is more precautionary," Mick shrugged. "I'll be further back and out of sight."

I looked at him, wondering what he meant by that. Everything was supposed to play out like it always had, except Alex had said a bigger deal meant looking like a bigger operation. It's difficult to be a bigger deal or deterrent if you're hiding behind a hill.

"I thought your guy Felix knew these guys," I said. "We don't expect trouble, do we?"

"If there is going to be any trouble, I can't let you take any of these," said Will. "My dad would freak out."

"Relax, Will. There isn't going to be any trouble," Alex said. He was trying to sound cool while glaring at me. "Aren't these off the books anyway?"

"The handguns, sure, but the rifles aren't. They're just not for sale," said Will. "And even if they were off the books, burners don't work that way. Nobody wants to carry a gun connected to another crime unless it's a one-time carry, one-time use piece."

"There isn't going to be a crime," said Mick. "It's just a transaction."

"It's a drug deal. Pretty sure it's a crime," I said. I don't know why I said it. It fell flat, sucking the energy out of the air.

Brett was looking at the weapon Alex picked out for him. He was holding it sideways like they sometimes do in the movies. My bad feeling was coming back again.

"Why does your dad have burners anyway?" Brett asked. It felt like the right question at the wrong time.

"This is Vegas," Will said. "You can't own a gun store without them."

"Wouldn't the police get wise to it?"

"They're probably among his dad's best customers," Alex said. "Isn't that right, Jamie? You know what I'm talking about it."

"What is that supposed to mean?"

"Joke, brother," Alex said. "Man, everybody is so uptight today."

"Yeah, let's all put a lid on it. We know what we want," Mick said. "We need you to deliver, Will. Your cut will be five grand, in installments. That's for bringing the guns out and giving Brady and Jamie a ride home when it's over."

This part of the plan was new to me too. Nobody ever said anything about catching a ride home with Will.

"Since when?" I asked. "Why wouldn't I ride with you?"

"Lamer," Alex said. "What will these guys think if everybody starts pouring over some hill and loading up into Mick's car? You're so stupid sometimes, Brady. Let the adults work it out. Mick, I don't know why you bother with him."

I was still holding the Garand in my hand. If there was a clip on the table, I would have picked it up and pressed it into the chamber. Somebody needed to put him down.

"We don't know when and where the meetup will be, but Alex is right. We need three rides," he said. "But I'm done talking about it. It's giving me a headache. Alex, I hope you rolled a joint on the way over because everybody needs to chill out."

Alex did roll a joint on the way over and lit it up before we left the parking lot. Then we cruised around, passing it back and forth between the four of us while Brett leaned his head toward the passenger window. He had rolled it down, letting the heat in along with the breeze.

"I hope smokey bear don't pick up the scent," Alex said, adding a southern twang. "This here car has a honey bar."

Alex had been couching criticisms in bad jokes as soon as Brett expressed silent disapproval that we were smoking pot in a place he couldn't escape. Under other circumstances, he had resigned himself to not caring whether Mick or I smoked, but this was his first time confined in the car with four desperados, replaying lines from every stoner movie we ever saw.

"Hey man, how am I driving?" Mick asked with a laugh.

"Pretty good for a red light, man," Alex said from the back.

All of us laughed. Even Brett laughed, shaking his head in surrender or maybe it was a contact high.

"Single, stoned, and stupid is no way to go through life, boys," he said, embellishing a line from his favorite movie, *Animal House.*

When it was like this — five guys reliving little bits of movie magic — it was easy to forget how lousy the rest of reality could be. There weren't any threats of juvenile detention camps. Nobody was thinking of throwing a punch. The little brick layers inside us, who spent all their time building barriers over the course of our lives, were on break.

The world was perfect until Jamie tried to bypass me and hand Mick the second joint while he was driving. It was too short to pass, and Mick burned his fingers while reaching back to take it. It flipped over the seat and fell into his lap, singeing the hair on his legs. He scrambled for it, trying to knock it off onto the floor so it didn't burn him. I moved to help him too, leaning over to find it.

"Drive, man, drive!" Jamie yelled from the back.

I lifted my head up, looking first at Jamie, whose hands were pressed against the sides of an elongating face, eyes big and wide, mouth agape in preparation for a scream. Then I looked out the window as the car careened over the curb to avoid the vehicle in front of us. Mick stomped on the brakes, and we all lurched forward. Two more inches, and we would have been embedded in the light pole.

"I got it," I said, reaching down and picking it up while everyone else caught their breath. I smiled with a little sense of triumph until Alex brought me back to earth.

"You idiot," he said to me. "Why didn't you grab the wheel?"

"What?"

"All you had to do is grab the wheel while Mick grabbed the joint," he said. "And why was Jamie handing him the joint anyway? He should have passed it to you."

"I don't know." I looked at Jamie.

"Don't look at me," Jamie said, throwing me under the bus. "It didn't look like you wanted it,"

"What are you talking about?"

"You should have taken the joint, Brady," Jamie said, cool and aloof.

"You know what? I don't need this crap," I said, opening the door. "I'm out."

"Brady," Mick called after me. "Come on, man, get back in the car."

"I'll get back in when those punks get out," I said. "Otherwise, I'm walking home."

"Man, we all know it wasn't your fault," Brett added.

"Bye," I said and flipped Alex off. He flipped me off, too, amused but not angry like I was.

"Suit yourself," Mick finally said, giving up. "Come over whenever you get home."

"Yeah, maybe I got plans."

Mick backed off the curb and slowly pulled away, giving me time to reconsider. I didn't. So he tore away down the road as if nothing had happened. We were lucky nothing more did happen. But instead of being grateful, Alex had to find some way to pin it on me, as if it was my fault, always my fault.

He wasn't alone in thinking so. My mother told me the same thing every day. If the bathroom I shared with my sister was dirty, my fault. If there was a ring on the coffee table, it was my fault. If my mother and George got into a fight, it was my fault. If we got caught having a party because I let Jamie's dad in the house, my fault. If Mick crashed his car, it was my fault. It was my fault I was walking home alone again. It was reflexive. For me. For everybody. So what?

I didn't care anymore. Let it be my fault. It was easier than letting it become something else. It was easier than being told it was all in your head or that nobody was blaming you when it was clear everybody was blaming you.

The last school clothes shopping spree was like that. My mother was digging in her purse for her keys, trying to remember where she had parked the car. I was carrying all the bags and boxes of clothes, both arms full. My sister was skipping along between us.

Tab saw our car first and started running toward it, jumping out without looking both ways. I somehow managed to grab her hand and yank her back, boxes and bags being dropped in the process, but not before the squeal of tires cut through the afternoon air and an older woman, with salt and pepper hair like my grandmother once had, yelled out to be more careful.

My mother said she was sorry and then turned to face me. I thought she would thank me for saving my sister, so I smiled a little, trying to convey that I understood what a close call it was. She slapped me instead.

"Why weren't you watching your sister? She could have been run over," she said.

My face was hot. She struck the smile right off it. My eyes welled up, but I kept my composure and bent over to retrieve the packages, which were mostly my sister's clothes anyway.

"My arms were full," I said to the sidewalk. "I didn't see ..."

"Stop making excuses," she said. "We both know it was your fault. You just better hope nothing is damaged."

Later that evening, she brought it up at the dinner table for George's benefit. When I complained my arms were full, she brushed me off and said nobody was blaming me.

I never went clothes shopping with her again. Instead, I resigned myself to wearing whatever generic clothes she brought home after guesstimating my size. What did I care? It wasn't like she would grab anything off the rack from wherever my friends shopped. My sister might have enjoyed trendy stores, but I was limited to Sears and J.C. Penney, which was still a step up from the hand-me-downs my grandparents had arranged in Ohio. But that was a given. They were poorer than my parents.

I didn't care. After selling for Alex, I could buy my own clothes. Sometimes Mick and I went to the mall and shopped for hours since money wasn't a problem. Neither were the girls who were out of our league. We tried to flirt with them anyway, being bad boys and all.

Sometimes they would talk to us if they wanted a Coke or something. Most of the time we wandered around, eventually migrating over to Spencer Gifts. We would spend an hour or so in there, laughing at all the stupid stuff they stocked: a mug with a lime on it that said "Suck It," choker collar necklaces with pentagrams, fart machines, and plastic poop.

We were always tempted to buy some of it but stuck to the band T-shirts if we bought anything. Then it was just a matter of sneaking one or two into the wash at a time so my mother didn't notice. If she did notice, I always told her Mick gave it to me or it was bought with lawn-mowing money.

"Hey, mind helping us with some directions?"

I was so lost in my thoughts that I hadn't seen the car pull up beside me. I looked over. There were two older guys in a black and gold 1978 Oldsmobile Cutlass. The guy asking me was older. His skin was wrinkled by age and too much sun, hair pushed back, and unembarrassed by where his hairline started.

I couldn't get a good look at the driver but, like the older guy, he wore a button-down shirt over a white tee. His eyes were unseen behind sunglasses. I could see their sports jackets laid flat in the back seat, which is how people in Vegas minimized creases in the heat. Nobody drove around wearing a coat in the summer.

I looked up and around for the first time. I hadn't been paying attention to where I was walking. I had just been walking. I was still walking now, the car trolling alongside me.

"So is this the part where I tell you that I don't talk to strangers?"

He chuckled and gave his partner a playful shove. "Tommy, get a load of this kid," he said. Then he turned back to me. "What? Are you ten? Come on, help a guy out."

"You can't really get lost in Las Vegas," I said. "All the casino streets run east and west. Drive until you run into one of those and you'll find your way."

"Nah, this ain't that easy," he said. "I'm looking for someone's house. Maybe you know him."

"I doubt it."

"What's the name, Tommy?"

"Brady. Brady Wilks," he said.

"Yeah, that's it," he said, taking a toothpick out of his mouth. "You know Brady Wilks?"

Hearing my name come out of his mouth stopped me in my tracks. I instinctively reached my right hand to my back pocket, looking for the knife I sometimes carry. It wasn't there. I was too quick when I rushed out of the house.

Whatever good feelings had dulled my senses earlier had gone, wiped away by one micro trauma after the next. My heart was pounding as my head exploded with scenarios, figuring out what to do. I could run or fight off every instinct in my body and try to play it cool.

"Never heard of him," I said.

He smiled and looked down, head shaking. Then he pointed at me with his toothpick.

"Hey kid, do you know why I have this stupid toothpick hanging out of my mouth?"

I shook my head.

"I'm trying to quit smoking," he said. "At my age, it's no good for me anymore."

I looked at him dumbly. I didn't get it.

"You might want to find something like a toothpick, too," he said. "Maybe then you can quit with the lying. Because those, those lies, I can guarantee they aren't good for you at your age."

My head was screaming to run, but my feet were anchored. They already knew that running wouldn't do me any good.

"We already know who you are," he said, smile gone. "So relax before you pee yourself. You're not in any trouble."

"What do you want?"

"You're friends with Andrea Bigelow, right?"

"I wouldn't say friends, exactly," I said. "I know her, sure."

"Not friends, eh? Well, she thinks differently, which is good for you."

"Yeah?"

"It seems Miss Bigelow almost had her purse stolen by some tools, and you, I'm told, though I can't imagine it, no offense, got it back for her," he said. "Her dad, Mr. Bigelow, appreciates your kindness to his daughter and asked me to give you something."

"What's that," I said, trying and failing to relax.

"Well, it's a funny thing, you see. Sometimes when certain guys drink at a bar in this town, they might buy a round or two or whatever. So, the other guy, the one getting the drink for free, might give him a marker — a token of appreciation for, like, buying a drink," he said, hands waving in the air like he was conducting an orchestra. "So, let's say they go to a bar another time, and the guy with the marker is running a little short on cash. All he has to do is put the marker on the bar, and he won't pay for drinks for the rest of the evening. Pretty darn cool, if you ask me."

"I don't follow you," I said.

He flipped a silver coin to me. It was about the size of a silver dollar, but it wasn't American.

"Mr. Brady Wilks," he said, drawing his words out as if I might not understand him. "Mr. Bigelow asked me to tell you that the next round is on him."

I didn't say anything. All I could do was look at him with a blank face.

The toothpick, now back in his mouth, was replaced by a white business card. I reached for it. He pulled it back.

"Kid, I have to admit you don't look like much," he said. "But let me add I'm impressed by the way you took on those three punks, the way Miss Bigelow tells it, to defend her honor and her property. I appreciate it. And Tommy here appreciates it too. Thank you."

"I do," Tommy said. "Good job, kid."

He held out the card again. I took it. And with a wave of his hand, the car pulled away and down the street.

I stood there for a moment before looking at the card. There was nothing printed on it, but he had written his name and number on the back. It read Moe Dentz.

I rolled the coin in my fingers before dropping it into my front pocket. The card I slipped into my back pocket.

If this were Dungeons & Dragons, the encounter would have been similar to being given a life debt but then finding out it was being offered by the guild master of thieves or assassins, which would make the debt a bit too risky to claim.

Unfortunately, this wasn't a game, which meant it was a dangerous favor to own. My fault.

I got my bearings, doing what I told Moe and Tommy to do when I thought they might be asking for directions. I walked a block north until I ran into one of the major east—west streets and headed toward home. I had chores to do before my mother would let me go out with Cheryl.

CHAPTER 8

WHITE PUNKS

When I got home, I didn't go over to Mick's house. I started tackling my chores one day late because we had taken the trip up the mountain yesterday.

There were house rules. Unless other plans were made, cleaning day was Saturday to free up the weekend. Plants were watered. Shelves were dusted. Ashtrays emptied. Bathrooms cleaned. The kitchen was wiped down. Vinyl floors mopped. The trash was taken out as needed. The lawn was mowed, except in the summer when it went brown and dormant in the heat.

It took me a few hours to finish because I never knew when my mother would pull a white glove inspection. I didn't want to take a chance today because I had blown off doing the work in the morning, and she didn't have anything better to do.

Her work was already done. She did the laundry, and I lucked out, consolidating my clothes the day before. George had vacuumed the rest of the house, which was carpeted in a brown and rust-flecked shag, except the bathrooms and bedrooms. Mine was blue. My sister's yellow, stained by the previous renters because they used to park motorcycles in the house. My parents' room and the guest bedroom were dark browns. Sometimes his job was delegated to me, but not today.

Most weekends I was supposed to make sure the dusting
was done before the house was vacuumed because dust travels
downhill. She said it was pointless to sweep and then knock
dust all over the floor. It was also one of a hundred corrections
she was trying to instill in me because my grandmother was lax.

"Aren't you a house on fire today," she said, creeping into
the kitchen while I was mopping the floor. "You must want
something."

"No, no," I said, huffing feigned exertion. "Except, maybe
going out tonight."

"Next door again?" she asked but didn't want an answer.
"You spend too much time over there."

"No, not with Mick," I said.

She looked surprised, disbelieving. "Who?"

"Oh, no one, really," I said. "Just some girl I met."

"You ... you met a girl," she said, huffing it out like a joke.
"I'd like to see that."

"Um, maybe," I said. "So, can I go?"

"I'll think about it," she said but then reconsidered. "Yes, if
you help inventory the camping equipment for Girl Scouts. We
have that trip coming up."

"Yeah, sure." Whatever it takes.

My sister was in Girl Scouts, and my mother had become
the troop leader because nobody else could possibly do it right.
So I had become a de facto part-time assistant troop leader,
helping about a dozen of my sister's friends earn badges. I
qualified because I had been a Boy Scout in my other life.

The last badge I helped them earn was a theater badge, directing a play I learned in high school called *Us and Them*. It was a short one-act play about two groups of wanderers who agreed to share a region divided by a line. As time passes, the line becomes a fence, and the fence becomes a wall, and the wall becomes a symbol of mistrust between them until a war breaks out.

They performed it in the backyard to parents who were shocked by how well they did. They surprised me, too, in a way, because the theater was a new interest of mine, one of the few things in my life that didn't include my friend group.

I had stumbled into the theater by accident. All the physical education classes were full my freshman year, so I enrolled in the only thing left — speech — a class I laughed out loud about because I thought it was for kids with speech impediments. This mistaken idea was dispelled the first day when the teacher, Ms. Loretto, rapped a cane on the house seats of the high school theater to get our attention.

Speech, I learned, wasn't about learning how to articulate. It was about speaking in public — which was one hundred percent the opposite of anything I wanted to do. Except, this fiery and passionate teacher with hawkish features, oversized glasses, and blue jeans had a way of getting under our skin. She convinced me to try out for the school play.

Us and Them was the second play in which I was cast. The first was *Flowers for Algernon*, the story about a mentally challenged test subject who is given an experimental treatment to become a genius. I was simply cast as a partygoer who spoke no lines other than "rhubarb" and "turkey feathers, my dear" to create the illusion of background chatter.

But coupled with Ms. Loretto's mantra that you can do anything — anything — you want in your life, I was transfixed by both her and this idea. It gave me hope that there was an entire world of possibilities out there, and maybe I was just waking up to them.

I was so excited that I laid it out for my mother one afternoon. She scoffed at me.

"You don't get choices in life," she said. "I never did. You play the hand you're dealt."

The shared epiphany spiraled into an argument that lasted a few hours. My mother didn't like the idea of a teacher filling my head with what she considered nonsense.

Ms. Loretto wasn't the only one who had. My seventh grade reading teacher challenged me to read *Dune* after I finished a book report on the thinnest book I could find. It was about a kid who was moved to an arid, barren world surrounded by a deadly desert. He seems too frail for his fate until the sleeper awakens.

After reading the book, I would sometimes walk out to the edge of town and stare out at the desert between the suburbs and mountains framing Las Vegas, looking for some smoke signal or wormsign that the life of Paul Atreides could somehow be mine. I felt the same way about Charlie in *Flowers for Algernon* too, until the end. The play was a tragedy.

Cheryl came by shortly after we had finished dinner — green peppers stuffed with rice and hamburger — as the sun set. That's how the town rolled. Most things happen after sundown when the heat becomes bearable. Most things means a bunch of kids get together somewhere, play loud music, and drink large quantities of alcohol.

"Hey, she's here; I'll see you," I said, loitering at the door for permission.

"She isn't going to come in?" They were in their respective stay-at-home spots, George on one side of the couch watching something on HBO and my mother reading a book on the other.

"Nah, we have to get going," I said.

"So, when can we meet her?"

A million years would be too soon, I thought.

"I don't know," I said, fidgeting with my feet. "Can I go?"

"All right," she said, head back in her book. "Just remember that Cinderella's carriage turns into a pumpkin at midnight, and so do you."

"Got it," I said, making a peace sign before turning out the front door. I was free.

The top of Westcliff. The top of Ann Road. The top of Craig. The top of any street would do, as far west as any dirt road could take you once the asphalt ran out.

At the top of any one of them on any given night and sometimes several of them, a few dozen cars overloaded with passengers would line up along desert washes and empty out. A steady procession of partygoers walked a little further up from their rides, teenage pilgrims drawn to a bonfire of wooden pallets and a steady stream of drinks — draft beer or booze — poured into a never-ending ocean of red plastic cups. They were passed around until everyone had one or two in their hands, kids paying a two-buck cover charge until the alcohol ran out or the cops ran them off.

Either scenario usually played out around midnight, sooner if the music from whatever car had the loudest stereo system was too loud and bothered the outliers who owned edge-of-town homes. Even if most homes were a mile or so away from wherever the pile of stolen store pallets was lit, the ominous red glow of flames licking the horizon and ululating chants of the Human League or John Cougar would unnerve them.

It unnerved me. Cougar was fine, but the infusion of synth-pop masquerading as rock was also a reminder that the kids who fanned out to the edges of our bowl-shaped town weren't from the same tribe. The music my friends played was louder, harsher, and about living harder and faster on our own terms instead of those laid out by someone else — the lie we told as we altered our heads with chemicals in defiance of everything.

I didn't complain. I would have tagged along with Cheryl anywhere, even if it meant the moon. What did I care if she clung to what had become the last remnant of her high school experience? I was happy enough to be with her.

"Isn't it great?" she asked, pulling me through the core to get closer to the fire.

"What? Oh, yeah, the party," I said. "Sure."

She grabbed two off-loaded cups from a line forming near a keg. For every four cups passed into the party, two were poured down a funnel and into some kid's gagging mouth, a stunt that delineated who was cool. First person to puke wins.

"All you have to do is open your throat," I mentioned to Cheryl, pointing at the kid.

"That's all?" She gave a playful shove. "Some kid tried a butt chug last year."

"Come on," I said. "That's a joke, right."

"Swear," she said, holding up three fingers.

"I don't know what's harder to believe," I said. "That kind of craziness or that you were ever a Girl Scout."

She put a finger to her lips like it was a secret and backed up closer to the fire, moving to the music, arms up in the air with one hand still clutching the drink. I followed her silhouette like a pup being led on a leash, moving awkwardly to the alien beat of some tainted love.

This was a different side to Cheryl, which didn't fit neatly within her friendship with Denise. These kids, a combination of jocks and student bodies, could be her people as Mick's were mine. It fascinated me, this idea that she walked between two worlds with ease.

As we moved to the music, another guy started edging his way in with us. He was tall and lean with feathered hair. His short-sleeve shirt was untucked and unbuttoned, except for two buttons framing his light blue denim shorts. His hair was sun bleached, a faint shadow on his jawline placing him at around seventeen or eighteen years old.

What bothered me more than the intrusion was Cheryl seemed to be inviting him, turning her body away from me and toward him. I curled my hands into fists, waiting for her to say something, but she never did. It wasn't until he moved in closer, much closer than I had been, that I took action.

I reached out with my left hand and pushed against his right shoulder. It wasn't a shove as much as a push, but my message was clear. He put up his hands in surrender, smiling as Cheryl reached over to move my hand away.

"Brady," she said, laughing. "It's okay. I know him. He's a friend."

"Hey," he said with astute confidence, making me the third party.

"Brady, this is Greg, an old friend of mine," she said. "Greg, this is Brady. He's sort of my wingman tonight."

"Wingman?" Greg said, lighting up. "Like Herbert to Pip?"

"Good one," she said, laughing along and turning to me. "We had literature together. Herbert and Pip are from *Great Expectations*."

Her favorite book. Somehow the explanation didn't make me feel better after being introduced as anything but her date.

"Hey man, it's cool," he said. "Cheryl and I are just friends."

"Who's all here?" she asked.

"Cory, Val, Krystal..." he said. "Everybody's here. Come on."

"Yeah, cool," she said, grabbing my hand and tilting her head in his direction.

I pulled my hand away and pointed to my cup, shaking it as if it were empty.

"I'll catch up," I said. "I need a refill."

"Are you sure?"

"One hundred percent," I said as I sank into the crowd behind me.

I navigated toward the keg, knowing that being in a drink line creates the appearance of belonging, even if you don't belong. It's part of the art of being a perfect wallflower, something I hadn't had to do in a long time. I was part of the action when I was with my friends. Here, I was another face in the crowd, being pushed and bumped as bigger, older guys jockeyed to get their dates drinks.

Aside from the ring around the bonfire, inching closer to feel the heat as if it wasn't hot enough already, most broke off into loose clusters to talk to each other and about each other. Three guys are trying to work up the nerve to talk to a bunch of girls, but only one of the guys is interested in one of the girls. The other two are trying to size up who they might be stuck with for the rest of the night.

Another pack of kids is gravitating around someone's new Trans Am, a gift for his seventeenth birthday. The dork decided to drive it up here into the desert just to show off.

In another clump, some average-looking girl tries to calm another kid down. He's agitated that his girlfriend drifted into the arms of some other guy. He's oblivious that the one in front of him has crushed on him since grade school.

I sympathize, given I've lost Cheryl to a crowd of stumbling, mumbling posers, trying to find their place in the world of hot-boxed cigarettes smoked by people who don't smoke. They're supposed to be superior classmates, but all I see are drunks and wannabes.

"Brady, is that you?"

I turn toward the tug on my shoulder just as the kid manning the beer tap overfills my cup. Calvin Reynolds was a sophomore I met in theater class, but he tended to stick to the technician side, running spotlights and soundboards. As with the other tech kids, he's like me, more comfortable in a heavy metal setting. He buys weed from me every now and again.

"Hey, Cal," I say, feigning disinterest, so he doesn't know how alone I feel.

"What are you doing here, man?"

"Oh, I came with someone."

"Far out," he says with a squint to his eyes, looking for someone who isn't there.

"She's over there somewhere, saying hey to old friends," I said, motioning to a throng of kids.

"Right on," he says. "Hey, you should come with me. Daniel has something heavy you should try."

I scan the party crowd and don't see any sign of Cheryl, so I gulp down a quarter of the cup to keep it from spilling it all over myself and nod along like an idiot. The beer is warm and starting to go flat.

Cal leads me to a dark blue Camaro and tells me to jump in the back on the passenger side. He climbs in behind Daniel in the driver's seat. Nathan, a kid I don't know but know of, doesn't seem keen on letting me in, but Daniel assures him I'm all right, and he inches the seat forward so I can squeeze by.

Squeeze is the operative word because Ruth Harding, one of Alex's regulars, is already in the back seat, making room for me and Cal. She's already wasted, head lolling back and forth between being awake and unconscious. She recognizes me, though, reaching over to give me a soft hug. She's wearing too much makeup, deep red lipstick, and thick eyeliner.

"Brady, baby." She squeals in delight. "I've always liked you, Brady."

"Hey, Ruth," I say and press into her without returning the hug.

The car feels claustrophobic. The windows are down, but the music outside is muted, and the air inside is heavy with something I can't place.

"Light it up," Cal says. "Brady has to try it."

Nathan starts reloading a pipe he pulled out of the glove compartment.

"What is it?"

"Hash, but not your daddy's kind," Daniel says. "Nathan bought it from the City of Angels last week."

"It's going to knock you off your feet," Cal says. "Heaven."

As Nathan takes the first hit, I watch the flame disappear into the opening of the pipe, the mesmerizing curve of a blue flame. He hits it hard, passing it back to Cal. Cal pushes it over to me, skipping his turn and ignoring Ruth, anxious for me to try it.

I know it's going to hit me harder. Hash is a resin made from a gum that the cannabis plant produces instead of the leaves and flowers. I don't hesitate to take the pipe and lighter, despite feeling trepidation about smoking something outside of my control.

"Nothing else in it?" I asked just before pressing my thumb down on the dial.

Nathan waves a noncommittal hand. Cal snickers. I hit it, a deep, long inhale that burns a little more than I expected. I hold it in but then cough a bit, prompting Cal and Daniel to laugh. I hit it again, this time willing myself not to cough so I could save face in front of these amateurs. And then I pass it to Cal.

"Brady," Ruth reaches for the pipe as I pass it and then leans into me. "I've always liked you, baby."

Her hand is on my leg, running up from my knee. I want to push her off, but the hash and whatever is in it hits hard and fast. Everything feels slower, brighter, and safe. I'm drawn to the dash's colors, and the flame on the lighter as Cal takes a turn.

I'm happy for the first time since arriving here with Cheryl, sinking into my corner of the backseat with Ruth starting to kiss my neck. We're all laughing as the pipe is passed around in the car. I'm not sure what we're laughing at, but it was something I said.

"It's good, right?" Cal asks as if he needs an answer.

"Yeah, wow," I say. "You got this in California?"

"Sure, man," Nathan said. "But it's not, like, from there. It's from somewhere else, somewhere exotic."

"Like Thailand?"

"Yeah, tie-one-on-land," Cal snorts.

It's not funny, but I laugh anyway. My head is lighter, and I'm thirsty. I don't remember drinking the rest of my beer, but the cup is empty. The urge to leave starts creeping in, and I swear that someone is calling my name somewhere outside.

"Hey man, thanks a lot," I said. "I better cut out, though. I came with someone."

"There's nothing for you out there, man," Cal said. "Stick with us."

"Don't go, Brady," said Ruth, reaching out and then drifting again.

"Come on, Nathan," I said, pushing up on his seat. "Come on."

"All right. Chill out," he said, pulling his seat forward and opening the door.

The night air was still warm but felt cool once I was freed from the confines of the backseat. I held onto the car to maintain my balance, trying to establish where I was in relation to everything around me as the ground shifted beneath my feet.

Looking toward the valley, I could see three sets of reds and blues rolling up to the party, handheld spotlights on each squad car cutting through the desert on either side as they advanced up the hill. From the heart of the party, kids were starting to thin out, trying to find whoever brought them up or renegotiating a new ride because they were drunk, lost, or got into a fight with other friends or steadies.

I almost asked to catch a ride from Daniel since I was one of these lost souls. But then I heard my name called again. It wasn't just in my head. One of the girls coming down from the bonfire was Cheryl. I leaned in the car window before breaking away.

"You guys will get Ruth home, right?"

"We'll get her there, sure," Daniel said, laughing.

Cal and Nathan laughed too. I almost suggested she come with me, but I had no idea how that would sit with Cheryl, who just locked eyes on me.

"Brady!"

"Just making sure my friend gets home," I said, tipping as I let go of the car for support. I waved to her. "She's wasted."

"You're wasted," Cheryl said, offering herself as support.

"I am wasted," I said, smiling with a sense of pride. "Not as wasted as Ruth, though."

Cheryl looked in the Camaro, where Ruth was now sprawled over two seats, her head in Cal's lap. Cheryl shook her head.

"We've got to go," she said. "The cops are coming up the hill."

"Right there," I said, pointing down the hill with a finger revolver. "Here they come to save the day. Five-o."

She pulled me toward her car, nearly pulling me off my feet. It was down the hill more, a few hundred feet away. I turned to give Cal a final farewell salute, letting Cheryl navigate us through all the other kids trying to find their cars — some walking, some running, all of them stumbling. Headlights reflected off a rising tide of dust, making it harder to see as we traversed the path.

I was grateful Cheryl had the good sense to park with the front of the car facing east, down the hill. Behind us, teenagers trying to make tight U-turns created a bottleneck that the police would have to untangle for an hour. They would likely let everyone go as long as no one flaunted alcohol or tried to argue with them.

I thought we were safe when we made it to the Pinto, but it had taken us too long. When I poured myself into the passenger seat, the first police car had stopped parallel to Cheryl's car door. She gripped her steering wheel with white knuckles. The

118

flashing reds and blues outside alongside her and out the front window were blinding.

"You been drinking tonight, miss?"

"Me, no," she lied. "I'm just here to pick up my kid brother."

He shined a flashlight into the car toward me. I covered my face.

"All right, you drive safe," he said. "A lot of these kids have had too much to drink."

"Yes, sir, officer," she said. "You might want to check that Camaro up ahead. A girl in the back seat could use a safer ride home."

"We'll take a look," he said, turning off the flashlight. "Get him home and be safe."

The squad car pulled forward. We had to wait for the other two to follow before Cheryl could safely pull out and start down the hill.

"Why'd you do that?"

"Do what?"

"Narc out Daniel and Cal," I said.

"We're out of here, aren't we?"

I didn't have anything more to say about it. It was a close call, but we were out. A thick cloud of illuminated dust rose in the night sky. I imagined it looked like an alien invasion or military operation if you looked up at it from one of those outlier homes. I don't blame them for calling the cops.

"You know what to say when a cop asks how high you are?"

"No."

"You tell him he got it wrong. It's 'Hi, how are you?'"

She laughs, easing any fears I might have had that she was pissed off at me.

"You are so wasted," she said. "Maybe we should stop for coffee or something."

"You're the captain."

"I waited for you, but you never came looking for us."

"Yeah, I dunno. I was getting a refill and got disoriented."

"I highly doubt that."

"Then Cal spotted me. They were lighting up some hash and invited me along. It felt more like my scene."

"You didn't save any?"

"Pipe," I said, as if that explained everything.

"We'll drop by the 7-Eleven," she said. "I'll get you a coffee and some gum."

"Visine?"

"Glove compartment."

"Thanks," I said, digging into it. "So, you don't think of me that way, do you?"

"What way?"

"Like a kid brother."

"Let's save that conversation for another night."

The coffee woke me up but didn't do anything for my head. We sat in the parking lot, taking sips and talking about all her other friends and their plans. Some of them were headed out of state. Some were staying home. Some were learning vocations like being hair stylists or entering hospitality like casino workers or becoming construction workers. Las Vegas seemed to have an eternal hunger for those things. Hundreds of jobs here don't require a college education.

It felt good when it was just her and me, without all the background drama and distractions. I hadn't felt that way with anyone since I left my grandparents — like I fit someplace. Who knew it would be in the passenger seat of a Ford Pinto, owned by a girl who was too old for me and way out of my league?

"Did you hear me?"

"Sorry, I was just thinking," I said.

"Do you need my help walking up to the door?"

"No, I've been walking in drunk for a while," I said. "I know what to do."

"You're not just drunk," she said.

"It's cool. I'll just walk in, complain about being tired, and screw off to my bedroom," I said. "It's the safest way to play it tonight. But you might want to pull in front of Mick's place just to be safe."

"Why's that?"

"If I don't make it," I said. "I don't want them to think you dropped me off. I'll tell them we got separated."

I almost fell asleep on the short drive between the 7-Eleven and my house. The caffeine wasn't strong enough to bring me back from wherever the hash had taken me.

A small surge of adrenaline kicked me when I felt the car stop. It was showtime, and I had to pull myself together. I huffed and opened the door, but she called me back before I could exit.

"See you," she said, placing her hands on either side of my face and kissing me.

It wasn't a peck but a deep kiss that stretched out for minutes. It felt so good that leaving was the last thing I wanted to do. We started to pull away, but I kissed her again, three small parting kisses that I had been practicing for years.

"Good night, Cheryl," I said.

She laughed. "Sweet dreams, little brother."

I waited a minute for her car to turn right around the horseshoe corner before heading to the front door, almost falling into the bushes that divided Mick's house from mine. I hadn't come home this wasted in a long time, using his house as a crash pad instead.

The best way to play it was to be bold by walking in and taking a seat in the chair that flanked the couch where they sat. Most nights, I was home free if I could force myself to engage them, tell them about my uneventful night, and watch a little television. But I was too wasted to try it tonight. I opted for the fallback plan. Brush them off like I had a bad night and go straight to bed. Do not pass go. Do not collect $200.

I traced the house with my left hand to the front door. Looking in through the window, I could see they were in the same seats as when I left. George was watching television with a whiskey sour on the table next to him. My mother alternated between a book, a Pepsi, and a cigarette.

The doors were left open, so I pulled the screen door out, slipped in, and hung on the front door. As the screen door slammed behind me, I crashed into the house with a plan to head for my bedroom to the right.

"Fun night?"

"Heya, I'm burnt out and hitting it," I said, head down and avoiding eye contact. "Tell you tomorrow."

Somehow I missed the hallway and hit the wall instead, bouncing off it and turning toward them to explain. Except, I didn't have an explanation.

"You've been drinking," my mother said. Her voice was flat.

"No, I haven't been drinking," I countered, feeling my words slur.

"Then you're on drugs," she said.

"Okay," I lied. "I've been drinking. I drank way too much. Can I sit down?"

"You better," George said. "I think you'll fall down if you don't."

Was he laughing? He was laughing. Unbelievable. So was she.

"Is this going to happen every time you go out with Cheryl?"

"No, no, we were separated," I said, trying to remember if I ever told them her name. "This happened after Cheryl."

"Separated?"

"Yeah. It happened because we were separated."

"Like a spat?" George was intrigued.

"No, not a fight exactly," I said. "It was just a bad night. Can we leave it at that?"

"Fine, Brady," she said, cigarette smoke curling around her head. "Go to bed. We'll talk about the consequences tomorrow."

"Thank you," I said.

"Thank you," she said. "At least you didn't lie this time."

She didn't know when I was lying because I was always lying. I even lied to her when I didn't have to. When you live with someone so unstable, lying is always the best option, like crawling to my bedroom was the best option.

But I didn't do it. I picked myself up and stopped by the bathroom first so I could throw up. I don't know what was in whatever I smoked, but it made this one of the worst nights of my life. And somehow, it was also one of my best.

CHAPTER 9

DOG HOUSE

It was the third day of my seven-day restriction when I received an unexpected reprieve. My mother allowed Lewis Barnett to come over to get a book I had borrowed from him before school broke for the summer.

She liked Lewi and wished I hung around with more kids like him. Lewi was a year ahead of me in school but had also taken speech as a prep class for college. I almost invited him over to play Dungeons & Dragons once or twice, but he seemed too straight to be a good fit with Brett and Mick. He most certainly wasn't a good fit with Alex.

So like most people I knew from school, he was more of an acquaintance whose house I visited once or twice to play a board game or a few hands of low-stakes poker. He was the oldest in a big family, so it was always easy to get a game going, with one of his brothers my age and two sisters, one and two years younger. There were more Barnetts than those four, but the rest were too young for me to pay attention to them. Eight wasn't enough.

"Did you like it?" Lewi asked, leaning against the door to my room.

The Black Cauldron wasn't the *Lord of the Rings* or even *The Sword of Shannara*, which Terry Brooks ripped a bit from Tolkien's story, but one of its messages stuck with me.

There is no greater love than to lay down your life for your friends. It makes you think about who your friends are.

"Pretty good," I said, holding it out for him. "Easy read."

"That's true," he said. "It always reminded me of eating Turkish delight. Classic fantasy. You really need to read *The Lion, the Witch and the Wardrobe*."

The Chronicles of Narnia was his favorite series. I always hesitated to dive into it because there were seven books. Maybe it was a commitment issue.

"What are you working on?" he asked, looking down at my drawing.

Drawing was one of the things I did when I was on restriction. What else could I do? I would read, draw, and build out the world for an ongoing Dungeons & Dragons campaign that Mick and I hardly played anymore. The characters were all alive to me but stuck in suspended animation.

"Just a character from the campaign," I said. "I started a couple days ago."

It was a life-sized scale drawing of a woman, leaning forward, one arm above her head on a tree branch to steady herself. At a glance, nobody would see her as a fantasy character. It was only on closer inspection of her eyeshadow, jewelry, and a thin braid holding some of her hair back that it became more apparent. The drawing stopped at her waist, but someone savvy might notice the top of a sword hilt.

The drawing's outline was light. I had been working on coloring her in all morning, finishing her skin and some of her hair. I crosshatched most of it with colored pencils, but her hair and areas like the rouge in her cheeks would be blended later.

"It's great work, Brady," he said, searching for conversation. "Hey, we're going to get a poker game going in a couple days if you can make it."

"I don't think she'll let me off that easy," I grumbled. "Four days and counting."

"What did you do anyway?"

"I came home drunk, and they caught me," I said, snickering. "I mean, walking into the wall didn't help."

"You didn't?" His eyes were wide in disbelief, the corners of his wispy mustache curled up with his lips.

"Guilty as charged, man," I said. "What can I say? If you're in Rome, you gotta drink like the Romans. We were at the top of Ann Road. Ever go?"

"Nah, I only have a beer or two when I drink so that's not my scene," he said. I didn't know he drank.

"Right on. Maybe I can host the poker game some Saturday afternoon the next time I'm not grounded."

"I won't hold my breath," he said.

"Bring your sisters," I said, but then tried to qualify my invitation because it sounded so weird. "More coin for the kitty."

"I'll bring Flynn too," he said. "I know plenty who would make it. Give me a ring."

I told him I would but didn't walk him out. I wasn't ready to have another conversation or confrontation with my mother outside of seeing her at the dinner table where there were witnesses. She had more barbs when we were alone, except when she wanted to embarrass me. Sometimes she would play up how she was giving me the silent treatment, talking to me through George while visiting her friends. Sometimes she posted a sign that said "pigs" on the bathroom door, making it a point to tell people that she meant pig, singular. The boy had poor aim, she'd say, as if that explained everything.

Given the alternatives, I was glad to wait out the rest of my restriction in solitude. The only time I struggled with room or house confinement was in Ohio. I had accidentally put a dirty knife away. She had warned me there would be an inspection after I put the dishes away and I missed an offensive water spot. She went on and on about about it because I couldn't see it. That was the problem, she said. I was blind to filth.

The punishment was room restriction for a month. When I made the mistake of expressing defiance — telling her I was enjoying my time reading books, drawing pictures, and playing with plastic army men and board games — she started taking everything out of my room. First the books, then the toys, and soon every pencil and piece of paper. I was left with a bed, dresser, four walls, and a window.

It was the kind of punishment nobody believes until she boasts about it. She enjoys being a "tough love" mom, which is why I was grateful that this restriction was just another vacation.

Then again, for all I knew, the week-long restriction was a stall until she could do something more drastic, like registering me for that camp. Anything was possible, which might have explained why she was granted visitation rights. Maybe this was my last chance to say goodbye before I disappeared for the rest of the summer or maybe forever.

I dated a girl in middle school who was sent to a similar camp. She came back more messed up than when she left. It makes me wonder if some parents ever realize that they're part of the equation. Maybe what some of us are trying to escape isn't responsibility as much as the crazy-making imposed upon us. Wrong, do it again.

"Aren't you the popular one today," she said from the same place Lewi was standing just a minute ago. "Why don't you come out? Cheryl's here."

"What do you mean 'here?'"

"What else would it mean? She's here in the living room," she said. "She called earlier today to see if you were all right. She's the reason I allowed visitors today. How else was I going to meet her?"

So that's what this was about. If I had a line of coke, I would have hit it right then and there in front of her. It's the only way to escape this kind of crazy-making.

"All right," I said, trying to keep my composure. "Let her know I'll be out in a minute. I just want to clean up a bit."

"Fine with me," she said. "We were having a nice conversation anyway. She's lovely."

I didn't waste any time after she left my room. I kicked off my sweats and grabbed a fresh shirt and shorts. I dropped by the bathroom, glancing at the door to make sure no signs had been put up while I wasn't attentive, and ran a comb through my hair.

When I came out, I found my mother sitting at the dining room table and Cheryl looking at some pictures on the wall. She was looking at a sketch of Norman Rockwell painting his own self-portrait.

"This is very good," Cheryl said. "Did Brady draw it?"

"Oh no, none of his work is that good," she said. "I drew that one to teach him a lesson."

"A lesson?"

"There will always be someone better," she said. "I hadn't drawn in years, but it all came back when I sat down to do it. "

"Mom," I said.

"Speak of the devil," she said. "I shouldn't tell that story. He's still sensitive about it."

"Mom!" I said.

"All right, I'll give you two some space," she said, amused and waving her hand as if shooing a fly away before another thought occurred to her. "Maybe you should invite Cheryl over for dinner."

She retreated to her room, which I knew wouldn't hold her interest for long. In this house, it wasn't the adults who holed up in their rooms. Kids did it by themselves or by order.

"Sorry about that," I said.

"You don't have to apologize," Cheryl said. "She seems cool enough."

"If you say so." I never argued with other people's assessments. It was a losing battle.

"I don't know what the picture thing was all about, but she put an ashtray out for me," Cheryl said. "She's not all uptight."

"If you mean that they gave me a beer on New Year's Eve when I was eleven, and I danced with their drunken friends around a wall that separated the kitchen from the living room in our Ohio apartment, then no, I guess not. But if you mean measuring how close the garbage is to the top of trash can, you know, to determine whether it needs to be taken out or if you're wasting bags, then you might think twice."

"You're making that up," she said.

I desperately wanted to change the subject.

"You didn't come over to talk about my mom, did you?"

"No, I wanted to make sure you're okay," she said. "I shouldn't have dropped you off like that."

"What? You didn't have a choice. It was like ten to midnight. A few more minutes and it would have been off with my head anyway."

"I guess. I just felt guilty afterward," she said. "I wasn't exactly sober."

"I didn't notice. I pretty much stumbled in, got sick, and was busted. Not necessarily in that order."

"So you're public enemy number one, now? Not too shabby," she said, teasing me. "And yet, here I am. In your house. Visiting the prisoner. Bearing gifts."

I hadn't noticed. She had a book in her hand. *Great Expectations* by Charles Dickens.

"Oh, thanks," I said, feigning interest in the cover. "What do you want to do?"

"I don't know. Give me the tour."

There wasn't much to show her, but I gave her one anyway, steering clear of the hallway that led to my parents' bedroom and guest room. My mother had to be lurking in one of them.

The single-story layout was simple. The living room with the front door entrance faced south. The dining room was open to it, directly north, and framed most of the backyard, with a sliding glass door that led to the back patio. The kitchen was to the left of the dining room. My parents' room, and the guest room, were to the right.

My room and my sister's room fed off a hallway to the right of the front door. The guest bathroom was divided into two adjoining rooms. One with a vanity and a toilet, which was closest to our rooms. The other had a vanity and bathtub with a shower, closer to the guest room. When my sister and I were younger, I used to chase her and her friends through the adjoining bathrooms. But like most of our activities together, we outgrew it.

"Your sister has a bigger room," she said.

"She picked first," I said. "So I picked this one."

There wasn't any scenario in which I would have picked a room next to my parents, but where the choice paid off was my window. From here, I could exit the house with no one noticing. Had I picked the other room, the only escape route would have placed me in the backyard, right next to my parents' windows.

As soon as we walked into my room, I grabbed the sweatpants lying on the floor and tossed them in a hamper. She smiled at that and then scrutinized the surroundings.

"I thought you said you weren't very good," she said, looking at the drawing on the floor.

"It's something to do," I said. "Nothing serious."

"I think it's pretty good," she said. "No bed, huh?"

"The couch is longer than a twin. So when they bought a new couch, I convinced them to let me have this one."

She ran a finger over the spines of some books on my shelf, nothing of interest to her, I was sure. She was probably disappointed that her gift didn't fit so she moved on, evaluating the dozens of cassettes I owned.

I had grown the collection by convincing kids to join the Columbia House mail order offer. You could buy twelve cassettes for a penny if you bought four more at regular member prices in a year. There was also a four-cassette bounty for every friend you referred.

She knew all the bands, but it's what she didn't expect that she picked out. I buried my head in my hands and groaned.

"Barry Manilow?"

"It was one of the first cassettes I owned when I was a kid," I said. "I don't listen to it anymore, but I have a hard time parting with things."

"You're blushing," she said.

"I haven't had a girl over in a while." My mouth was moving but I didn't understand what I was saying. "Most of the parties are next door or somewhere else."

"At the Copa, Copa-ca-bana." She sang, laughing, sliding it back into place. "You don't have to feel embarrassed with me. I think it's cute."

Cute isn't a word I want to be associated with me when I'm supposed to be a bad boy. I felt exposed, realizing that Cheryl was starting to see me for the boy I was and not the guy she had come over to find.

"Maybe we should go back into the dining room so I can bum a smoke," I said.

"I didn't think you smoked cigarettes," she said.

"I don't want a full cigarette. Maybe just a hit."

"Okay, but it depends," she said.

"On what?"

"On whether you invite me over for dinner."

It was the worst idea in the world, but I did it anyway. I was in the passenger seat of a car destined for a collision, and there was nothing else to do but close my eyes and try to relax for the impact. We weren't having anything special. Shake' n Bake pork chops, peas, and mashed potatoes for everyone except my sister. When Tab didn't like something, they made her a hot dog. It's what the kid ate four nights out of seven.

Cheryl and I set the table, laying out five place settings on a rectangular, Formica-topped table that seats six. George would sit at the head of the table, his back toward the kitchen, my mother to his right and my sister next to her. Cheryl sat on George's left, across from my mother. I sat next to Cheryl, across from my sister, creating this weird sort of "kids at the end of the table" vibe that I knew Tab would take advantage of by kicking me under the line of sight.

George was his usual cool and aloof self, breaking the ice by acting like having company was as alien as a salad sandwich. He settled into his chair, giving Cheryl a quizzical look as if he had to take a moment to figure out this new arrangement with an extra person sitting at the table.

"I don't remember having another daughter," he said. "Hi, so who are you anyway?"

"This is Cheryl, George," I said. "Cheryl, George is my stepdad."

"Okay, if you say so," he said, holding up a hand and giving her a tiny wave. "Hi, Cheryl. I would have worn something more formal if I knew we had a guest. But no, not really, I wouldn't have."

The long hair, the beard, and his borrowed jokes were all part of the charm. They were among the reasons that almost all my friends thought my parents were laid back and cool, with a strange hippie vibe. They weren't hippies. They were better defined as barflies, with George looking for laughs and my mother providing them.

He was never the problem unless you became the brunt of his jokes. Sometimes he asked my mother to cut me some slack. If I wasn't already enrolled in the camp after coming home drunk and stoned stupid the same day I was threatened with it, he was the likely reason. But other than that, he mostly deferred to my mother to raise me as she wished.

"So, tell me, Cheryl," he said. "What do you think of the dope problem?"

"Excuse me?"

"You know what I think? I think we have too many dopes."

He always won people over. My mother could too. She seemed elated that Cheryl was here, pivoting George's opening into a game of twenty questions. She asked how long her family lived in Las Vegas, what her dad did for a living, and where she went to high school. When Cheryl mentioned graduating, I could have fallen out of my chair.

My mother just moved on to her next questions, whatever they were, but I could see the gears in her head working this idea over and over. The more she thought about it, the more her smile tightened like a catapult. Once it reached critical tension, whatever projectile she had loaded would be impossible to stop.

"The pork chops are delicious," Cheryl said. "Thanks again for inviting me over."

"Hey, don't look at me," George said. "I just live here."

My mother laughed. "Thanks for accepting the invite," she said, pausing for a second before making an addition. "So, let's talk about the elephant in the room."

"Elephant?" Cheryl had no idea what was coming.

"This isn't a safari," I said, shaking my head. "No need to talk about it."

My sister saw her opening. She kicked me and smirked. Tab didn't know what was coming, but she knew it would be good.

"What's an eighteen-year-old woman doing with a fourteen-year-old boy?" she asked, still smiling. "That's what inquiring minds want to know."

Tab didn't know what our mother was saying but laughed anyway. I didn't. I felt myself shrinking in my chair, dying inside. It wasn't the first time. It wouldn't be the last.

"I mean, he can't even take a driver's permit test yet," she continued, but Cheryl didn't miss another beat.

"Oh, it's not like that," she said. "We're just friends."

"Friends?"

"Yes," Cheryl said. "We met because I'm friends with Denise. You know her, the brunette who lives across the street?

Anyway, Brady and I started talking about books like *The Hobbit*, *Lord Foul's Bane*, *The Shadow of the Torturer*, *Nine Princes In Amber*, you know, all that fantasy stuff I know I shouldn't like as a future lit major, but it's a guilty pleasure of mine. It was nice to be able to talk to someone about so many. He's got quite the collection."

I was sure she hadn't read any of them other than *The Hobbit*, but she must have remembered the titles when she skimmed them in my room.

"Yes, he loves his little fantasy books," she said. "True story. I enrolled him in a book-of-the-month science fiction and fantasy club once and told him I would buy whatever the book-of-the-month selection was if he promised to read it. He didn't take me up on it. He was too stubborn and wanted to pick his own books. Can you imagine?"

"Mom," I said. It came out in a whisper.

"Oh, come on, Brady," she said. "Your friend gets the joke of it."

"All I can say is that if you ever want to offer me the same deal, sign me up," Cheryl said. "Can I help you clean up?"

"Thank you, Cheryl," she said. "Brady, you should invite your friend over, and the four of us will play Bridge. We haven't found anyone who plays in Vegas since we moved here, and it might be a fun change of pace."

"Sure," I said.

Cheryl was a good sport and kept the charade up while they cleaned up the dishes together, with my mother trying to reel Cheryl in as her new friend instead of mine. My mom washed. Cheryl dried. I was relegated to carrying the plates in and scraping them. George resigned himself to the couch. Tab ran off to play in her room, sticking her tongue out at me as she left.

I didn't care. I was too busy thinking of the fallout. If we had any chance of being together before, it was over now. Never mind that all my friends were older, or I felt more mature than most of my classmates. This was going to be a problem.

Cheryl confirmed my suspicions as she left. George gave me permission to walk her to the Pinto, but Cheryl stopped me halfway down the drive.

"You should have told me you were fourteen," she said.

"I'm sorry," I said. "I don't feel fourteen, and I'm closer to fifteen anyway."

"Everything makes more sense now," she said. "You know, I thought you were at least sixteen and maybe a little shy, but you're just a kid who's over his head, with me, with those friends of yours, with everything."

"Come on," I said. "I'll make it up to you."

"Yeah, how are you going to do that, exactly?"

"Nobody has to know anything," I said. "We'll just keep things about us between us."

When she looked at me, I could see her eyes had welled up. Her lips moved to one side of her face, fighting back the urge to cry in front of me or out of fear I might hug her.

"Damn it, Brady," she said, turning toward her car. "I was really starting to like you."

"Cheryl?"

"I'll see you later," she said. "I have to think about all this."

There was no fanfare when I went inside. I looked at my mother and George in their respective spots on the couch and feigned a thank you for having Cheryl over. I didn't react when my mother said she had thanked Cheryl for giving me a ride home the other night, another lie uncovered. I didn't care. My heart was breaking.

I shut my bedroom door and lay on the couch for a few hours, listening to Roger Daltrey sing "Behind Blue Eyes" a dozen times, rewinding the track every time the cymbals crashed at the end.

When I gave up on making myself feel worse, I exchanged the tape for *Led Zeppelin IV* and fell asleep. It wasn't until later, when the rest of the house had also slipped into slumber, that Jamie knocked on my bedroom window. The deal was going down.

CHAPTER 10

NOWHERE LAND

Mick was driving his car with me riding shotgun and Jamie in the back seat. Brett left with Alex, who was driving his primer gray Impala.

The last time I had ridden in the Impala was the same day Alex ruined its fading baby blue paint job, taking an exit ramp too fast and shredding the passenger side against the guard rail. We were laughing as he did it, showers of sparks dusting the right side of the car.

Mick was in the passenger seat that night. I was sitting behind him, rolling up the window to prevent any hot metal shavings from flying into the back seat. The first time was an accident, but it became a game. Alex would accelerate, weaving into the guard rail and turning the steering wheel just enough to match the curve without losing contact or control. We told him how bad he was messing up the car; he'd laugh and do it again, hands tight on the steering wheel and mouth agape in manic amusement. It was hilarious. It was terrifying.

The plan was to meet up with Will at the site, some remote location in the desert, pass out the handguns and rifles he had borrowed from his dad's shop, and then drop Jamie and me behind the hill where the deal would go down. While we climbed to the top of the hill from its backside, Alex and Brett would park for the meetup, and Mick would ride somewhere further out.

"Hey, look at Jamie," Mick said, smiling and throwing a thumb to the back.

Jamie was asleep. Somewhere between our block and riding out into the blackness of the desert, he had stretched himself across the back seat and faded away. I didn't know how he did it.

"Like a baby," I said. "Wish I could, but I'm too keyed up to sleep."

"He was freaking out, so Alex gave him a few ludes to calm down."

"I thought we were doing this deal straight?"

"Come on, Brady. It was just a couple quaaludes. He'll be fine."

I didn't like the way he shrugged it off. He was too cool about it.

"What, you took some too?"

"Just one to take the edge off."

"Sure seems like a big deal," I said. "None of this is going like we talked about."

"What do you mean?"

"Remember when Jamie and I were supposed to be deterrents — two guys with rifles standing on a hill? Nobody is going to see us standing up there at one in the morning."

He didn't say anything for a minute. He kept his eyes on the road, watching the Impala's tail lights in the distance and waiting for Alex to turn off the paved road.

"It's not too late, you know," he said, quieter. "You don't have to do this."

"Of course I have to do this."

"No," he said. "I could drop you out at the turnoff and come back and get you when it's done. Alex won't even miss you."

"I'll pass on being left in the middle of the desert, thanks."

"Sometimes I wish I could take it all back, you know? Like, things would be so different if I never invited you out back to get high or introduce you to Alex or cut you in on anything. No offense, man. But you're just a kid."

"Now you sound like Alex," I said, snapping. "Who's to say I wouldn't have gone this way on my own? I'm only two years younger than you, anyway."

"Maybe, but I can tell you go along to get along," he said. "You do it because you're trying to be a good friend, maybe a better friend than I've been to you lately."

I didn't like it when Mick got this way. Nobody did. It was unfair, but big kids aren't allowed to act like kids, as if maturity can somehow be measured by feet and inches. Mick wasn't the sentimental type, but there seemed to be more going on inside him than the quaalude. It made me wonder if he was afraid, or already regretting whatever came next.

"Come on, man. We go way back. Remember when you found Spot in the bushes the night after he died? Nobody understood why you felt the way you did when you lost your dog, but I did. And when I need to get out of my house or lose my head, you're there for me with a place to crash. We get through things together. Nah, you don't have to feel bad about anything. I had my own reasons to go along before, and I have my own reasons to be here now."

The enigma wasn't lost on me. Nobody wants someone like Mick to be soft, but they always want a kid like me to be. Skinny kids with glasses are supposed to be easy marks, book smart, and street stupid. That's the funny thing about labels. None of them are ever right, but people will tell you to pretend they are. And, if you aren't careful, you'll convince yourself that you are whatever label they assign you.

I didn't like how we were doing it, but I wanted to be here. Money has a way of leveling the playing field. A few thousand dollars muted any threat of being sent to a juvenile camp. It allows us to wear whatever we want to say to the world. It means getting a girl's attention if not the girl. Get enough dough, and it's easy to set priorities and face the world on new terms.

"Cheryl. She's one of them?"

"If she'll ever talk to me again."

"What happened?"

"Same thing that happens here, all the time," I said. "She thinks I'm too young."

He jeered me. "You are too young. What is she? Eighteen?"

"Hardships have a way of making you older than your age, Mick."

"I suppose."

"Six months ago, your biggest worry was whether your overman might survive falling off an ice ledge while looking for a frost giant lair. Now, we're driving into the desert to pick up two bricks of heroin. Tell me you haven't aged six years in six months."

"I've never thought of it like that."

"I have. What else are you going to do locked in a room for a month?"

"Yeah, I know you've been through it even when you lived in Cleveland, but sometimes you say and do stupid kid things too."

"Like this isn't one of them," I huffed. "Hey, Alex is making the turn."

I had seen the brake lights before the blinker as the Impala made a hesitant turn off the asphalt and down a dirt road. Mick followed. Within minutes, all we could see was a trail of dust ahead, green and brown sage scraping against his car, and the road becoming increasingly treacherous with uneven dips and bumps. Jamie woke up, half dazed and wondering how close we were to somewhere.

"We're going somewhere," I said. "We're going nowhere."

"These are the kinds of places my dad told me about when he worked vice," Mick said. "Smugglers cross the border from Mexico and then daisy chain it deeper and deeper into the United States. The ones who make the first crossing don't know anything. They're just told to drive somewhere and make a phone call. Then people on this side of the border tell them where to drop it so dudes like the ones Felix is introducing to Alex can deliver it. They do it that way so if the law catches someone, the mule won't have anything to say."

"Don't you ever worry about your old man finding out?" Jamie asked, sitting in the middle of his seat and leaning over into the front.

"There was this one time, Brady was there, so he knows, we weren't sure where we were going to get high. So Alex took us to a playground near the community center off Jones. It was right across the street from a precinct."

"Yeah, I remember," I said. "We climbed up into the slide fort and smoked a pinhead right there, overlooking the squad cars."

"Man, you guys are nuts," Jamie said.

"Nobody wants to look in their backyard," Mick said. "Besides, my dad isn't the same go-getter he used to be. He's coasting along as a desk sergeant and pulling in plenty of overtime."

"At least he's in the picture," Jamie said. "I haven't seen my dad in five years."

"What? Wasn't that your dad who came looking for you the other night?"

"No, man, that was my mom's boyfriend," he said. "Don't let him fool you. He's slick."

We were a few miles off the road, and I could tell our collective hearts were beginning to work overtime, with whatever drugs they had taken wearing off. The brush had started to thin out along the dirt road, which had been reduced to two ruts traversing hills instead of a long open valley.

"Did you guys really think that was my dad?" Jamie asked, more to break the imposing silence. "He doesn't look anything like me."

We all laughed, releasing some growing tension as we passed a bent, long-forgotten mile marker. In the distance, the headlights illuminated the Impala, brake lights flaming red and motor running. A few hundred feet to the right in a small gully by a clump of mesquite trees, we could see the ghostly outline of Will's truck.

I was the first to step out of Mick's car to greet Brett, who had also gotten out.

"Where's Will?"

"I don't know. His truck is empty," Brett said. "Alex is going to pull around, and then we're going to take a look around."

From what we could see, the entire area between the high beams was heavily used, flattened by footprints and tread marks. Homemade burlap backpacks littered the ground. A few feet away, tangled in some barbed wire, was a sleeping bag.

I thought of the guns, imagining them confiscated by the cartel, and Will gagged somewhere out in the middle of the desert, being accused of a double cross.

Will emerged from a shallow wash with a hoot. "Will you all look at this crap?"

"Whoa, where did you come from?" Jamie had joined me while Mick waited in his car.

"I went down there to take a leak," he said. "It didn't seem like a good idea to leave the truck running or the lights on. Come on, give me a hand."

The three of us walked over to the truck with Will. From inside the cab, he pulled out a knapsack with two handguns, the Beretta and Walther PPK.

"These two are for you and Alex," he said, handing them to Brett. "They're loaded, so be careful. I have the rifles in the back. You can give Mick his gun, but we might as well keep your gun secure until I take you around back."

"Thanks, Will," Brett said and then tipped a baseball cap and exaggerated a West Virginia accent. "Well, boys, I guess I'll see you on the other side."

"Roll a natural twenty," I said, which was game slang for a perfect hit, the kind that severs heads with the right weapon.

Will pulled the Weatherby from the back and held it out, not sure who would take it for Mick.

"You go," Jamie said to me. "I'll wait here."

I walked back over to Mick and opened the rear door on the driver's side. I slid the rifle into the back across the seat.

"Don't drive too fast," I said. "I'm sure Will wouldn't want it tossed around back there."

"No worries," he said. "I'm going to head to a turnoff we passed about a half-mile back and see if I can get a good angle. We got about an hour. Be cool, Brady."

"Right on," I said. "Be cool."

Mick put his car in reverse and turned around, kicking up dust again and adding to what Alex had also stirred when he turned the car around to face the direction we had come. He figured that pointing the Impala straight out was his best bet if anything happened.

I gave the Impala a little wave and shielded my eyes until Alex turned off the headlights. He was smoking, dangling the cigarette out of the driver's side window between drags, something I'm sure Brett didn't appreciate. But what was Brett going to do?

Alex was the boss tonight and, technically, he would be every night until he made his investment back. And that's why I envied Brett. He was lucky. He wouldn't have to put up with selling it. He'd be home in a week or so, waiting for a money order.

I almost walked over to the Impala, the open driver-side window beckoning to me, but then decided against it. I didn't have anything to say. I wasn't here for Alex, and I had already wished Brett good luck. It would be over in less than an hour, and all our lives and fortunes would change.

"You boys ready?" Will asked before directing us to get into the cab. We were as ready as we would ever be.

Even with Jamie in the middle, the truck felt spacious — more than capable of taking us to the position Alex had mapped earlier in the week. To get there, Will drove past the Impala and a little deeper into the foothills past the clearing, driving off the road and circling back around behind the incline that would give us a sight advantage over the clearing and gully.

Like Alex, Will made a U-turn so he could find the road when it was safe to leave. Then he hopped out of the truck, expecting us to follow his lead. We did, circling around to the back as he unpacked the other two rifles. He handed Jamie the Remington and then held one out for me. It wasn't the Garand. It was the M16.

"I said I wasn't going to take it," I said flatly, holding my hands up as if the weapon had been sitting on a stovetop too long.

"It wasn't my idea. But Alex did say you would say that," said Will. "Look, Brady, I don't care, but Alex told me that if you didn't take a gun, you should consider yourself cut out. So take it, don't take it, I don't care."

"Nobody is going to need an M16 tonight," I said. "It's stupid. This is just Alex trying to harass me again."

"Whatever," Will said, still holding it. "Not my problem."

"Heck," Jamie interjected. "I don't care. I'll take it."

We both looked at him, neither of us comfortable with the idea.

"You all said it yourselves," Jamie said with a broad grin. "You won't take the M16 and I want to take the M16. I wanted to take it from day one. Here, you take the Remington."

I didn't like it, but I didn't have much choice unless I wanted Alex to get the better of me. Remingtons were fine guns. It wasn't as nice as the Garand, but still a fast shooter, accurate, and nicely balanced.

"It has ten rounds," Will said to me before turning to Jamie. "I don't like this, but the M16 has a 30-round magazine. Come here and I'll show you how to use it, not that you'll be using it."

Will gave Jamie a crash course in using the lightweight weapon, showing him how to take the safety off and set it to semi-automatic firing. He also showed Jamie what to do if a round failed to load, pressing the forward assist. It took a couple minutes because he didn't need to learn anything else. Neither gun had any additional clips.

I didn't need any instructions. The Remington was self-explanatory. The only noticeable difference was that Will's dad had replaced its floor plate with a detachable 10-round magazine. It was ten times more ammunition than I needed.

Like the Weatherby, it was a hunting rifle, but this one lacked a scope.

The hill wasn't steep, maybe four or five hundred feet. I led the way, Jamie following close behind as I tackled the lowest angle with the least amount of blowdown. We hadn't thought to bring a rope.

I wish I had seen the terrain in the daylight because trying to climb it without having a complete picture of the slope felt stupid. Neither of us had dressed for hiking, but at least I was wearing jeans. Jamie was wearing street clothes, basketball shorts, and Vans.

Off to our right, as I climbed, I could hear rustling in the sage. It was probably a desert mouse or chipmunk, but the sound was still menacing, matching our movements and stopping when we stopped. As long as it wasn't a snake or coyote, we'd be okay scrambling over rocks with rifles slung over our backs.

"We should have brought headlamps," I called back to Jamie, more to hear my own voice than anything else.

"This sucks, man."

A general uneasiness began to seep in as the hill steepened toward the top. The speed of our ascent felt sluggish and unnatural. It reminded me of rock scrambles in Red Rock Canyon when we went hiking, but this terrain wasn't as tricky. It felt like climbing toward a void, my one free hand grasping at nothing but empty air.

Making it to the top of the ridge didn't do anything to ease our disorientation once I turned off the flashlight. Will had turned off his truck below us on the sloping side, and Alex had turned off the Impala's lights on the steeper side. If it weren't for the low rumble of an engine, I would have been lost.

By trying to not focus on anything, I could see Jamie scamper up to my right in my peripheral vision. It was a trick I learned as a Boy Scout. The scout master had told us our eyes are more sensitive to dull light and motion along the edges. I didn't know if it was true or not. What was true was that I could also make out the horizon on the other side of the clearing. A sliver of moonlight created a silhouette of the ridge line.

"Man, I can't see anything," Jamie said, shuffling closer to me.

"Me neither," I said, deciding it was easier than trying to explain anything.

"So what do we do now?"

"Wait, I guess."

"And then what?"

"I don't know, Jamie. I guess we'll be able to see more when the dealers get here. Their headlights should light up the whole area."

As I said it, I couldn't help but think that this was a stupid location for a meet. Aside from being well-used, hills on either side of the rough road were problematic. Anybody could set up an ambush on either side. It's what I would have done had this been a Dungeons & Dragons campaign and the players were meeting a dubious source. Even lowly orcs or goblins could give a torch-carrying group of adventurers some trouble in a place like this.

I glanced over at Jamie. He was still breathing heavily from the climb up. I suddenly didn't feel good about him sitting close to me with an M16. Too many things could go wrong.

"I don't think it's a good idea for us to clump together," I said. "You should move over more to the right and lie down instead of sitting up."

"I don't know, man," he said. "I'm wearing shorts."

"Just do it," I said. "And I don't think we should talk anymore. I'm starting to get a bad feeling about this."

The bad feeling came from my realization that the location wasn't as stupid as we had been. Alex agreed to meet in the dead of night in a place these dealers knew too well. So we might have been packing, but none of us were crack shots, and Jamie had never fired a gun. We weren't dressed for the desert. We didn't pack water. We hadn't thought about walkie talkies.

Our best bet was that everything would play out as smooth as Alex said. They would hand him the drugs. He would give them the money. They would leave first, and then we would all pack up and go home, thousands of dollars better off than we had ever dreamed.

So it all rested on Alex. He was the same kid that drove his car into a guard rail for kicks. The same kid who got a jolt out of smoking dope across from a police precinct. The same kid who wanted me to camp out with an M16 while I watched him do a drug deal. I'm glad I didn't have the bigger gun.

CHAPTER 11

NUTHIN' FANCY

Two cars pulled into the clearing, a black Grand National followed by a blue Chevy Nova. We knew they were coming long before Alex did, their high beams cutting a path through the desert for what felt like an hour. Alex saw them a few minutes before they arrived, flashing the lights of his Impala as they turned the last slight bend.

Both cars stopped on either side of the dirt road, angled inward so their headlights illuminated the Impala and blinded Alex and Brett. Jamie and me, we could see everything. The entire clearing was awash in light.

Nobody moved for a few minutes, a standoff of sorts until Alex decided to make it happen. He turned off his car and opened the driver's side door. Brett mirrored him, slowly exiting from the passenger side with a backpack in hand. He held it up.

Alex walked toward the other two cars, about twenty paces from the Impala. Brett followed, trailing six steps behind.

I don't know if Alex coached him to do it this way or not, but it seemed like they had done this a hundred times before. They appeared relaxed; my heart was pounding hard enough for both of them.

Alex stopped, holding up his hands in a gesture of goodwill. I took aim at the Grand National. Its doors opened first, with the driver and passenger getting out in much the same way Alex and Brett had done, except it was the driver who carried their backpack.

"Oh man, this is really happening," Jamie whispered to me.

I shushed Jamie and told him to cover the Chevy. A third guy was emerging from the passenger side, which probably meant there were four of them all together.

Alex seemed focused on the Grand National's passenger. He was the smallest of the three who were visible. I assumed it was Felix, recognition lighting up in their body language. They clasped hands and leaned in toward each other.

I couldn't hear anything, but their gestures told the story. Felix introduced Alex to the man with the backpack. He didn't look out of the ordinary. He was just a man wearing a burnt orange polo shirt. He had wavy black hair, a mustache, and some scruff under his chin. He and Alex clapped hands and started talking, with Alex more animated than usual.

I imagined the conversation was straight up. The middleman was talking about the product, and Alex was talking about cash in hand. This wasn't a one-time deal, but a first-time deal if everything went well. A two-hour drive and a fifteen-minute meeting were all it took to become major players on the west side suburbs of Las Vegas.

I glanced at the third man, who hung back from the exchange. There was no question he was packing. He wore a striped paisley-patterned shirt with his cuffs unbuttoned. The shirt was untucked over tan pants, and he stood with his legs shoulder-width apart, hands folded in the front. He was a soldier, unflinching except for the occasional adjustment of a belt holster hidden under the shirt.

I took slow, shallow breaths, in through my nose and out through my mouth, trying to keep calm. It wasn't working. I felt a strange sensation being up here, removed from everything going on below me but somehow standing right in the middle of it. My finger kept moving back and forth from the stock to the trigger.

None of those war movies I watched growing up on the living room floor of my grandparents' home could have prepared me for this moment. Every cell in my body was telling me to shoot, yet I knew there was a good chance I would freeze up if I had to do it.

I dissociated him from being human and then reminded myself that he was human. I could do it if I had to, but I would regret it all the same. Or maybe I couldn't do it after all, and the regret would be that I was nothing but a lousy kid playing deadly games in the dark.

When I returned my gaze to Alex and the middleman, their conversation was winding down. Orange shirt held the backpack out. Alex took it, unzipped the top, and looked inside. He nodded at the contents before holding it out for Brett. The two of them exchanged bags.

Alex's bag was a black rucksack emblazoned with a giant Rolling Stones logo, Mick Jagger's lips and protruding tongue. Leave it to Alex to pick out something that smacked of a joke.

And it was a joke. From this distance, I could see the orange shirt's body posture change as he opened the bag. His shoulders were confident when he felt its heft, and then slumped in disgust and confusion when he looked inside. Something was wrong.

"Oh no, Alex," I said. "No, no, no."

"What?" Jamie said. "What's wrong?"

"He never had the money," I said.

As Alex's left hand came down from passing over the sack, his right hand came up with the Beretta. He pulled the trigger just as the orange shirt looked up to ask if Alex was stupid. The unasked question was answered before the man's lips could move. The bullet punched in his forehead, dead center. Then Alex shot him again when he hit the ground.

Brett and Felix reacted to the first unexpected ear-splitting retort of the Beretta like a mirror image before taking different actions. Brett ducked, dropped the bag, and scrambled to grab a handgun tucked in his belt. Felix ducked and tried to spin away toward the Grand National for cover.

It was too late for Felix. As he ran toward the car, Alex shot him three times in the back.

Paisley shirt didn't waste any time drawing his weapon and firing at Alex and Brett as he back-peddled toward the Chevy for protection. Brett danced with every crack, throwing his hands up in the air as if they could ward away the bullets. Alex never moved. He just stood there like a grinning idiot before pivoting to level his gun on the last man standing.

Alex never had to fire. Two more shots broke the air in overlapping succession, snaps that were more distant and unforgiving. The first bullet hit the paisley shirt square in the chest, knocking him over. The second, coming from a different direction, tore into Brett, somewhere between his chest and collar bone, spinning him around like a rag doll. He dropped his gun and fell to the ground.

As paisley shirt also fell, the Chevy's engine roared to life and lurched forward with the intent to run Alex and Brett over. As soon as it did, Jamie stood up to my right, flipped the M16 to fully automatic, and unloaded his entire clip in the car with three successive bursts.

The rounds punched into the hood and roof of the Chevy, taking out one of the headlights and shattering the windshield. Jamie was screaming as he did it, a wild crazed war cry that jolted me out of my paralysis.

"Get down!" I yelled at him as whoever shot Brett turned their attention to us. "They see you!"

Jamie flopped flat on the ground, grunting as he landed on the rocks and desert shrub. Several bullets whizzed past our area in steady succession, hornets in the night. Two ricocheted off the ground, one dangerously close to me, kicking up small stones. I fired the Remington in response, aiming toward the muzzle flashes I had seen in the distance.

"Stay down," I said, huffing at Jamie but he wouldn't listen.

"I'm out and out of here!" Jamie screamed, throwing the M16 down.

He stood straight up and started down the hill toward Will's truck. The shooter took two more shots, missing him. So I pulled my trigger twice in response. Mick had started firing on that position, too, trying to confuse the shooter as to which one of us might be a priority target.

Neither one of us had a prayer to hit him, but we did a decent job at distracting him. Alternating fire gave Alex enough time to get Brett off the ground and over to the Impala. Once they were inside and driving away, I slid to my right and retrieved the abandoned M16. Unlike Jamie, I didn't stand up. I rolled onto my butt and scooted down until I was sure my head was out of the line of fire.

Then I scampered down the hill toward the truck below. Will had already started his engine. Jamie was screaming, his shorts had gotten stuck on a sagebrush while he slid toward the headlights. As soon as he was free, he was bounding down the slope again.

"Wait for me! Wait for me!" he yelled, voice heaving.

"Hurry up!" Will yelled from the cab. "Back of the truck. I ain't waiting!"

I was twenty feet behind Jamie and closing, trying to balance myself between a run and a skid down the hill. The truck was already moving by the time Jamie reached it. He threw himself over the tailgate and into the back.

When I hit ground level, I had some distance to make up and broke into a sprint, catching up as the truck started to traverse the terrain. The guns went into the back first, and then I clung onto the tailgate, my feet trying to find the back fender as the truck labored across the desert in search of the ruts that had led us behind the ridge.

Once on the dirt path, I secured the guns and rapped on the truck's rear window. I thought this would be a good time for us to climb into the cab, but Will wasn't having it. He wasn't going to slow down or stop for anything.

"We don't have time," Will said. "Hang on. We're getting out of here!"

It was a good thing Alex had already driven out of the clearing because Will gunned the engine, expecting the shooter was waiting to take another shot. Jamie and I expected more gunfire too. We pressed ourselves against the inside of the truck bed, expecting to become targets as soon as the truck was exposed to the light. But no shots came.

The whole area was obscured by a cloud of dust that the Impala had kicked up, and now Will was adding to it as we barreled past the dead Chevy and now empty Grand National. Looking back, I noted the carnage we were leaving behind.

Four dead bodies and one dead vehicle. They had been stupid, but so had we. None of us considered that the cartel might have positioned their own precautionary shooter or shooters on another hill.

More horrifying was the idea that Alex had betrayed us as much as them. The consequences were exponential. Someone had seen us, and they were still out there. They would know the Impala and come for it. And in coming for it, they would be coming for Alex. And in coming for Alex, they would be coming for the rest of us.

Will must have been thinking the same thing because he meant it when he said he wasn't slowing down. He kept speeding up. He hadn't seen Brett hit like we had, but he may as well have. He was panicking and pushing his truck harder.

With each successive turn, we found ourselves skittering across the back of the truck and bouncing off the bed with every dip or hill. The worst of them launched us as much as six inches into the air, with every landing hard, bare skin on metal. I was pounding on the cab in between the jolts of terror, but it wasn't doing any good.

"We're out! We're out! We're out!"

I said it over and over, and Will waved me off as the truck ripped across the desert road, stones and dust flying up in a cloud of debris behind us. I could hear Jamie praying for it all to be over as the truck bucked and spun. But his prayer wasn't working. Every impact seemed to come faster and harder than the last until I was convinced that I would fly right out of the truck bed the next time I was airborne.

I had no choice but to put my faith in the guns, grabbing onto their straps and trying to maintain a low center of gravity. Jamie put his faith in the side of the truck, burrowing his fingers into the grooves that ran alongside the bed frame. It was a mistake.

On one of the bumps, Jamie was bucked feet-over-head. The last things touching were his fingers, clasping a tiny slot meant for a camper shell. He couldn't hold on. As I reached out for him, the world slowed to a near standstill. I was too late. He flew out, discarded into the desert.

"Damn it, Will!" I screamed, pounding on the back of the cab again. "We lost Jamie, man! You have to stop! Please, Lord, stop!"

I didn't know what else to do, so I kept on pounding and yelling, standing up in the bed so I could beat on the cab's roof despite the risks. I was crying now, hysterical about everything that had gone down. Brett being shot. Jamie being lost. Alex throwing us to the wolves. The relentless roar of this runaway truck.

A few minutes later, Will did slow and stop. He slid open the window in the back of his cab, panting as if he had been the one in the back, holding on for dear life instead of me. He was crying the adrenaline out of his body; slowly grasping that his worst fears had come true.

"I'm sorry," he said. "I'm so sorry."

I think we were all sorry. But I'm not sure we knew what we were sorry for other than allowing our lives to fall so far away from our control.

"Just turn around and go back," I said. "We have to find him."

We did find Jamie a couple miles back. His prayers might not have slowed the truck down soon enough, but someone or something had protected him. He was cut up and bruised, but he said no broken bones. I didn't believe him. People who fly out of truck beds die all the time.

Jamie chalked it up to landing on soft soil and sagebrush. Will swore he wasn't going as fast as we thought. I still thought it was a miracle. That, and Jamie probably had a concussion.

He wasn't acting like himself. He was more relieved that Will came back for him than upset by the recklessness. Of course we came back, I told Jamie. We didn't have a choice. He would have died out here if we hadn't.

A silence fell upon the three of us after I said it. Maybe we had just postponed the inevitable. He was going to die anyway. We were all going to die anyway.

CHAPTER 12

DON'T FEAR

Real bullets don't behave as they do on television, piercing the tissue and embedding themselves into some muscle so a doctor, medic, or tough guy can pop them out with tweezers for a souvenir. No, they dislocate limbs and shatter bones, turning someone's entire body into a weapon as little bits of matter become projectiles. They fly around on the inside doing more damage like dominoes.

By the time Alex helped Brett to the Impala, he was fading. The bullet had hit the spot where the collarbone meets the sternum, shattering parts of both and sending pieces of bone into Brett's throat and left lung. It had also dislocated his shoulder, fractured two ribs, and lodged on the inside of his scapula.

When he fell, he fell hard, breaking an elbow and fracturing his skull. By the time Alex arrived at the medical center with a made-up story, Brett was in and out of consciousness as dark circles appeared under his eyes and liquid drained from his ears and nose.

Alex said he ran into the hospital, yelling for help. He said that someone — probably a rancher — had taken pot shots at him and his friends while they were out night hiking.

Shortly after two attendants walked out to assess Brett, one ran back in, calling for a gurney and more help. The emergency room lit up, doctors and nurses following alongside as they wheeled Brett from the parking lot into surgery. Everyone else made phone calls or paged specialists. He needed them all.

Alex stayed in the waiting room for a few hours until Mick arrived. He wanted Mick to stay with Brett once he came out of surgery. Someone needed to coach him on the story Alex told. It was a good one. After taking his statement, Metro dispatched officers to question the alleged shooter, a rancher with a predilection for discharging his weapon anytime he saw trespassers.

Alex knew the police would come up empty, but he didn't care. He wanted the police as far away from the actual site as possible, and the rancher lived in the opposite direction. So the story was, as Mick told me, that the three of them — Alex, Brett, and Mick — went night hiking north of town like they sometimes do. It's a great place to see the city lights.

They had done it many times before, but this trip was different. Someone, a rancher, they assumed, mistook them for trespassers, even though they never climbed a fence or came across any markers. Frightened by the first shots and disoriented, they ran toward the rancher, one of the bullets hitting Brett. After that, the shooting died down enough for Alex and Mick to help Brett back to the car.

The story wasn't perfect, but it didn't need to be. Everyone was focused on Brett. He was in serious condition, and his parents were hundreds of miles away in West Virginia. Without any family in town, the hospital bent the rules and let Mick sit with him after surgery. When I arrived, Mick told them I was family and could take his place so he could get some rest.

As far as anybody knew, I was at home and sleeping like a baby when Brett got shot. Earlier that day, my mother unknowingly became an alibi if I needed one. She busted into my room, waking me up from a bad dream, and telling me that Mick's mom had told her something frightful.

"Thank goodness you were on restriction," she said, an unrecognizable look of concern painted across her face.

"What are you talking about?" I mumbled, turning away from her to keep any bruises under the covers.

"There's been an accident," she said. "Brett's been shot, and he's at the hospital. For a minute, I thought you snuck out with them."

"What? Who? Why would I do that?"

"It doesn't matter," she said. "You're here. You're safe."

"You're saying Brett's been shot?" I sat up but kept the blankets close, feigning embarrassment so she wouldn't come over and hug me. It almost looked like she wanted to, a sympathetic stranger in my room.

"Yes, he's at UMC," she said. "It doesn't look good, Brady. Mick's with him right now."

"I have to go see him," I said. "I feel like I should be there."

It was the one thing I could think of to get out of the house, wanting to know how badly Brett was hurt. I also realized they had come up with a story, and we had to get it straight. She told me to slow down, get dressed, and we would talk about it. It was aggravating. She promised to take me, but not until late afternoon.

I tried to make the best of it, pulling together a few things. I had this dumb idea to bring a few things from Dungeons & Dragons along, like the descriptions of a few magical items his dwarf had picked up while Mick played for him. I had also drawn a few new pictures to show him. In our campaign, Gimli had risen to become the King of Lortmil Mountains. So that's how I drew him.

All this was before I knew how badly he was hurt. None of it was needed, at least not for Brett. There was no turning back the clock to a time when our biggest problem was whose character should open the trapped chest after we failed to disarm it. The best I could do was read to him while he slept or sit and pray, something I hadn't done since I was ten.

It was after my mother dropped me off that Mick filled me in on everything I missed before he went home. I was glad it was him. I don't know what I would have done if Alex had still been at the hospital. Brett was here because of him.

"Don't look at it that way," Mick said. "Alex saved his life."

"Are you kidding me?"

"After everything went bad, he kept his cool. He was being shot at and still got Brett out of there. He got it all — the gun, the heroin, and the cash."

"I was there. I'm not so sure it was in that order."

"Does it matter?"

"I'm also not sure he had any cash either."

"What makes you say that?"

"Mick, I already said it. I was there. I saw it go down. The guy in the orange shirt opened the bag and saw something was wrong. That's why Alex shot him and then shot Felix."

"No, the other guy drew first. You must have missed that when you panicked."

"I didn't panic."

"What else would you call opening up with an M16 on fully automatic?"

"That wasn't me. It was Jamie."

"Jamie?" This surprised him. "Why would Will give a gun like that to Jamie?"

"I wouldn't take it." I shrugged. "I told Alex I wouldn't take it, so I didn't."

He considered this for a minute, scratching the red stubble on his chin. I could see him rewriting the chain of events in his mind. Alex drew his gun. Alex kills the middleman and Felix. The third man fires his weapon. Mick takes him down. Then Jamie opens up with a machine gun before we started firing at the hidden shooter.

"That makes more sense," he said. "So the guy in the polo drew on Alex, and then Jamie panicked."

"Are you even listening to me?"

"What, Brady? What do you want me to say?"

"He's no hero Mick. He screwed us."

"Well, that's not even important right now," he said. "All you need to remember is that three of us went hiking to see the lights. You knew because we asked you to go, but you couldn't because you were in the doghouse. Then some stupid rancher started shooting at us. At least we think it was a rancher. It could have been anybody."

"Yeah, sure," I said, but I couldn't let it go. "Jamie almost died last night, too, you know. Will freaked out and bounced Jamie right out of the truck bed at what felt like sixty or seventy miles per hour. He almost bounced me out too. So it could have been me. It almost was me."

"I'll talk to them," he said.

"So that's it?" He didn't bite on my exaggeration.

"Yeah, that's it. Oh, and Alex wanted me to give you this."

He tossed me a small plastic bag. I didn't have to look to know. I shook my head.

"So that's the way it is," I said. "All business."

"That's the way it is," he said.

"Brett is fighting for his life, and we're selling dope."

I said it like it was the stupidest thing in the world, snide and sarcastic to get a rise out of him.

"I don't know what it is with you. You think we're going to sit around and roll dice after what happened?" His face was redder than his freckles, and he swept a hand toward my books and drawings on the service tray. "Grow up, Brady. We all wanted this to work. Brett doesn't want to live in West Virginia. Will doesn't want to work at Farm Basket. You got all that crap with your mother. Alex has his mom's deadbeat boyfriend. And I don't think my parents will last the year together."

"What?" I didn't know anything was wrong between his folks.

"Yeah, pretty sure my dad is having an affair," he said. "All those extra hours aren't overtime. Well, maybe some of them are, but not all of them."

This surprised me. I always thought of his parents as the perfect match. The cop and nurse, working graveyard shifts so that they could spend more time together. Never mind what we did there, Mick's house always seemed stable.

"I'm sorry, man," I said. "I didn't know."

There was a time I would have known. He used to tell me everything.

"Now you know," he said. "Look, it doesn't matter why it happened. All that matters is that we keep our stories straight. A rancher shot Brett. And when somebody else asks about what Alex did, and they will, Alex didn't have a choice."

"It will be our word against the guy who shot Brett," I said.

He tightened his lips and ran his fingers through his wavy hair. He had lost his patience with me.

"You guys didn't think any of them were going to make it out of there," I said to break the silence. "Did you?"

"I'm too tired to keep this up," he said. "Just go along to get along for once."

He didn't say anything else. He just shook his head and left me with the steady, quiet thrum of Brett's breathing. I looked over at him — raccoon eyes, bandages matting his hair, oxygen pumped into his nose — and wondered if he had known.

The way Brett fumbled for his gun, I assume he didn't. The way Mick fumbled the conversation, I assume he didn't either. Maybe Mick might not want to admit it, but Alex committed us to a very dangerous game, much more dangerous than orcs and goblins, giants and dark elves.

Drug cartels had this weird, one-off symbiotic relationship with Las Vegas. Several kingpins and bosses considered it their second home, running millions of dollars through the casinos. The Mob didn't want them dealing in town, but they weren't against treating some of them like royalty, guests taking up residence inside two-story suites along the Las Vegas Strip. On occasion they made the news, like the one that murdered a federal judge in San Antonio a few years earlier.

I kept thinking that if they could kill a federal judge like we saw they did on the news, it wouldn't be anything for them to kill any of us or all of us. They might not have owned Vegas like the Mob, but they were hard baked into its unraveling fabric. The only thing we didn't know was where Alex's connection fit. As Mick's dad liked to say of them — the Mob, the movie industry, the drug cartels, the feds, the corporate types — were connected in one way or another.

We heard about it every night over dinner. Mob men were becoming informants. Feds were on the take. The parents of movie actors bought guns for cartel hitmen. Big money was buying casinos with corporations. It was a wild ride like musical chairs. Everybody in Vegas understood this, and the safe play was to not talk about it. Let the big boys work it out and hope you are not around when a car bomb goes off.

As it turned out, I was glad I brought the game along after all. For the next couple of hours, I blocked everything else in the back of my mind and created a side adventure for Gimli and one of my characters, Argon. Argon was a high-level ranger, a cross between Aragorn from *Lord of the Rings* and Prince Barin from *Flash Gordon*. I played it as if Brett was right there with me, awake and as animated as ever when we played.

The thing about Dungeons & Dragons that parents or people who never played didn't understand is that the bonds you make during the campaign feel like any real-life adventure you might share with someone. The problem-solving, the imagined combat, and the conflicts between characters all play out in approximated real time, slowed down or sped up as needed.

Game play is a shared experience that you talk about the same way as any other memory, saying things like, "remember that time when you slipped off the ice ledge in the glacial rift of the frost giant Jarl?" Brett or Mick would remember because every character that was roped together almost tumbled over the edge.

Mick's character, Garth, and my other character, Spinner, saved the day. Being an overman with exceptional strength, Garth anchored the group to buy some time. Spinner was a brùnaidh, like a tiny house elf, only this one had studied magic and became a great wizard. When Gimli slipped, and most of the group went over the edge with him after failing saving throws, Spinner had just enough time to find the right spell.

Wasn't that the same scenario we were playing now? Brett had slipped over the edge, and we were all in danger. Mick would have to buy us some time while I found the right spell to save us.

"Remember the other time Gimli didn't make the saving throw?" I asked Brett. "You got so mad that you threw the dice at me."

It had come down to the same trio of characters fighting against a dragon I had created to be more potent than Tiamat, which was an evil dragon goddess with five different evil dragon heads. I had invented a new dragon because our characters had become so powerful that the challenge felt like it was waning. I named the dragon Sabazios and modeled him after an acid-spitting black dragon, only stronger. Gimli was the one who didn't make a saving throw, and he died, disintegrated in acid.

Never underestimate someone's attachment to a fictional character after they've played it for a couple of years. Brett was so upset that I had to send the characters on another quest after their loss against Sabazios. Their new goal was simple: resurrect Gimli. So we brought him back to life, but there was a penalty. Gimli had lost his primary weapon, the Axe of Dwarvish Lords, forever.

"You never had much luck with saving throws," I said to Brett as if he could hear me, trying to lighten my mood. "Maybe that's all you need now."

I rolled a twenty-sided die on the tray, and it came up a three, not enough to save anyone for anything. Startled, I swatted it off the tray and pretended it was still rolling so the three wouldn't stand. The die rolled across the floor and toward the door. I stood up to retrieve it, hoping for a better outcome.

"Lose something?"

Cheryl was standing in the doorway, smiling. She bent over and picked up the die.

"You didn't happen to see what it landed on, did you?"

"I didn't look," she said, crossing to me, oblivious. "Sorry."

"It's not important," I said. "I'm just messing around."

"More fantasy stuff?" She looked at the screens, figures, and dice I had out.

"Something we used to play together. I thought, I don't know, it might help somehow," I said, embarrassed. "What are you doing here?"

"I came by to apologize for the other night," she said. "Your folks told me you were here and might like some company."

"Yeah, maybe." I started folding the screens, closing the books, and stacking them up.

"You don't have to stop," she said, honing in on one of the portraits I had drawn of Gimli. "This is good. Have you ever tried drawing a real portrait?"

"I drew portraits of Kiss last year," I said. "Does that count?"

"I'd love to see them."

"I sold them to Trish Two for twenty, five bucks apiece," I said. "Too late."

"Is it?"

"What?"

"Too late?"

"The doctors say he'll come out of it, but nobody knows," I said. It wasn't what she was talking about, but I couldn't think about her and me.

"Your parents said a rancher shot him?"

"So they say," I said.

"But that's not what happened."

I shrugged and looked up at her. Why did she have to be so beautiful? Her face was so lively, even in the worst of circumstances. Her passionate mouth held a familiar smirk, played up by bright amber eyes always framed with light blue and green eyeshadow.

I didn't say anything to her, but she knew. She came closer to the chair and begged me to get up with her hands. I relented, and she hugged me.

It wasn't a passionate or playful hug but something altogether different. It was deep and firm, something reserved for people who have known each other a lifetime instead of days or weeks. The comfort of it, something I hadn't felt in so long, made me want to cry for Brett and, not only him, for everything I had lost over the last five years.

"I thought you could use it," she said, giving me a final squeeze before she let me go.

When she did, we stood face to face for a minute, and she reached up to wipe an errant tear from one of my eyes. I didn't know it was there, but her pouty smile assured me it was all right.

"He's your friend, Brady," she said. "We don't always recognize how important our friends are until we come close to losing them or lose them outright."

"Yeah, I suppose."

"That's why I'm here," she said. "I don't know what we are exactly, but I spent the night thinking about it, and I'm not ready to say goodbye."

"I'm glad you're here," I said, trying to regain control of my feelings. "Brett isn't the best conversationalist right now."

She laughed at that and then suggested we head down to the cafeteria, saying the change in scenery might refresh my spirits.

She was right. Sometimes a Coke and a smile can do wonders for your disposition.

We didn't stay in the cafeteria very long. I didn't want to leave Brett alone. I didn't like the idea of him waking up with nobody around, never mind the mission of story collaboration that Alex and Mick had assigned me.

When we weren't talking, having Cheryl around inspired a casual confidence that comes from knowing the end game might be better than the middle. There was a way out of the fog, and she was the beacon.

"One of these days, you'll have to teach me to play," she said, paging through one of my books.

"Sure, what would you be?"

"Maybe a bard," she said.

I laughed. "Nobody's a bard."

"No? Aren't they a jack-of-all-trades?"

I rolled my eyes. "It's never helped me."

"Funny," she said. "You don't strike me as someone who can play a lute."

"You got me," I said. "I cannot play a lute."

"I'd play one," she said. "Sometimes storytellers are the only people who can save us."

We talked for a bit longer about the merits, or lack thereof, of bards. She almost convinced me there was a place for them. Then we both fell into a quiet meditation; our chairs pulled close enough that our legs were touching. We just sat there like quiet guardians, overlooking Brett, and the room returned to a near silent state like before she arrived. I could have stayed there with her all night.

When Mick returned to the hospital, he was rested and refreshed. He was surprised to see Cheryl but accepted she was my ride home. He told us Brett's parents were on a red eye flight, so the hospital might not be as lenient about visitors tomorrow. There was nothing we could do except wait and see.

Cheryl took me home and waved goodbye from her car. She had some things to take care of in the morning and needed to get home. We didn't kiss or anything, but she suggested I give myself a break and go to the drive-in with her. I reminded her that I was on restriction, which made her laugh.

"I talked to your mom," she said. "Not anymore."

It didn't make sense, but what does when you follow your heart?

CHAPTER 13

BETTER RUN

I didn't sleep well after Cheryl dropped me off. There were too many loose ends, and I kept running them over and over. I know Mick said he would talk to Jamie and Will, but I felt like I needed some time with them too, especially Will.

Sometimes Will got up early to work on his car, a '72 Duster he never drove because the engine needed so much help. We teased him, saying he should trade it for a Hoover. He could push it faster and the garage would be cleaner. Win-win.

Will's house was different from most. It was the split-level facing south on the closest inside corner of our horseshoe-shaped street, but with a detached garage around the corner. It faced west. So while he lived next door to Mick, we always thought of Will as living around the corner. Nobody ever knocked on his front door. We just caught him in the garage with the hood of the Duster up.

Not today. The garage was shut. I thought about waiting around a few minutes when I noticed the weathered reddish-brown Volare with a tan vinyl roof. It was parked a few houses down the street.

As I squinted to get a better look, it pulled out, creeping away from the curb and toward me. I couldn't make out any of the occupants. As it approached, I could hear the music. It was

Spanish. I didn't understand the words, but the singer's heart was breaking. *Él me mintió. No me amaba, nunca me amó.*

Mine started pounding as the Volare angled toward me instead of staying on the right side of the street. I took a step back, a bad feeling spreading up from my toes into my stomach. I turned around, picking up the pace in the opposite direction.

As soon as I rounded the corner, I heard the car accelerate, so I broke into a run but not home. I cut across Will's lawn to the fence between his and Mick's house.

Will had one of the few houses in the neighborhood with a wooden fence instead of cinderblock. It made it more difficult to climb, my feet scrambling to find a foothold, splinters threatening my fingers as they gripped the top of the fence. My adrenaline helped me over, my feet landing on Will's doghouse before I jumped down into the backyard alongside the house, startling his two pit bulls.

They were closer to the garage on the opposite side of the yard when I came over the fence. Both of them lurched back in surprise and bounded toward me. I had maybe a half-second before they recognized me or ripped me apart.

You hear about this kind of stuff on the news all the time. Pit bulls maul nosy neighbors and unsuspecting owners. They snap arms, tear flesh, and go for the throat.

"Horus, Hathor," I said in a stern exhale. "It's me! You know me!"

Both slowed at the sound of my voice, and I held out my hand so they could sniff it. I half expected Horus to sink his teeth into the flesh, but he gave me a gentle lick.

"So good to see you, boy," I said, reinforcing the connection. "So good to see you."

They pushed past me and climbed up on the doghouse Will had built between his home and the side wall fence they shared with Mick's family. Hathor was growling at the wooden section I had climbed over. Horus started barking at something on the other side.

I slid around the back corner of the house. If one of the car's passengers took a look, they wouldn't see me. They'd only see two very unhappy pit bulls who weren't interested in having any more uninvited guests.

"Come on over," I whispered to myself. "I dare you, double dare you."

Nobody was coming over. With the dogs there, they wouldn't chance a look.

"Dude, what are you doing back here?"

Will was standing at his back door, holding half a grapefruit in one hand and a spoon in the other. I stood up from a squat and brushed off my pants as if this was the most natural encounter in the world. His mouth was drawn up into his familiar goofy half smile as if everything in life had a punchline.

"Hey, Will," I said. "Guess I'm interrupting your breakfast."

"You're lucky you weren't breakfast," he said, motioning to his dogs as they came back around when they heard his voice.

"These cuties? Nah, they know me," I said, reaching down to scratch Horus behind the ears. "Don'tcha?"

"Well, you're here," he said. "Want to come inside?"

"Thanks."

The back door was three steps up to a small patio because the kitchen was on the high side of the split-level. The mess in the sink reminded me that Will and his dad had been on their own for the last few years. Dishes were stacked, waiting to be washed.

"Mick said he talked to you yesterday," I said. "So I thought I would stop by."

"Yeah, we talked."

"You cool with everything?"

"Mostly," he said. "It's probably smart Alex is dumping his car, but I don't like the idea of him keeping the Beretta for a while. I'm already in deep, losing the M16 like I did."

All of this was news to me. I didn't know where to begin.

"I saved the M16," I said. "It was latched in the back of the truck with the Remington."

"Sure. It's also a murder weapon. Same with the Beretta and the Weatherby. I haven't figured what I'm going to do yet, but I better have it figured soon. My dad will notice them missing more sooner than later."

"What if we go out there and clean up the site?" I asked. "Then there's no evidence."

"The site's already clean," he said. "Didn't Mick tell you?"

No, he didn't tell me because Cheryl was standing right there last night. So I didn't know anything. Will must have seen it on my face because he made a muted snort like it amused him. He knew more than me for a change.

"Alex went back out there after he left the hospital. Everything was gone. The cars, the bodies, even that stupid sleeping bag that was left behind," he said. "Weird, huh? And then Alex got weirder on me."

"Alex? He talked to you too, not just Mick?"

"Yeah, Alex. He started going off about the Golden Rule. Do unto others as you would have them do unto you. Except he says it differently. He says: 'Do unto others as they do unto you.' So if I treat him badly, then he won't treat me with consideration. He says that, right now, all of us are under his spell or protection or something like that. Isn't that your Dungeons & Dragons stuff?"

"No, Alex doesn't like D&D," I said. "That's his Church of Satan stuff, except he's not a member. He likes to pretend."

"Pretend or not, it sounds pretty stupid to me," Will said. "Pisses me off a little. I wouldn't be involved with Alex if it wasn't for you and Mick. He's a loose cannon. Same with Jamie."

"They're Mick's friends, not mine."

"Tomato, tomahto," he said. "We don't choose our family, but we sure as heck choose our friends, and you've chosen yours. Speaking of which, you didn't tell me why you were in the backyard."

"Oh, it was nothing. I saw a car I didn't recognize and got spooked."

"Well, next time, come up to the front door," he said, smirking. "I wouldn't want Horus and Hathor to hurt you by accident. Dogs don't recognize people by their faces as much as our voices and smells."

"Sorry, I'll keep it in mind."

"You do that," said Will. "You can also tell Mick that when I get the Beretta back and my cash, I'm out."

"Sure, anything else?"

"Not to be rude or anything, but yeah ... I got to get ready for work."

"Okay." I started toward the front door.

"Oh, one more thing. It's something my dad says: 'If the devil can't make you bad, he'll make you busy.'"

"What does that mean?"

"I don't know, but it sure seems like someone is keeping you busy."

"I guess," I said. "I'll see you."

It was strange seeing Will agitated instead of his usual, affable self. I didn't like it. When people get nervous, they act out of character. That was the last thing anybody needed.

I let myself out, taking a long look out the front door to see if the Volare was still out. It wasn't there, which was a relief. I pulled the door shut and headed home, my head turning everything over and over. I didn't need another distraction.

There was too much I didn't know, and Mick hadn't had the chance to tell me. Murder scenes don't clean themselves.

I was having a hard time wrapping my head around the idea. I hadn't thought of it as a murder scene. Until Will called it that, it was just a place where things went sideways. But he was right. It was so much more than that. We murdered people. They were bad people, but I don't think that matters.

Thinking about it made me unsettled, a queasiness I couldn't shake. I didn't know anything about those guys we left in the desert. Not even Felix, which was just some name Alex called his source.

It gave me the urge to stop by Mick's house, but there wasn't any point. His car was gone, and his parents were home. They were probably having breakfast for dinner or already sleeping before their next twelve-hour shift. I never understood how people could live like that, but Mick summed it up yesterday. They didn't do it well.

I decided to go home and call the hospital. Maybe I could ask my mother to take me over for a few hours since Cheryl wouldn't be around until later. My mother might be agreeable if I promised Cheryl could pick me up from the hospital. It would save her a second trip.

When I cleared the oleanders between Mick's house and mine, I heard someone approaching to my right. They weren't walking. They were running. My first thought was it was one of those thugs from the car, so I braced myself and turned around with my hands up and ready.

It was Jamie. He had run up to me, chest puffed up and arms slung back, a cast on his left hand. I guess he had been hurt after all.

"Hey, man," I said. "You scared me for a second."

"Yeah, you should be scared," he said, scowling at me. "You should be wetting yourself, smart-mouth punk."

He gave me an unexpected shove. It wasn't a hard push, but the cast was sharp, and it unbalanced me. He wasn't playing around.

"Whoa," I said. "What's going on?"

"What are you doing telling people I panicked?" He bared his teeth at me. "I didn't panic. You panicked. You and your little pop gun. You didn't shoot anybody. I did."

"What are you talking about?"

"I'm talking about me saving the day and you not doing anything except running your mouth," he said. "I think it's time someone shut it for you."

"Forget it," I said. "I'm not fighting you."

"Right, because you're all talk," he said. "When it went down last night, you choked. I was the one who saved Alex and Brett."

"If you say so."

"I do say so," he spat. "So stop talking smack about panicking. I didn't panic. You did."

"Okay, hero," I said. "You saved the day. See you around."

I didn't give him a chance to respond. I turned back to my house, putting up a hand and giving him a little wave. It made him furious. He started circling me in a lazy arch and jumping up and down like a movie prizefighter. I ignored it, but he kept following me up the driveway, taunting me to turn around and fight him.

"Come on, Brady," Jamie said. "Chicken. You chicken?"

I wouldn't take the bait. So he decided to make a move. He came up from behind as I cleared the driveway and gave me a shove. I flew forward into the front windows. The panes of glass buckled, rattling the house. I could see my mother startled, leaping up off the couch before I spun around and chased Jamie into the street.

"You want to fight so bad, bring it," I screamed at him. "Come on!"

He threw a weak jab with his right, and I knocked it away and then another. I could hear my mother coming out of the house and yelling nonsense at us. She sounded like those wailing Iranians we saw on the television news sometimes. She wanted us to stop, but it was too late. When Jamie threw a glancing blow off my chest, I punched him in the forehead with my right hand and then in the stomach with my left.

We may have been evenly matched in size, both lanky kids, but there was no mistake about who had more experience in a street fight. I punched him again, and he dropped to a knee, cutting it open on the asphalt. He started to get up, so I hammered down on his head and shoulders, stopping when I felt my mother grab my right hand as I cocked it back for another swing.

"Brady, that's enough. Get in the house right now!"

"Yeah, Brady," Jamie said, wiping blood from his lip. "Listen to mommy."

"You too, Jamie," she said, snapping at him. "You go on before I let him beat some sense into you."

Jamie started to say something but changed his mind when she let go of me. Her face twisted, transforming into a banshee all too familiar to me. She was taunting him, ready to chase him across the street and into his home. He didn't argue anymore. His expression softened, and he started to walk home.

"This ain't over, Brady," he said.

"Oh yes, it's over," she called after him. "Don't come back except to apologize."

Any thought that my mother was an ally was dismissed by the time we reached the front door. She didn't want to hear it, she said, before I could say anything. I was relegated to my room to calm down.

"I don't know what you were thinking," she said. "You almost went through a window."

I shut my door before she could say anything else. Jamie didn't hit me hard, but he did get in one lucky swing, a glancing blow with his cast. It made my cheek sting. The spot was tender now, but the skin didn't break. I lay back on the couch in my room, kicking my feet over the armrest and covering my head with a pillow.

I was stuck in my room again. I had come to think of it as a desert island and the few things I owned had washed up on the beach.

It wasn't much, marginally more than I had when I lived with my grandparents. Aside from fantasy books and D&D manuals, I owned a stereo I once placed on layaway until I earned enough money to pay for it by mowing lawns and renting pencils in the sixth grade. I had a small television with three channels on a good day.

I was more likely to play music than watch television. But more valuable than either possession was a ream of paper and colored pencils. They helped me to escape to different times and places when I couldn't leave out the window. And when things felt bleak, I set the paper aside and drew lines on my forearms with a hunting knife.

I wasn't interested in any of those things today. All I could think about was the wild look in Jamie's bloodshot eyes. He didn't see me as much as he was obsessed with the thought of me and what I had done or didn't do, said or didn't say. Then I wondered what fueled his rage. Fear? Guilt? Anxiety? Drugs?

I didn't know. All I knew was that our pact was fractured, inside and out. Brett was unconscious. Will was out. Jamie was unhinged. Mick was beguiled. And Alex? He was the one keeping us busy.

I pushed the pillow off my head and unfolded my hunting knife. If the Volare drive-by wasn't random, none of us had a chance.

CHAPTER 14

TOO LATE

Everything feels different when my mother lets me out of the box. She doesn't even say a word about it, too busy tittering over Cheryl knocking on the door and asking if I was home. I could hear them from my bedroom.

"Are you wondering if he can come out and play?"

I could tell my mother had had a drink or two. It wasn't something she did at home in the afternoon. Maybe the fight shook her. I didn't know. I wasn't going to ask.

"We had plans to see a movie, Mrs. C," Cheryl said. "I thought it might be good to give him a break from worrying about Brett."

"Aren't you the mothering type," she said. "Fine, as long as you don't split up. I don't need him coming home drunk or stoned again."

"It's just a movie. Double feature."

"Curfew is midnight," she said absently. "It might not be for you, but it is for him."

"Understood."

"Has there been any word about Brett?" I asked, emerging from my bedroom to break the tension. "Hey, Cheryl."

"Hey."

"He's unconscious but stable," my mother said. "George said his parents made it in on their flight. They're probably there now. I don't really know. I get little bits from different people but never the whole picture."

"I was thinking about stopping by the hospital," I said. "Today's out, but maybe tomorrow."

"We'll see," she said.

"All right," I sighed. "Do you mind if we get going?"

She stopped me before I could make my escape and put a hand under my chin. She was looking at my cheek, still crimson and puffy. She bit down on the inside of her mouth, a habit that made her face contort. Then she ran her thumb over the wound. She made sure it stung before releasing me.

"Have fun," she said, waving me off.

"Night, Mrs. C," Cheryl said.

We were halfway to the Pinto when Cheryl asked me what that was all about. I pushed her off, saying I didn't want to talk about it around here. I didn't want to talk about any of it anywhere, even if the fight and last few days were the only things I thought about.

Our first stop was the 7-Eleven between my house and hers. We were trolling for beer.

She parked to the left of the store by a dumpster, just out of sight from the clerks inside. We waited, the radio on low, and the window rolled down, looking for the right guy to come along. They were almost always the same, men between forty and fifty who could pass as aging bikers, heavy metal heads, or long-time construction workers and car mechanics.

Anybody else was suspect. Sometimes the Las Vegas Metropolitan Police Department would set up a sting outside places like this one. If they weren't sending in an underage narc to catch clerks selling to minors, then they were trolling parking lots for kids like us who asked sympathetic drinkers to buy a twelve-pack or case of beer in exchange for a six-pack. Anyone with a close-cropped haircut was out. Clean-cut cowboys were out. Seniors who were spooked and would tattle to the clerks inside were out.

"Are you going to tell me?"

"It's nothing," I said. "Jamie tried to push me through a window."

"That doesn't sound like nothing," she said.

"It wasn't much of a fight." I looked out the window.

"Did you get hurt anywhere else?"

"Not really. See for yourself."

I turned to face her, leaning in so she could get a better look. She ran a couple of fingers over it, and I pulled back. It stung from my mother pushing on it.

"Let me guess? I should see the other guy."

"Something like that," I said. "Jamie blew the whole thing out of proportion."

"What?"

"It's all so stupid. I told Mick how it all went down, and Jamie disagreed."

She didn't have to ask me. She wanted to know what really went down. The next question was already resting on her lips.

"You were with them the other night, weren't you?"

I let it hang in the air without saying anything for a minute. I looked out the window again to bide my time, wondering how I might change the subject.

"What about that guy?"

He was a big guy with a gray beard and long hair. He wore a mechanic's shirt, now unbuttoned and untucked, revealing a sweat-stained wife beater. He had an uneven, loping walk, which seemed to preclude him from being an officer of the law.

"Yeah, he might be right."

Usually Cheryl, or whoever was doing the ask, would call a guy like this over to the car before they went into the store, but his stride put him inside before we could call him over. Not wanting to miss the opportunity, Cheryl got out of the car to tap him on the way out. It wasn't ideal, but we didn't want to miss the opening of the movie.

She leaned against the building, right next to the glass doors covered with point-of-purchase posters and for-sale signs. She wore short denim cutoffs that made her tan legs look longer. Knowing that her ask would come with a healthy dose of flirting, a pang of jealousy crept over me.

He lit a cigarette ripped from a fresh pack when he came out, which gave her an opening to ask him for a favor. He almost said no, pointing to his freshly lit smoke, but Cheryl charmed him with a sway of her hips and a smile on her lips. She offered him two cigarettes from her pack to make up for the trouble and enough to buy a six-pack for himself.

When the arrangement was made, he took the smokes she offered and crushed out his own, dashing back into the store with some excuse that he almost forgot the beer his old lady asked him to bring home. I didn't know if there was an old lady, but it didn't matter.

He came up with a twelve-pack in one arm, a six-pack in the other. He made it a point to keep the change. Beggars can't be choosers, he might have said to her with a gruff huff. She didn't care, taking the twelve-pack in both hands and walking over to the car. She passed it in through the passenger window for me to place in the back on the floor and cover it with a blanket.

Cheryl had already stashed a bag of homemade popcorn behind the driver's seat. Mostly, the West Wind Drive-In didn't care what smuggled concessions were in the car, but they frowned on extra movie-goers getting free rides in the trunk.

Mick and I had done that a few times with random friends, but it was never us in the trunk. Not only were we too tall, but we wouldn't see any humor in being "forgotten" stowaways, locked away for an extended stay. But for whatever reason, we always got a good laugh when someone else was pranked — let out an hour or so after being snuck inside.

We arrived with plenty of time to spare, cars still lined up in front of six glowing arches that reminded me of a McDonald's knock off, except they were red Ms with round golden bulbs illuminating the two-lane entrance to one of three screens. You picked your movie, picked a lane, and then drove under one of the arches, hoping the best spots weren't taken by the time you found your way inside.

We were lucky. Cheryl found one toward the back with a little more elbow room, but not so far back to risk a back-row motor home looming over us for the duration. She parked, and we positioned the tin-soaked metal speakers on either side of the car to hang in the windows. We left the windows down, planning to roll them up again when the movie started, just enough to create the illusion of privacy.

She had picked the movie *Poltergeist*, a horror film set in newly minted suburbia just like the ones that had started to fill in the empty lots that checkerboard our neighborhoods. Slate siding and asphalt shingles were being upgraded into uniformed painted stucco and terracotta clay tiles. The newer Vegas communities weren't unlike those in the movie. These new homes were dressed up with a southwestern desert flair.

The second film was a tagalong B-movie horror flick called *Venom*. Neither of us had heard of it, but it didn't matter. We'd enjoy a beer buzz, socialize over most of the double feature, and then cut out early to avoid a mass exodus of impaired drivers. I had that dumb midnight curfew to think about too.

The movie's opening epitomized suburbia with Craig T. Nelson crashing out in front of a television and a golden retriever scavenging for food while everybody sleeps. There isn't a hint of anything unusual at all, except for a goofy-looking kid that most people thought was cute. She talks to the electronic snow on the television for a few seconds.

She wasn't the first kid to peer into the on-screen static after the broadcast ended. Everybody I knew did it when we were kids, looking for weird shapes or secret messages, which is why Spielberg used this collective experience to artfully capture our attention before descending once again into a montage mirror image of an Americana fishbowl. Bicycles, football games, neighbor disputes, dead pets, and goldfish. Everybody was chasing the same stupid things.

But then the parents did something unexpected once they retreated to their room for the following evening. JoBeth Williams lights up a joint, and once again, I find myself face to face with real-life problems before the story has time to hook us.

"Are you going to tell me?" Cheryl asked, passing me an open Miller Genuine Draft.

"Tell you what?"

"What really happened to Brett?"

I took a swig and looked out the window. She should have picked the special John Carpenter double feature instead.

"Look," I said. "*The Thing* is playing on the other screen."

"Come on, Brady," she said. "You can trust me."

Trust is a fragile thing, hard to share and easy to break. It takes a great leap of faith to surrender your deepest vulnerabilities to another person in the hope they'll keep your secrets without judgment. My grandmother was the one person who never broke my trust.

"Yeah, I was there."

"I'm sorry," she said, placing a hand on my shoulder. "What happened?"

I looked at the screen. JoBeth was showing Craig how their dining room chairs move from one side of the kitchen to the other on their own. He kept looking for strings because there are always strings attached to things. Then JoBeth places her daughter in the same spot, and the dopey kid slides across the room in a football helmet.

"When I was a little kid, like eleven, there was a carnival held across the street in a supermarket parking lot. The most exciting ride was the hammer, two whirling pods that spun you in a circle. One of the carnival game attendants dared me to ride it ten times to win a piece of carnival glass, a little green vase. Has something ever come into your life like that? You know, deep down, it's wrong, but it tickles you in the pit of your stomach, so you don't want it to stop until it's too late," I said. "It was kind of like that. We all rode out into the desert together, looking for an easy payday, thinking we were somehow special, invincible. But we weren't so special. The deal went bad, and everybody started shooting."

"Shooting?"

"First Alex opened up and then everybody."

"Like a gunfight?"

"More like a war movie," I said, shifting in my seat. "I was on a ridge with Jamie. And the other guys had someone on a hill too. That's who shot Brett. Brett didn't see it coming. One minute Alex was shooting people, and the next minute, Brett was hit and lying on the ground. Then everybody started shooting. Mick took someone down. I'm pretty sure Jamie did too."

"And you?"

"Yeah, I was shooting too."

"Oh, Brady," she said with a gasp. "Did you kill somebody?"

"No. I mean, I don't know," I said. "It was dark, and I was shooting at whoever hit Brett. I never saw him, only muzzle flashes. But does it matter? We're all part of it."

"I think it matters," Cheryl said.

There was a storm on the screen. People were screaming. A tree was trying to swallow the goofy girl's brother.

When I closed my eyes, I could see those men from the cartel screaming just like the family on the big screen. I could see it that way, but none of them screamed. Nobody had any time to scream except Jamie. Jamie was screaming like a madman and unloading everything he had with three bursts of a machine gun.

"I don't know," I said, reaching into my pocket to pull out the plastic bag Mick had given me. "Here's the carnival glass."

I tossed it on the center console between the car's emergency brake and stick shift. Cheryl picked it up to get a better look.

"This is what you were after?"

"All for that."

"It looks like cocaine, except brown," she said. "What is it?"

"Heroin," I said.

"The next big thing," she whistled. "Ever try it?"

"No," I said.

"Do you mind?"

She looked into my eyes when she opened the baggie, waiting for me to give her permission. I wanted to push her hands away and kiss her, pressing my lips against hers, but all I could manage was a mischievous smile. This was more about her and me being together than the proposition. I was too lost in her smile to stop it from happening, so I let it happen.

She scooped some of the power out with a fingernail, breaking the connection to snort it. She did it again, this time holding her hand out to me. The tickle in my stomach told me everything I needed to know, but it wasn't about the high anymore. I couldn't deny this experience with her. I drew her hand to my face and inhaled. My nose tingled. It didn't burn as much as cocaine.

"How long do you think it will take?"

"Maybe five minutes," I said, watching her take another dip.

I could already feel the effects as all the pain points I was living with began to float away, small orbs dancing above me and out the window. Go into the light. Go into the light, little troubles. There is no place for you here anymore.

Cheryl was talking to me, but I couldn't hear the words. I felt warm and happy, zoned out on the idea of kissing her again. She was smiling at me, calling my name. I couldn't answer her because I was too busy trying to figure out why every time felt like the first time with her.

A friend of mine once told me that a woman always knows when the kiss is coming. It never made sense to me because I never knew when I would kiss someone. Sometimes I would force myself to make a move, but I felt too good to force anything right now.

Her words were like the movie, drifting further into the background until only Cheryl and her parted lips were left. I leaned over and kissed her, and she kissed me back.

We were kissing, hands gliding over each other's bodies like we had never allowed them to do before. It felt right. Everything felt intensely right, as if we were lying on a cloud, floating over a parking lot of cars, unaware that we had ascended to someplace better.

"I love you," I said.

But I don't know if I ever said it. Somewhere between our drinking and kissing and petting, I wondered if the intense pleasure I felt was from being with Cheryl or if it was the heroin. I couldn't tell the difference, but it didn't seem to matter to either of us as our skin flushed, our hands grew heavy, and the tin of the speakers faded into the night.

We woke up sometime after the second movie ended to a flashlight being tapped on Cheryl's fogged window. She pulled her shirt down and I straightened up, sweeping some empty beer bottles into the back.

"Movie's over, lovebirds," said the voice on the other side of the glass.

"Sorry." Cheryl rolled down the window. "We fell asleep."

"You kids today," said the security guard, pointing. "Show some self-respect."

I zipped up my pants, numb to whatever I couldn't remember. Cheryl started the car and drove toward the exit, trying to regain her orientation before heading toward my house.

"Hey," she said in a daze.

"Yeah?" I answered, expecting her to ask why her shorts were unzipped like mine.

"Do you think we could do that again sometime?"

I didn't know what she meant by that. I hedged.

"I hold the key," I said and pocketed the baggy. "So the door's always open."

It was such a corny thing to say, but she laughed anyway. And then I laughed right along with her. We rode the cloud for a few more miles before the living room lights at my house came into view, and all those little troubles started to find their way back into my life. I scratched at one creeping up on my arm and took a drink of warm beer to quell the growing nausea in my stomach. My mother was awake and waiting.

CHAPTER 15

THE KNIFE

A light tapping on glass woke me up from a hazy sleep. At first, I thought it was the security guard at the drive-in movies again, rapping on the car window. But I wasn't in Cheryl's car anymore. I was at home, lying on the couch in my room and enveloped in a fog.

I glanced over at my flip clock. A little after three in the morning, someone was at my bedroom window.

I usually slept naked under a comforter, but I hadn't bothered to undress after coming home from the movies. So there wasn't any need for modesty as I sat up to face the silhouette peering in my room from the side yard. The only thing I had to overcome was the hole in my memory. I didn't remember anything after Cheryl pulled up to the house.

The realization gave me a jolt of anxiety, and I sat up, trembling and nauseous. I might have thrown up if it wasn't for the visitor. I tried to focus on my window instead of my missing memory. I told myself to deal with one problem at a time and cracked the window.

"What?"

"Hey man, it's Cal."

"Cal?"

It wasn't out of the ordinary for buyers to drop by my window when the house was dark, but Cal never had. I hadn't seen him since the bonfire party got busted, and then me along with it.

"Hey Brady, you got any dope?"

"Let me check," I said, rubbing away the sleep from my eyes.

I never kept much at home, preferring to hit Alex up when I knew someone wanted to buy. The little bit I did have was kept in a box, tucked up under the couch in a small hole I had cut into the foam above the web spring. I reached under and retrieved it.

"Yeah, I've only got a gram left. You can have it for a couple bucks," I said, and then remembered the baggy in my pocket. "I got something else too. It'll blow your mind."

"Yeah, what is it?"

"Brown sugar."

"No way."

"You can have what's left for, I dunno, ten bucks," I said. "And I'll throw in the gram."

The sale would be a loss, but that was the point. Alex had Mick pass me a bag as a sampler. You use them to introduce a better high to trusted customers. I didn't consider Cal trusted, but he was all right.

"Just pass me a ten through the window, and you can take it all."

"I don't know, man," Cal said. "I'm not the one buying it. Nathan is."

"Is that right?"

Nathan was the one who passed me the hash that night. Looking back on it, I was sure it was laced with something.

"Yeah, man," Cal said. "Why don't you come out and talk to him."

"Seriously, I just want to go back to sleep," I said. "Ten bucks or no deal."

"Come on, Brady," he said. "Nathan's parked across the street. It'll only take a minute."

"He won't come over?"

"You know how he is," Cal said. "Do me a solid."

This is the part of the job I hated the most. Everybody wants a favor in the suburbs. They want you to float them for a week. They want you to meet someone, so they look important. They want you to go out of your way, like pushing is akin to hanging your head out of a drive-up window and asking someone if they want extra ketchup.

"Yeah, all right," I said, sitting up and scratching my head. It ached.

I slid the window open and popped the screen off. Then I walked up the sofa like porch stairs, ducked through the window, and jumped down onto the grass next to Cal. He was mesmerized by my exit, swift and silent. I had done it a million times.

"Where is he?"

"Right across the street."

Nathan wasn't alone. He was leaning against the back of a big boat of a car I had never seen before with two other guys. He watched me cross the street, smiling at me with arms folded across his chest. The other two ignored me. They were smoking cigarettes, looking down opposite ends of the road — one with a mullet and another with a shorter punk cut.

"Man, Cal," I said. "I don't appreciate unknowns rolling up on my house."

"Sorry, Brady," he said. "I'm very sorry."

The way he said it should have tipped me, but I wasn't feeling like myself. So I walked right up to Nathan and held up the two bags, one in each hand. I must have looked annoyed because his grin quivered, and it took an effort to maintain it.

"This and this," I said. "Ten bucks."

"Ten bucks for this and that," Nathan parroted me. "That's the best you can do for me after you ratted me out to the cops?"

"Cops? What are you talking about?"

"I'm talking about someone telling the cops to pull Dan over," he said. "They busted all of us. The Camaro is still impounded. Ruth's parents put her in rehab. And I already had a warrant out."

I looked at Cal. He shrugged and looked down, not wanting to look me in the eyes.

"You're on board with this?"

"They went right for Ruth, man," he said, kicking the asphalt. "Somebody tipped them."

"Yeah, well, it wasn't me," I said. "The only rat here is you, Cal. This is my home, man. Not cool."

A switchblade snapped open behind me. I should have known. Nathan couldn't care less about the dope.

"I really don't have time for this," I said. "If you got busted, it's your own fault."

One of Nathan's friends, the bigger of the two, circled around to block my path between the car and my house. He was a big kid, taller than me by four inches and thirty pounds heavier. I might have blown past Cal, but this kid — with a tapered haircut, short in the back and brushed forward over his forehead — had a punk vibe about him. This wasn't his first shakedown.

"The pot, the smack, and a pound of flesh," Nathan said. "Then we're even."

I dropped the bags in one pocket and pulled my knife out of the other — a folding hunting knife. There wasn't a snap, but they were unnerved by how fast I thumbed it open and positioned it in my fist, blade down and thumb capping the handle.

"You're making another mistake," I said. "I'm not afraid of blades."

Mick owned dozens of throwing knives and switchblades. When it was just the three of us — Mick, Brett, and me — we'd spend some afternoons messing around with them.

Most of the time, we would play mumbly-peg. You must flip a knife off your hand in various positions so it sticks into the ground. We added a twist. The knife had to stick between the opposing player's feet. If your knife was the one that didn't stick or, if you flinched at any time, you got a point.

The person with the most points had to watch the winner pound a stick in the ground, hammering it in once for every point racked up by the loser. Then the loser would have to pull the peg out with their teeth.

I lost twice. The first time was when Mick taught me the game and another time when Alex played. I kept flinching because he was trying to hit my feet.

Nathan had a tense, hesitant look on his face. He held the stiletto with his thumb on the bolster, which told me he might have been in a knife fight maybe once in his life. Most fighters use a grip similar to mine but with the blade forward and the thumb wrapped around the handle.

Holding the blade like he did gave him a weak grip and an exposed forearm. He started circling with the stiletto fully extended, assuming I wouldn't move into his range since he had the reach. He was right. I didn't want to do anything until he made a mistake. So I circled along with him while he tested out some weak jabs.

His friends took new positions, like three of four posts in a boxing ring. The two kids I didn't know were eager and hungry-looking. Cal was the exception. He was frightened, having never seen anything like this before. This wasn't a typical fight where everybody drew in and started screaming for someone. This was something else, and everyone was quiet. None of us wanted unwelcome attention.

"We don't have to do this, you know," I said, sizing him up.

"Oh, we're doing it," he spat at me and lunged high to the left.

I dodged his knife and punched him in the forehead with my fist holding the knife. Then I landed a second blow to his side with my left while sidestepping his attack. I waited for him to recover, maintaining my defensive stance.

"You've done this before." He smiled at me.

I didn't answer him, but he was right. I had done this before, long before meeting Mick or knowing anything about Dungeons & Dragons. A knife wasn't just some flashy menace in midwestern cities like it seemed to be in the desert. Any kid who explored the woods always wanted one to wear on their belt or in a boot.

Nathan kept on with the same tactic. He would jab with the knife a few times and then attempt a slash. I avoided his attacks, dodging them with a sidestep or jumping back out of the way. A few times, though, I threw a few punches before retreating. I didn't want to hurt him as much as convince him to give up. He must have known any of those punches could have come with cuts.

Any chance he would give up disappeared when the punk stuck his leg out and tripped me from behind. It threw me off balance, and Nathan took full advantage, slashing my exposed shoulder. It felt like someone snapping me with a wet towel, one rolled up tight into a rat tail. The cut wasn't deep, but it was bleeding.

Drawing first blood gave Nathan a boost of confidence, negating all those punches I landed. He waved the knife with wild arches. Any one of them could open up another cut. So I knew I had to put an end to it.

When Nathan overextended on the next jab, I pushed his arm in toward his body with my left hand and cut downward with the knife in my left, cutting his forearm and forcing him to drop the stiletto. Then, staying outside, I spun around and dragged the blade across his leg above his knee. It hurt him bad. It was over.

As he collapsed to the asphalt, I came up from the attack erect and face to face with the punk. He was smiling at me. I didn't know why until I felt a hard punch to my leg. The kid had drawn his own knife and plunged it into my quad.

We both looked down at his blade, two inches or so deep. The sight of it made me feel weak in the knees. I took a stumbling step back as he pulled it out. It gave with a little effort. There was blood, but not as much as I would have thought. The punk was going to come at me again when I heard a familiar voice command him to stop.

It was Mick. He ran up and threw a hard right into the back of the punk's head. Then he was on him like a giant, slugging the sense out of him.

Mick wasn't alone either. Jamie was all over Cal with a wild barrage of roundhouse punches, cutting the kid's face with his cast. And Alex was swinging a baseball bat at the mullet kid, who was holding up an arm to fend off any swings while trying to help Nathan back to the car. I wanted to get up again, but I couldn't manage it. So I pulled off my sleeveless shirt and tied it around my leg wound.

It would have been more of a brawl had they expected it, but they hadn't expected it. I hadn't expected it. For all their faults, I was thrilled to see them. My friends were here.

Nathan, Cal, and the mullet had taken refuge in the car, intent on starting it up and taking off as Alex took a few swings at the hood and headlights. As soon as the mullet got it started, he peeled off down the street, leaving us in the rearview and deserting the punk outright.

"I saw what you did," Alex scolded him. "That was a cheap shot and we're going to make sure you don't do it again."

I was barely on my feet before I could see what Alex meant. Mick had laid the kid out in the gutter, and Jamie was holding his arm up on the curb. The kid, tough a few minutes ago, was crying now. A dark stain appeared on the front of his jeans.

"I'm sorry. I'm sorry. I'm so sorry," he pleaded with Alex, who was a taking position over him with the baseball bat. "You don't have to do this."

"I'm not going to do anything," Alex laughed with a hiss. "He's going to do it."

Alex held the bat handle out to me, and I took it. It was clear what he wanted me to do, but all the fight had already fled from me. Hurting this kid after Mick had beaten him bloody didn't feel noble.

"We don't have to do this," I said. "He's right. Let's let him go."

"Come on, Brady," Jamie said, a grin spread from one ear to the other. "Do it."

It was so strange seeing him here, on my side. A few hours ago, he tried to put me through a window. None of this made any sense, so I had to put a stop to it.

"No."

"I'm not asking," Alex said.

"We already won," I said.

"Alex is right," Mick said. "We can't have people cruising our block."

I flipped the bat around in my hand again and held it out to Alex. Instead of taking it, he pulled out the Beretta from the back of his pants and pointed it at the punk.

"If you don't break his hand," Alex said. "I'm going to shoot him."

The kid was whimpering. His sobs were quiet and steady, helplessness draped over him like a body bag as he accepted the inevitable. If I didn't hurt him, Alex was going to kill him.

"Man, I don't get you or Brett," Alex said. "We save your lives, and now you want to question us?"

"What about Brett?"

"In and out of consciousness and confused, but not out of the woods yet."

"He told his parents he was buying drugs in the desert," Jamie said. "Alex told his parents he was confused because he did drugs in the desert. First-timer bull. That's the only reason we're not all busted yet. They haven't told the cops."

It was too much to take in under the circumstances. I felt lightheaded. All I wanted was to call it quits and sleep it all off, assuming I didn't bleed to death.

"What's going to happen, Mick?"

"I don't know, Brady," he said. "One problem at a time."

"All right. This problem's over," I said, pushing the bat toward Alex again.

"No, Brady," Alex said. "You're not hearing me. This loser isn't the problem. You are the problem."

"What's that supposed to mean?"

"If you don't break his hand, somebody's going to hell. And maybe it won't be him."

I looked at him. He had a crazed look in his eyes again, bloodshot and hungry. He enjoyed this, all of it. He'd shoot us both and smoke a bowl, no problem. I appealed to Mick.

"You going to stand by?"

Mick didn't say anything. He turned his head away, so he didn't have to look at me. The momentary rush I felt when they came to my rescue was turned on its head. I wasn't saved. I was enslaved.

"You're really going to fire that thing in this neighborhood?"

He snickered, slurping up the spit from the corners of his mouth, and cocked the gun. It wasn't pointed at the punk anymore. It was pointed at me.

"I hate you," I whispered.

"I don't care."

I stood on the sidewalk and swung the bat three times, a meat tenderizer ignoring any bone and softening the meat. He wouldn't use it any time soon, if ever.

The third time I hit it, he let out one last wail before all his anguish was swallowed up by silence. Now it was impossible to tell what was and what wasn't broken by the end of it. His fingers dangled from a swollen stump.

Mick picked him up and pushed him down the street, telling him to get out of here while he still could. He took off in a stumbling jog, cradling his ruined hand. Part of me wished I could go with him, not to help him but to help myself.

"Good boy," Alex said, reaching for the bat.

My grip tightened around it. For a minute, I wondered if I could knock the gun out of his hand and take him out. The eyes under his aviators invited me to try, but a couple of porch lights turned on — nosy neighbors to the rescue.

"I'll take your soul another time, lamer," Alex chuckled. "We've got to fly."

Alex grabbed at the bat, and I released it. He and Jamie headed toward Mick's house. Mick turned to me before following them.

"You need stitches," Mick said, pointing to my leg. "Figure out a story."

"Mick?"

If I ever needed a friend, it was now. He shook his head.

"Look, I'm sorry, but we're in a different league now. Go home."

I did as he said. I limped to my bedroom window and managed to climb up and into it. I didn't bother retrieving the screen. I fell onto the couch and tried to come up with a story. The first one that came to mind was "let sleeping bears lie."

CHAPTER 16

HUSH NOW

I remember a black-and-white photo of my mother and me with Lake Erie in the background. It must have been October because she was wearing a windbreaker, and I was bundled up in a gray sweatshirt with a hood. It was cold but not winter coat cold.

Her head leaned in over mine, one hand pressing me into her. She was smiling at whoever was holding the camera, a sly one, like she shared a secret with the photographer. I was looking someplace else, rubbing sand off my hands as she smothered me for a staged shot on one of her rare visits.

Sometimes I would think about that picture when I couldn't fall asleep in the extra bedroom at my grandparents' home, wishing for it to be real. It wasn't until I lived with her that I understood it could never be real because something was wrong with me. She told me as much when I helped her dust and organize three huge bookshelves in her bedroom after we made the move from Cleveland to Las Vegas.

She had come across a folder with an assortment of drawings and letters, handwritten pages with heavy cursive writing. It wasn't her writing. Hers was always light and dramatic with circular flourishes. This writing flowed with sharp angles and tight curves, an artist's handwriting.

"Those are some stories your father wrote," she said, reading my mind without looking at me. "I saved them for you in case you ever wanted them."

"What are they about?"

"Dark things," she said. "Death, isolation, betrayal. Your father was a sick man."

"That's not what grandma said," I said. "She said he was a very talented artist."

"Your grandmother wanted you to idolize him, but it's important you erase those ideas right out of your head," she said. "Because sometimes the lines between genius and insanity become blurred, and your father crossed over."

"I don't understand."

"One of the stories is about a dying raven, pages and pages of everything it sees while it lies on the sidewalk dying, ants already working at its carcass, maggots burrowing in its flesh. Do you want to read a story like that?"

"I guess not," I said with a cringe. I didn't know what else to say.

"There's another story about two lonely white finches who hear each other's song and fall in love against all odds. They do everything together for a while, making the most beautiful music you've heard — long, sharp, cheerful little cheeps," she said. "One day, the female finch tells the male finch that she is pregnant. The two of them, along with all the other white finches, have a glorious celebration, flitting between the golden leaves of an Indian summer. None of them have a care in the world until the day the baby finch is finally born under the darkening winter skies. To everyone's surprise, the baby finch isn't white like its mother or father, but black as a starless night. The male finch is furious. He assumes his soulmate had an affair with an inferior black finch. He threatens to kill her and the baby for the treachery until an early winter storm provides a revelation."

"What was it?" I hung on her words.

"When all the white finches tried to take shelter from the storm, nobody would take her and the black baby finch in," she said. "So the two of them were caught out in the storm. As the wind and freezing rain pelted the pair of them, the female finch's feathers began to turn from white to gray and then to the black of night, just like the baby finch. She had tricked the white finch into loving her by painting herself white, months before they met."

"That's terrible."

"Terrible because you're the black baby finch," she said. "But sometimes I wonder if it wasn't him who lied to me. It's one of the reasons I'm so hard on you, Brady. I'm working against those bad genes he gave you. I know they are there, too, because you look just like him. Black as a starless night."

Her words were cold and lifeless as if she had accepted my presence as a punishment. Somehow, it was her fate to suffer me. I tried to change the subject.

"Are the drawings his too?"

"Yes and no," she said, holding one up. "They're my drawings, but then he took them from me and added hard shadows, darkening them with emotional distress. 'There are no lines in art,' he told me. 'Only shadows within shadows.' Sometimes he would force us to go with him into remote, isolated areas, just to watch him paint clouds or barns or trees. Even though I had some talent, he said I could never understand art like he did. How could I? I was the black finch that tricked him, and you were the proof."

I pushed the papers back toward her, a knot growing in my stomach. I hadn't known any of it, but it made sense. All those problems I had at school, all those fights I used to be dragged into, all those breakdowns my grandmother suffered while undergoing cancer treatment. It all came back to the darkness in my heart.

"I don't think I want these," I said. "I don't think I want anything from him."

"Oh, Brady, you just made my day," she said. "Maybe there is hope for you after all. Tell you what? Why don't we burn them all up when we finish the shelves? Deal?"

"Deal," I said with the smile she expected.

She gave me a fist bump and tousled my hair. We burned his art and papers a few hours later, but it didn't work. It might have been the happiest I remember her being with me, but my heart felt darker and heavier than ever.

It felt just as heavy now. I had invented the story that I was going to tell my mother when I woke her up. There was only one problem with it. The punk stuck me with a blade thinner at the spine than my knife. If anyone was going to believe me, I had to stick my knife into the wound and make it match.

I put a towel under my leg and a belt between my teeth. I wasn't sure what the belt would do, but I had seen it enough in movies and on television shows to think it was important. Bite down on this, they always said. I bit down.

I wanted to do it fast, one quick jab in and out. But then my brain betrayed me with another piece of television medical trivia. If I severed the femoral artery, I would bleed to death within a few minutes. She wouldn't get me to the hospital in time. Or maybe I would pass out before I could wake her up.

I imagined my mother opening the door in the morning or early afternoon, wondering why I hadn't gotten up. She would find me lying in a puddle of blood, a knife sticking out of my leg with my hand resting on the self-inflicted wound. She would never see that coming — me, scrapping her advice to cut my wrists down the vein and going for the femoral artery instead. Maybe she could give me extra points for originality.

Or maybe not. I had to be careful. I didn't have a clue where the femoral artery was or how close the punk came to clipping it. I went slow instead.

The first inch wasn't as difficult as I expected. There was no resistance. The blade slipped into a hole that was already there. The second inch was more difficult as I came to the place the two knives didn't match up.

I felt pressure in my leg before the skin started to give. It didn't hurt as much as I thought it would so I kept going. I half-expected it to squeak like a knife sliding into a block of cheese but since there was only a dull throb, I pushed it in deeper, wondering if I should keep going until it hit the bone.

No, I decided. Some people think the best lies are big lies, but they're not. The best lies are those wrapped in so many layers of truth that you can't find the lie anymore.

"Mom," I called out to her from the doorway. I never called her mom anymore unless something was wrong. "Mom."

"Brady?"

"Mom? Are you awake?"

"No. I mean, I am now." She wasn't happy. "What is it?"

"Um, I have something to show you?" I didn't know what to say.

"What?"

"I have something to show you. It's really neat, um, important."

"It's four in the morning."

"You're going to want to see this."

I could hear her putting her robe on, quiet enough that George wouldn't wake up but huffing enough so I would understand she wasn't happy. It was like an early warning siren. If she was unimpressed with whatever I woke her up for, I was dead or might as well be dead because she would dish out the deadliest restriction imagined.

Funny. I was standing outside her door with a towel wrapped around a knife wound, and I was more terrified by her reaction than the injury.

"Go into the bathroom so you don't wake George," she said.

"I don't want you to freak out so I'm not turning on the light until I tell you," I said.

"What is it?"

"I've been stabbed."

"What?"

"I slipped getting up to go to the bathroom and fell on a knife. It stabbed me."

She turned on the bathroom light. I was holding the towel tight around my leg, but a streak of blood ran down my shin to my foot.

"Oh my God, Brady," she said, the wind sucked out of her rising anger.

"I'm sorry about the towel," I said. "I didn't think. I just had to grab something."

"Oh my God," she said again, unable to find the words. "Let me see it."

I undid the towel and showed her the wound. The bleeding had slowed, but it hadn't stopped.

"It's still bleeding," she said. "I have to take you in for stitches."

"You mean the hospital? I don't think we have to, do you?"

"What kind of mother would I be if I didn't take you in? A pretty piss poor one."

"Yeah, I suppose."

There it was. It wasn't about me anymore. She fled the bathroom and returned to her bedroom to get dressed in jeans and a T-shirt. She didn't bother to write a note.

My story was stupid. I didn't realize how ridiculous it sounded until we were in the car and headed to the hospital. She wanted to know how it happened, and I had to tell her three times before she could wrap her head around it.

"I got up to go to the bathroom and slipped on a piece of paper," I said. "And then I fell on my knife. I don't know how it happened, only that it must have been propped up on a shoe or something."

"This doesn't make any sense. Why was it out?"

"Oh, you remember when Lewis dropped by a few days ago? He was playing with it and must not have put it back."

As absurd as it sounded, a lie wrapped in a few truths is infinitely more plausible than the alternative she could not imagine. She knew I left drawing paper on the floor. She saw Lewi visit with her own eyes. It was a dumb story, but the simplicity of it beat out the more complex truth by a mile — a couple punks cruised our house seeking revenge, and I willfully climbed out my bedroom window to accommodate them.

The doctor who saw us in the emergency room was less convinced. But like my mother, there weren't any other facts to provide him further speculation, except one. He asked me when she left to use the bathroom.

"You know, you can tell me anything," he said. "If you need help, this is the time to tell me."

"No, I'm fine," I said. "It happened just like I said."

He squinted at me. Then he rolled up my shirt sleeve and showed his disappointment by dabbing at the slash with antiseptic, pushing twice as hard than he had to.

"So, did you cut your shoulder before or after you fell on the knife?"

"I don't know how that happened," I said. "Earlier in the day, maybe?"

"It doesn't need stitches, so I won't say anything," he said. "But I do pray you know what you're doing, kid."

"I never know what I'm doing."

"Apparently," he said, placing a Band-Aid over it and rolling down the shirt sleeve.

My leg took thirteen stitches, inside and out. He wrote prescriptions for pain, Tylenol Codeine Four, and something to help me sleep. My plan was to refuse them. I didn't trust prescription medicine. Who knows how it might react with whatever else was racing around in my body? I didn't know why he wrote it up. It didn't hurt much.

My mother, always better in a crisis than the everyday, said we should stop at White Cross Drugs to fill the prescriptions anyway. I asked if we could stop in at UMC and see Brett before we did. Valley Hospital was a block away from UMC, where Brett was being treated. It didn't make sense to me, but the general rule of thumb was you went to Valley if you had money and UMC if you didn't.

The exception was Flight For Life. Everybody in need of emergency medical helicopter transports went to Valley Hospital. It was the only place with a helipad.

My mother put up some weak resistance. She wanted to pick up the prescriptions at White Cross Drugs and get home before the sun came up. But to the wounded goes the spoils. I convinced her to drop me off, get the prescriptions filled, and then pick me up after.

"What about visiting hours?"

"Come on," I said. "It's a 24-hour town. Besides, nobody says anything if you look like you belong there."

I pointed to the bandage wrapping my leg. She still didn't like the idea, but she was feeling sentimental. I could tell because she always dialed back on earlier times when she felt this way.

"You really scared me tonight," she said. "I haven't been this afraid for you since I came home to the old apartment and found you sitting outside, bloody and bruised."

"When those kids jumped me for lunch money?"

"Yes," she said. "It was terrifying."

"I didn't know you were scared," I said. "You never said that before. You only wondered what the neighbors might think."

"That's not fair, Brady," she said. "We all do our best. Besides, I never understood why you wouldn't just give them the damn money anyway."

"It wasn't their money," I said. "And tomorrow? They would've just done it again to me or some other kid."

"I see your father's temper in you. He was always so intense." She frowned. "All right, maybe seeing Brett will do you some good. Empathy. Look it up later when we get home, and maybe you'll understand what you're always putting me through."

I knew what empathy meant, but I wondered if she did. It's one thing to imagine what someone might feel like when they're going through something, but it's something else to feel what they do. I don't know. Maybe I was becoming numb to everything. When someone assaults you with their fears every day, you tend to put up barricades. Mine were a mile high.

"Thanks for letting me see him. I'll be back down in thirty."

She wanted to say something else but didn't. She lit another cigarette instead and tucked it between two thin, colorless lips and drove away.

UMC had visiting hours, but nobody cared unless you caused trouble. I slipped past the empty security booth and took the elevator to Brett's room. There wasn't anyone behind the nursing desk on his floor either. They must have been busy with other patients, waking them up to take sleeping pills and a dozen other things they were always accused of doing.

I blended in and eased into his room, hoping his parents hadn't spent the night. They hadn't. The room was empty, except for Brett. He had an IV line running to his arm and was on oxygen, but the more intrusive ones like the endotracheal tube, were gone.

Alex had said he wasn't out of the woods, and maybe he wasn't. They were still monitoring his heart and other functions like brain waves or something.

He looked more peaceful than on my last visit, with some color coming back into his face. He didn't look as swollen but still sported raccoon eyes. It might take a few days or weeks before they faded.

I stood over him for a few minutes, waiting for him to notice me. It was a dumb idea, but I tried to will him to sense me standing there and wake without me waking him up. I timed my breathing to his own, slow and shallow.

Seeing him asleep in the hospital bed felt like looking at the past, a time Mick and I didn't belong to anymore. Unlike us, Brett was just a normal kid looking for the next laugh he could share with friends.

Last year, it was his idea to dress up as Quasimodo and climb up on the roof of his house so he could throw a straw man down as trick-or-treaters approached it, looking for Mick — dressed up as Frankenstein's monster — and a few pieces of candy. My job, when I wasn't running around like a wolfman, was fetching the body for the next group of lions and tigers, fairies and witches.

It was a fun night. Every time he tossed the body down, the trick-or-treaters would scatter. Then they would look up at the hunchback silhouette dancing on the roof and start screaming. Mick and I would bust a gut. And Brett would call down, cursing us for spoiling the spookiness for the kids. We couldn't help it. He made a good monster.

"When one does wrong, one must do it thoroughly," I whispered, remembering a line from the hunchback book. Looking at him broken in the bed said it all. We had become the monsters and Brett the victim of our folly.

I turned to leave, my eyes wet from trying not to cry. I could find no joy in our crimes. Brett was the kid, we found out later, who went door-to-door early on Halloween collecting candy just so the three of us had candy to give away.

"Mom? Is that you?"

I stopped at the door and turned around. "Hey, bud."

"Brady?"

"You know, breaking the rules," I said. "You need anything?"

"A drink," he said with a voice like sandpaper.

"Sure, man. Anything."

There was a Styrofoam cup on the table beside his bed. I put the straw to his lips so he could take a sip. His eyes opened, slits between the blackness, trying to see me.

"What are you doing here?"

"I don't know. I wanted to say I'm sorry. Sorry all this happened to you."

"Yeah ... and?" He forced a laugh and grimaced, choking on the laugh. "Nah, I'm joking. You, of all people, should be telling me, 'I told you so.'"

"I wouldn't say that." I tried to wipe my eyes dry. "But it looks like your seven years of college is down the drain."

He chuckled and choked again. "Oh, ouch. Don't make me laugh anymore."

"Right on. All you need to do is make a saving throw, and you'll be fine in no time."

"Oh great. I was never any good at those."

"I'll give you plus eight on the roll."

"You're a true friend to the end," he said. "I don't deserve it, I know. I always treated you like a third wheel, even though you knew Mick longer. Sorry about that. I don't know why I did. Maybe because you're younger than the rest of us, like his little brother tagging along. It never really hit me until I saw the way Alex treated you. He just stepped right in and took my place while you kept yours."

I never liked to think of it that way. Mick and I were best friends. It didn't matter who came into his life for a while. I'd been the constant. Maybe that's what made it, like Brett said. Mick and I were like brothers, and I was the younger one.

When I didn't say anything, Brett closed his eyes. I thought he would drift off to sleep again but he raised his hand and beckoned to me. He wanted me to come closer to the bed.

"I have to tell them what went down, Brady," he whispered. "My parents. The cops. I have to tell them."

My entire body tensed. If Brett did that, there was no telling what Alex might do.

"It's not a good idea, man," I said. "Alex ..."

"Forget Alex," he rasped. "It's not about him. It's about you and Mick. Do you think those dealers are going to let it go? We crossed them, and they'll be coming after us for the drugs, for the money, for revenge. So you got to tell them too. We need protection, Brady. You gotta tell them."

I had forgotten about the heart monitor, but it was making noise now. I started to back up, but he reached out and grabbed my hand. I wrenched it away and stared at him.

"You got to tell them, Brady," Brett said. "You got to tell them. You gotta tell them, Brady!"

He was punching the bed with his hand like a hammer, the one without anything attached to it. And he kept yelling at me. Saying the same thing over and over as everything in the room lit up, beeps and whirls and lights.

My own heart was racing. When I turned to leave, I ran into the nurse coming in. She looked at me, surprised and agitated.

"You're not supposed to be in here," she said. So I fled down the hall.

As I made my way back to the elevator, I could see more hospital staff headed toward Brett's room. I brushed past them all, head down and determined to escape. Except the elevator indicator wasn't moving. It was forever stuck on the third floor, and I had to get out. I ran toward a door marked stairs and pushed through it.

Inside the stairwell, I caught my breath, replaying everything that had happened in my head and trying to figure out what triggered him. What did I say or do? I couldn't come up with anything, and I couldn't think clearly in the hospital. I headed down the stairs, my leg throbbing, and out the front doors. My mother was back, waiting in the car.

"Did you see him?"

"Yes, well, no, not really."

"Brady," she said. "You either did or didn't."

"I did, but he was asleep," I lied. "It was like you said. They don't want anybody in there outside of visiting hours."

"One of these days, you'll listen to your mother."

"Yeah," I said, biting my thumbnail and looking out the passenger window toward the first signs of twilight.

"You all right?"

"Sure, why?"

"You look a little flushed," she said.

"It's probably the leg," I said. "Hurts a bit."

"Let's get you home then," she said. "We could both use some rest."

Before she pulled away from the curb, she reached out and put a hand on my forehead, tousled my hair, and combed some strands over one ear so she could see my face better. She had this weird, sly smile, like the one in that old photo, as if this was somehow a bonding moment between a mother and son.

Right. This was perfect for her. Her son was sitting beside her and in need of a mother's help. Some punk had stuck a knife into his leg, though she didn't know it. Another treasured memory when she kept me under her wing.

When we got home, I asked for a couple of pain pills. I didn't want them because the pain wasn't so bad. I had to take them. I needed the sleep.

CHAPTER 17

EVERY STITCH

I didn't roll out of bed until late afternoon, feeling washed out from the codeine and lack of sleep. My throbbing leg lost the argument with my growling stomach, so I stumbled into the kitchen to forage.

When I passed George in the living room, he said nothing. He was reading the newspaper, some story about a cop killed by unknown assailants outside of a diner in South Dakota. It was strange and unexplained.

He glanced up long enough to flash me a sardonic smile. I knew the look. He had something sarcastic to say about my so-called self-inflicted stupidity, something along the lines that I was brain dead, lying, or both.

As long as I didn't engage him about it, it was fine. He preferred being a mushroom — kept in the dark on most matters. Sometimes he went to bat for me, but mostly he was hands off. His childhood was unsupervised. He was one of three brothers who did what they wanted after their father died too young.

I heated up some seasoned hamburger we used for tacos the night before and tossed in a bowl of toppings. Having leftovers for lunch was a win because the alternative was often peanut butter and jelly or a slab of meat cut from a salami log. It also reduced the risk of a Tupperware potluck for supper, which usually consisted of whatever we didn't eat for two or three weeks straight.

It took a little bit of time for round two. George buzzed around the dining room table shortly after I sat down to eat. He couldn't contain himself.

"Your mom says you fell on your knife."

I took another bite, my gaze fixed on the taco salad. It was a lame attempt to give him nothing more than a nod of my head. He might understand, given a taco salad was considered a five-star lunch by any standard in our house.

"Huh. Do you mind telling me how you managed that?"

I swallowed and looked up at him, taking my time to clear my mouth with my tongue. He was grinning at me.

"I don't know," I said. "I was half-asleep."

"Right, you slipped on some paper," he said, amused. "And the knife was ... what ... balancing on the handle, so the blade was pointed up in the air."

"Well, I think it was propped up on a shoe or something."

"A shoe?"

"Or something."

"Right," he said, drawing it out like it was the stupidest thing he had ever heard. "And you expect me to believe that?"

"No, um, I don't know how it happened," I said. "I think Lewi left it that way when he was done with it. You know, just tossed it down or set it aside, so it was propped up somehow."

"By a shoe?"

"Or something," I said. "I mean, there were shoes where I fell. It could have been anything."

"It could have been anything, like propped up by a shoe or dirty clothes or a stack of books or some weird black magic like they have in South Dakota? Or, it could have been anything like you snuck out of the house last night and somehow managed to get stabbed?"

"It was really late."

"I don't care, but you tweak the screen every time you climb out the window."

I took another bite of my salad and shrugged my shoulders. It needed more hot sauce, but I didn't want to get up while he was standing there.

"I don't even want to know," he said. "I won't tell her but keep it out of the house."

"Yeah, sure."

That was George. He was one part cool, and one part didn't care. Cool, because he wasn't going to rat me out. Uncool, because for once in my life, I wished I had a real dad who would ask if I was in some kind of trouble or how he could help. He wasn't that. His most significant contributions to my life were a few random stories about how he and his brothers shot arrows at each other or blew up mailboxes with M-80 firecrackers. One time, they dropped a cherry bomb in an old milk chute, taking down their neighbor's wall and giving her dog a heart attack.

After lunch, I took a shower. I had to wrap my leg in plastic wrap. My mother told me the stitches might dissolve in water. I didn't know if she was telling the truth or not because she was always on me about using the shower and running up the water bill. She didn't understand why I took one every morning. She only took a shower every few days to avoid drying out her hair. I didn't have that problem with shorter hair.

I couldn't get a good angle to wrap my shoulder, so I didn't bother. If it scarred, it scarred. It could be a good thing if it did. Visible scars make people think twice; invisible ones not so much. They have it backward. Visible scars mean you've been in a fight. The invisible ones keep you in it.

When I got out of the shower, my mother called me into the dining room. Two men were sitting with her at the table, casual as can be. George was standing in the kitchen, pouring a drink. I immediately thought this was it. She had called child protective services, and these were the guys who would take me to the juvenile detention camp. It was worse.

"You might want to sit down," she said. "I'm afraid there's some bad news."

"Yes, you might want to sit down," the older one with a mustache said.

"No, I can take it," I said.

Neither looked like they would relent until I did as I was told. I crossed my arms instead. I wanted to take whatever they had on me standing up. I dared them to lay it on me, never appreciating their sympathetic glances until my mother blurted it out.

"Brett's dead," she said.

She said it as flatly as you might tell someone about a news story. Ozzy Osbourne bit the head off a bat. The Russians landed a probe on Venus. Gas prices are going up because we're boycotting Libyan oil. Your grandmother's dead.

She had told me that news the same way too. We still lived in Cleveland. I didn't even blink when she told me.

"No, she's not," I had said. "I saw her last month around my birthday. I'm going outside to play football."

The weight of it didn't hit me until I took my first step onto the snow outside. The entire world looked dead. It doesn't snow in Las Vegas, but sometimes the desert looks just as dead.

"No, he's not," I said. "I saw him last night."

The four of them just looked at me like I was a freshly lit fireworks fountain on the Fourth of July. Everybody knows something will happen as the tiny coil of fuse glows, but there is a hesitation when nobody knows exactly what kind of fireworks it might be. Will it be a small ribbon of lights buzzing around like bees, a wailing siren that forces you to press your palms to your ears, or an explosion that makes younger kids tuck their heads in the nearest lap?

It was a dud. When one of the officers apologized, I sat on the floor in front of them. I didn't scream or cry or explode. I just quietly surrendered and melted before them. No one moved to help me, just in case my fuse was still fizzling.

"They know you saw Brett last night," she said. "That's why they're here."

She brought me back. I was up on my feet again, ready to throw punches or cut out of the room. I scowled at them.

"What? You think I had something to do with it?"

"Nobody's saying that, son," said the mustache. "We were just wondering why he was upset with you."

"He wasn't upset with me."

"The hospital staff said Brett was upset when a boy matching your description left his room last night," said my mother. "Everybody is on your side, Brady."

"On my side?"

"They want to help."

"They want to help me? I don't even know who they are!"

"Easy, easy," said the mustache. "Let's start over. I'm Detective Clegg, and this is my partner, Detective Ward. This is just a routine, um, inquiry about the death of your friend. We don't think you did anything. We have questions because his parents filed a police report after his death."

"Why did they do that?"

The two men looked at each other, and then Clegg motioned to Ward. Ward sucked in a long breath.

"Brett told his parents that it wasn't a rancher who shot at them like your friend Alex reported," said Detective Ward. "Brett's version checks out. We interviewed a few ranchers and their neighbors around the area where your friends said the shooting occurred. Nobody recalled an incident or gunfire."

"Why would they say otherwise? It doesn't mean anything."

The younger detective ignored me. "So there is a good chance they were someplace else. Do you know anything about that? Where they were? What they were doing?"

"Brady wasn't even out with those boys that night," my mother chimed in. "He was on restriction. He came home drunk after going out with his girlfriend."

"Cheryl's not my girlfriend."

"She's eighteen, you know. Do you think she could get into trouble for traipsing around with him? Contributing to the delinquency of a minor? Statutory rape?"

"Mom!"

"Ma'am." Detective Clegg sighed. "This might be easier if we spoke to your son alone."

"Why would you say that? He's my son. I have a right to know what's being said."

George circled around the counter and put a hand on her shoulder. "Come on, honey. Let's move to the living room."

"I don't understand, that's all," she said. "I deserve an explanation. He's a minor."

"He's not in trouble. They want to know what he knows." George consoled her and then gently pulled on her chair, prompting her to stand up. As soon as they left the room, the detectives beckoned me to sit in her vacated spot.

"You can talk to us, son," Clegg said. He motioned to my leg. "If you need help, you can tell us."

How many times had I heard that? I knew better. There was no cavalry. The best they could do was whisk me away to child protective services. And then what? Find a foster home? I knew a few of those kids. They bought dope from us to dull the pain. No thanks.

"They can still hear everything in there," I said in a hushed voice, cocking my head toward the living room. "So keep it down."

"All right," said Detective Ward. "Do you have something to tell us?"

"Look, I wasn't with them, but they were probably out messing around with some guns, and Brett got hurt," I lied. "It's happened before, except we were only messing around with BB guns back then."

"So, the idea that it was a drug deal..."

"A drug deal? Yeah, right." I played it off like it was the stupidest thing I had ever heard. A big joke. "I'm sure the only drugs on them were whatever they smoked that night. And since Brett never really did anything like that, who knows what he dreamed up when he was unconscious?"

"All right," Ward said. "Then why was he upset with you last night?"

"Because I told Brett not to go out with them that night," I said. They weren't getting it, so I spelled it out slowly. "I told him, 'I told you so.'"

It made me sick to say it, all these lies, but it resonated. Both of them seemed to be put at ease as I confirmed their suspicions that there wasn't anything to what Brett told his parents. It was all a bad fantasy made up by a kid on morphine or whatever they were feeding him through an IV drip.

"That kind of makes sense," Ward said. "It fits with what the other boys are saying, except for this idea they were playing with firearms. Where would they get those?"

"Come on," I said. "You guys both know Mick's dad is one of you."

Ward nodded, but Clegg reacted differently. He swept his mustache down with one hand as he considered something that wasn't on the table. I couldn't tell what it was, but I could guess. If Mick had lifted some weapons off Big Al, these two guys would end up eating their own. Nobody does that in Las Vegas if they can help it. And if they can't help it, there are always unintended consequences.

"One more thing," Clegg said. "Do you know what this is?"

He tossed a small leather pouch with drawstrings on the table. I immediately knew what it was, at least I thought I did. I never used them, but it looked like a pouch some kids used to store their role-playing game dice. I had too many dice for that. I kept them all in an old wooden cigar box.

"A dice bag?"

"Dice bag?"

"You know, for Dungeons & Dragons and stuff."

Clegg shook his head, the corners of his mustache turning down in disappointment. He had wanted me to say something else. His mouth curled around the words like they were sour.

"It's a hex bag," he said. "Bad mojo."

"We found it at the foot of Brett's hospital bed," Ward added. "It was stuffed with hair, dirt, little bits of a bone, a needle, and a bent bullet casing."

"You wouldn't know anything about it, would you?" Clegg asked.

The expression on my face must have said it all because Clegg whisked it off the table and put it back in his coat pocket.

"I didn't think so," he said.

"Yeah, sorry." My head was pounding so I pressed down on my leg for a different kind of hurt. Only one person I knew would be stupid enough to believe in a hex bag. I could feel the color drain from my face.

"Maybe it's the meds," Ward said, standing up. "If you think of something else, give us a call."

"Wait," I said. "Aren't you going to tell me?" I threw it out there because this was my last chance to ask.

"Tell you what?"

"How did he die?"

"Sepsis," said Clegg.

"What's that?"

"It's not uncommon in a hospital," said Clegg. "It's an infection that runs away with itself, and all your organs start shutting down. Your friend, Brett, he was pretty banged up when he was admitted to the hospital. Maybe he was susceptible, or maybe it started during surgery. We don't know yet."

"Or maybe he was scratched by a dirty needle," Ward added. "Or maybe it was a bad shot or even the IV that was keeping him alive. Poor kid."

"The thing about his sepsis, though, the thing I don't like, was how fast it happened," Clegg said. "Usually, this stuff takes a few days, but hospital staff didn't even have time to react to it. He was fine this morning and then crashed in the afternoon."

"Was he alone?"

"No," Ward said. "He was lucky. That Alex kid, the one who brought him in and saved his life, he was with him."

I closed my mouth when I gasped, and my breath turned into a disgusting burp. Little bits of taco salad came up into my mouth. I dry swallowed them down, burning my throat again in an effort not to throw up. My eyes watered.

"You okay? Clegg asked.

"Yeah, I think so," I said, touching my leg. "Maybe it was my pain meds."

"Maybe," said Ward, tapping a card he left on the table. "Call us if you think of anything else."

I already had thought of something. My head turned in a thousand different directions as they thanked my parents and told them how cooperative I had been. My parents walked them out while I went into the bathroom and threw up.

CHAPTER 18

ONE WAY

I grabbed the knob and put my shoulder to the front door like I always did. On any other day, I'd walk right in like I lived there. In many ways, I did. When I wasn't on restriction, I spent most of my life at Mick's, protected by the safety of absentee parents.

Today wasn't one of those days. The door was locked, and it infuriated me. Mick wasn't going to keep me out today of all days. I pounded on the door, working myself into a fury until it opened.

"What the hell, Brady!" Mick towered over me in the doorway.

I shoved him inside with both hands, pushing him back into the living room. He didn't resist. He retreated backward, bumping into an end table next to his mom's favorite wingback chair.

"He was one of us!" I was crying. "Brett was one of us!"

I started pounding on his chest as the anger pent up in me over the last few hours boiled over. He didn't fight me. He deflected anything aimed at his face but took the body blows as they came.

"Did you know? Did you know he was going to kill him?"

"No, I didn't know," he said. "And I still don't know that's what happened. I haven't even talked to Alex."

"Bull!" I threw my hands in the air and circled the room. I wanted to smash something.

"He was my friend too," said Mick. "More mine than yours even."

"You don't get to say that!" I punched him again.

He took it, but I could tell I was getting to him. His lips were tight, and his eyes sharpened.

"I'm shook up too, man," he said. "But we don't know anything yet. The doctors said sepsis. That happens all the time in hospitals. My mom told me ..."

"I don't care what she told you," I said. "Did they show you the hex bag?"

"The what?" He looked at me like I had eaten rotten eggs.

"Hex bag," I said. "They found it in Brett's hospital bed. It was a little bag with bones and crap in it, and a needle — a freaking needle, Mick!"

"I don't know about any of that," Mick said, shaking his head. "I've got bigger problems."

"Bigger than Brett's death?" I was fuming again. "What's worse than that?"

"Nothing's worse than that," he said. "Everything's worse than that. It's over, Brady. My parents are getting divorced. That's why they aren't here. They got into a fight, and it was the last one. So yeah, this is the worst day of my life. Right now. Today. Happy? I lost one of my best friends and my entire flipping family along with him."

I blinked, disbelieving. His parents were the perfect match. They were both extra large and jovial public servants: the nurse and the cop. I never suspected anything was wrong between them until he mentioned his father's affair, late nights compounded with extra shifts that didn't exist. Somehow the two of them had become strangers.

"Funny how that works," he said. "You never know when it's the last of something until whatever it is is already out of reach."

He was right. The last time I saw Brett was last night in the hospital. I would never see him again. The last time I saw Mick and his family all together was at a barbecue around his pool last summer. I didn't give it a second thought until now. It had been a long time since our families had done anything as families.

"What are we going to do?" The mood of the moment had shifted.

"There's nothing to do," he said. "I'm getting out of here."

"What?"

"I'm out of here," he said. "They can take their choices and shove them."

"And go where? Do what?"

"I haven't figured it out yet," he said. "All I know is I can't stand the choices they gave me. Live here with my mom, move out with my dad, or join my sister at our grandparents."

Mick was always close to his mom's parents. Every other Sunday, the family — Mick's mom and her brothers — would congregate over there for a potluck. They were so used to seeing me around, I had an open invitation any time I could make it.

His grandparents also watched his sister on weekends and almost every night over the summer. It was her absence that gave us our freedom.

"I don't want to live with any of them. It's not like they really care, you know. They don't want me around. They have their own lives."

"There's no way your dad will let you get far. He'll call in your car as stolen."

"I'm not taking it. I've got friends. I've got connections."

"It won't work. He'll find you."

"I'll hitch my way out of here so he won't find me."

"Hitch across the desert? Are you crazy?"

We may as well have lived on an island surrounded by water. There were five ways out of this town: south to Los Angeles; southeast to Kingman, Arizona; north toward small desert towns like Beatty and Goldfield; northeast into Utah; or west toward a dead-end town my parents called Elephant-Fart, Nevada. Its real name was Pahrump.

"You'll be one of those kids they call throwaways," I said.

"Aren't you hearing me, man? I'm already a throwaway. Our whole family was thrown away. But I'll show them. I'm going to get out and make it in the world. Then I can tell them to stop looking at themselves and look at me. I'm doing things."

He was pacing around his kitchen. It was clear that he was scared, but he was excited too. He had this idea that running away would show them he wasn't just a child anymore. He could make his own choices if he didn't like the ones they gave him. I could relate.

My mother had told me so many times that I lived in her house, under her roof, on her couch, eating her food. It didn't matter if she was wrong or right. It was her way or the highway because as long as I was in her house, it was her rules. A couple times, I threatened to leave too. She told me not to let the door hit me on the way out.

"Give it a couple days, and we'll figure it out together," I said. "Maybe I'll go with you."

"No, man," he said. "I can't let you do that. You're too young."

"We're friends, Mick."

"Yeah, some friend I turned out to be." He sat down on a breakfast stool. "Some friend."

Seeing him crash like this filled me with regret. I wish I hadn't come at him like I did. He knew as much as I did, which was nothing.

"It wasn't your fault," I said, trying to snap him out of it.

"Do you really think Alex had something to do with it?"

"I don't know," I lied. "I thought I knew, but I don't know. Maybe it was Alex. But maybe it was just one of those things that happen at a hospital."

"You were right all along. I shouldn't have let Brett get involved. That's what makes it my fault."

"You couldn't have known what was going to happen. Alex turned the deal upside down."

"Except, I did know, Brady. I did know. Alex told me if he didn't like the deal, he was going to light them up and take the dope. He didn't say it was absolute, but I knew better. I could see it in his eyes when he said it, like it was the easiest thing to do."

I shook my head, glad to be standing behind him so he couldn't see my face. Mick had turned the heroin score into blood money just as much as Alex.

"I don't even want it anymore, any of it," he said. "You can have it, Brady. I only need just enough to get out of here."

I wanted to be angry with him all over again, but I couldn't be. I was too busy questioning myself and all the people around me. It was my fault Brett was dead just as much as anyone, which is why I felt so angry. We all have choices to make, right or wrong, and I had been making the wrong ones along with Alex and Mick and Brett and the rest of them.

I was just about to tell him I wanted out too, when we heard the whoop of a police siren outside. We both bolted up and ran outside to see what was happening. A squad car had rolled up next door, and Big Al, in uniform, was talking to Will's dad at the front door.

Mick called out to him. "Dad? What's going on?"

"Is Will all right?" I blurted out, wondering if the car trolling our neighborhood had returned and second-guessing whether I should have warned Will or not.

Big Al handed a clipboard to Will's dad and turned toward both of us, pulling his hands up for us to stop and stay back. We slowed down in front of the mountain. He looked bigger in uniform, the bulletproof vest adding another layer to his girth.

"Hey, boys," he said, greeting us like it was just another day. "Everything's fine."

My initial question was answered when I saw movement behind the curtains. Will looked out at us before disappearing behind them. He was safe, at least.

"There was a break-in at Mr. Haringer's this morning," he said. "They didn't get much, mostly the firearms he keeps in the back. He's going to give me an inventory of what's missing, and I wanted to give him a heads up that the ATF is coming out to talk to him."

"What was the siren about?" Mick asked.

"That was for your benefit." He sighed. "I wanted to make sure you are all right after everything that happened this morning."

Mick put his hands in his pockets. He didn't want to talk about it. I tried to bail him out.

"What's the ATF?" I asked.

"Bureau of Alcohol, Tobacco, Firearms, and Explosives," he said, answering me but taking in his son's demeanor. "It's a new federal bureau kind of like the FBI but focused on gun tracing and organized crime. Of course, if you ask them, they've been around since our country started taxing alcohol to pay for the Revolutionary War."

"Whoa, is that true?"

"What's true is everybody in law enforcement wants to expand their jurisdiction, and if that means you can concoct a story that your agency predates any publicly funded police force, then that's what they'll do. I mean, we all work together, but it's a crowded space with the FBI, ATF, DEA, U.S. Marshals, local police, highway patrol, and metro, you get the idea. And everybody seems interested in this break-in."

He wasn't going to say it out loud, but I already knew why. Everybody knew what was in the back of the gun shop. If someone targeted unregistered firearms, it might mean trouble for someone in the near future. We didn't need that kind of trouble.

"Why's that?"

"Somebody knew what he had back there," he said. "And they made a show of saying so, like they were sending a message."

Mick and I glanced at each other and immediately regretted it. Big Al straightened out of an otherwise relaxed posture. We had accidentally awakened his intuition.

"You boys don't know anything about this, do you? Hear anything?"

He was frowning, looking at us up and down like we might be perps. It made me uncomfortable that he was weighing our innocence and finding us wanting. The longer it took for one of us to respond, the more likely a shadow of suspicion would descend on us. I knew, and Mick knew it too, which is why he tossed a stick of dynamite into the conversation.

"The only criminal activity around here is your infidelity," Mick said and spat on the sidewalk. "So, to answer your original question, how am I doing? Bang off."

He gave his dad a one-finger salute and sulked toward the house. I turned to follow Mick but then hesitated as if I needed to be dismissed by this mortally wounded giant standing there with a wound more profound than any he had ever encountered in the line of duty.

"What happened to your leg, Brady?" he asked, recovering just enough to reanimate himself on unsteady feet.

"Oh, this," I said, shrugging. "I fell on a knife."

"Good for you," he said, not hearing me. "Look after Mick for me, will you?"

"Sure thing," I said.

He didn't make eye contact with me again. He just turned and ambled back toward Will's front door, which Mr. Haringer had left ajar before disappearing inside. When he didn't look back, I took it as my cue to chase after Mick.

I found him in his bedroom, stuffing clothes into a duffle bag. He was crying, and it unsettled me. His tears conjured a memory of Rosie Grier singing "It's All Right To Cry," even if I didn't understand the song beyond it being permission to cry — some 1970s psychobabble meant to take the edge off being a boy in the midst of changing times.

"See how he is?" he asked, punching some jeans into the bag.

"Your dad is a smart guy," I said. "What if we do know something about it?"

"What are you talking about?"

"Think about it. Somebody is tying up loose ends. The drug scene was cleaned up. The guns we used were stolen. Brett is dead. There was a car that didn't belong here trolling our street."

"Wait, what? When did that happen?"

"Yesterday."

"And you didn't say anything?"

"There wasn't any time to tell you," I said, pointing to my leg. "Cal selling me out to Nathan disrupted everything."

"What kind of car was it?"

"I don't know, a brownish Volare with four or five guys in it, maybe. I didn't stick around to find out. I ducked into Will's backyard."

"I thought you said Alex killed Brett."

I didn't know anymore. My head was turning in a million directions. Could Alex be behind all of it or some of it? It could be the cartel, but that didn't make sense. The cartel didn't make me break someone's hand in the middle of the night. The cartel wouldn't leave a hex bag if they killed Brett. That had to be Alex.

None of it fit. It was like working on three puzzles at once and not having a reference picture for any of them.

"I do. I mean, I did. I mean, I don't know, all right?"

"This isn't a game, Brady," Mick said. "You can't dungeon master your way out of it. Not everything is connected like one of your campaigns. Everything is crap, and it's blowing up in our faces. I don't want any part of it."

"You leaving isn't going to help anybody," I said. "If anything, it will put more eyes on us. The cops are going to start linking things together just like us, even if it doesn't fit."

He zipped the duffle bag closed and considered what I was saying. He had to see I was at least partly right. If the cops or ATF linked my leg, the gun store break-in, and Brett's death together, everyone would be questioned, and the truth would come out. Even if Mick and I kept our mouths shut, who knew what Will might say or Jamie, who seemed like a bigger wild card.

"What do you want me to do?"

"Give me a day," I said. "I have an idea. Maybe I can figure this out and fix it."

"Yeah, right," he said. "Even if you could fix it, it doesn't change the fact that my family, my life, is over."

He was right. I could do nothing about his family, just like there was nothing to do about my family. But unlike me, what made it worse for him was that he had a good one for so long. He lived with the illusion of a perfect family for sixteen years. I had envied him for it. And now, come to find out, everything he knew about his life was just as fractured as the rest of us.

Sure, he didn't endure the same kinds of problems I did, but he was being forced to choose one parent over another or move in with his grandparents and spend a couple years without any parents at home like I had growing up. It pissed me off that it might be Mick's best choice, and it pissed me off what parents did to their kids. They claim to be adults but never act like it.

"It's just a day."

He stuffed the duffle bag under his bed and ran his fingers through his hair. Then he looked out his window into the backyard.

"Remember last summer? We'd climb out there and jump into the pool. Why can't this summer be like that?" He breathed in and let out a long exhale. "I don't know, man. I'll try to give you a day, but no promises."

"Thanks, Mick. We're still in this together."

He sighed and then said he agreed with me, but I could tell he didn't believe it. I couldn't blame him. I wasn't sure I believed myself either. It was every man for himself.

When I got home, George told me Cheryl called a couple times, prompting Tab to sing about me having a girlfriend. I chased her into her room and told her to shut up because Cheryl wasn't my girlfriend. Although she was my girlfriend, sort of.

I wanted to call her back, if for no other reason than to hear her voice but I didn't have time. I had a different call to make. I turned the card over in my hand a few times before dialing the number.

It wasn't the card Officer Ward had left with me. Someone else had given me a card a few days ago. It was a guy who said I was owed a big favor. His name was Moe Dentz.

CHAPTER 19

BREAKING UP

Moe Dentz sent a car to pick me up the next day. It wasn't Tommy and the Oldsmobile. He sent another guy in a black Lincoln Town Car with a thin red pinstripe running the length of the car. It was an ugly mother of a hangover, and so was the guy driving it.

He told me his name was Sonny, a cliché cover if I ever heard one. Mobsters who picked cars for their trunk space were always called something like Sonny or Vito or Frankie. They all had the same stories too. Most old-timers migrated to the US from Italy and set up shop in New York City, while most new guys hailed from places like Milwaukee, Chicago, or Cleveland.

Sonny was a loud and proud new guy. He kept talking the entire trip, turning down the radio to hear himself talk. His story was a little different because it didn't start out with him bootlegging or hustling newspapers. He said he was just a dumb kid who didn't know what he wanted to do with his life after serving in the army.

"Wanna know why I took this job? I saw Coppola's flick, *The Godfather*," he said. "And then I knew, I just knew, this life was for me."

He worked his way around a few construction sites in Arizona until landing one that was a front. It was a golden ticket into a private club of sorts. Membership had been good to him, opening up doors to all kinds of jobs connected to horse racing, casinos, and discos.

"That's why Moe sent me to fetch you," he said. "I'm helping him work out some kinks at the Blue Derby."

The Blue Derby was a blue neon framed strip club located in the Naked City, a crime-plagued neighborhood north of the Las Vegas Strip with a mix of industrial businesses, low-cost housing, liquor stores, and strip clubs. The area got its name because so many show girls lived in the courtyard apartments and used to sunbathe in the nude for an even tan. But as they moved out and the strip clubs moved in, it took on a more nefarious reputation.

Sonny marshaled me past the doorman and into their 21-or-over lair with the wave of a hand. He sat me down at a table close to the bar in the back and patted my shoulder.

"I'll see if Moe is ready for you," he said. "And I'll send over a drink on the house."

The Blue Derby was nearly empty except for two men closer to the elevated stage than the bar. They weren't together. One of them was against the wall, leaning back and relaxed. The other was more eager, sitting next to the stage and leaning forward, peering up at one of two strippers working a pole.

It was surreal, stepping in from the daylight into this perpetual night, a dark room illuminated by soft neon, black light, and stage lighting. The tempo of the music didn't match the low energy of the emptiness — an old, sexy and soulful Barry White number — that the daytime dancers, bare chested, matched their moves to.

I squirmed in the chair, looking and then not looking at something that seemed too taboo to take in, like the half-clad showgirl statues that twirled around and around on the Tropicana marquee. I used to turn my head every time we passed them on the way to the airport.

When a drink landed in front of me, I was relieved. Twirling the ice around with a red stir stick gave me something to do besides ogle two topless women earning a few bucks before rushing out to pick up kids from elementary school. The drink smelled like pine needles. So did the third.

"Funny," she said, sitting in an empty chair beside me. "You look a little young to be a gin and tonic type."

She was young, much younger than the women on the stage, with tight waves of golden hair framing her delicate face. Her eyes were blue with tiny flecks of gold around the pupils. Her lips were red, a paler shade than you might expect in a place like this one. She was leaning in toward me, smiling, as if one of the hands holding her up would reach under the table and explore the seam of my jeans.

"Oh, I didn't order this," I said with a stammer. "It was on the house."

"A real VIP then," she said. "Nice to meet you, mister VIP."

Her smile was infectious, and an awkward laugh escaped me. I caught myself rocking back on my heels under the table and didn't know why, aside from her beautiful self-confidence.

"Yeah, no. I'm not a customer either."

"I see. A regular man of mystery." She rested her chin on her hands. "Don't tell me you just filled out a job application."

"No, nothing like that," I said. "I guess you could say I have some business here. Well, not here, but with someone who is here."

"So you are a VIP," she said, reaching over and giving my drink a stir. "That must be nice, coming to a place like this just to meet friends and talk business at your age."

"Me?" I said with a scoff. "How old are you?"

"Twenty-one, hon," she said. "Your turn."

"Beat you by a year," I said, lying in return.

She wrinkled her nose and rolled her eyes, never breaking the smile. Then she sat back in the chair and put one leg up on the adjoining one in front of us. My eyes gravitated to its bareness.

"I don't think so," she sang. "But I'll give you a pass on that one. There's nothing wrong with following the fantasies we want to believe in the most sensational city on earth."

"Thanks." The booze was getting to me. "So what do you do here?"

"Serve drinks," she said before pushing her lips toward the stage. "Dance a number or two, but it's too early for me to take a number, and too empty."

She was like a ray of sunshine bleeding into this dingy establishment, a bright glow that cut through the darkness just like the one that encompassed us every time someone opened the front doors. It was a reminder, just like she was, that beauty can be found anywhere if you look hard enough. Except I must have been lucky because I wasn't looking.

"You have a name?" she asked, all smiles again.

"Brady, Brady...," I said, cutting myself off before giving up my last name on the second introduction.

"Nice to meet you Brady, Brady," she said, mocking me with an outstretched hand like a princess. "Sandy."

I took it like a gentleman. "Is that your real name?"

"Would you like a better one?" she laughed.

I laughed, but her answer made me uncomfortable as if there was a good chance Sandy wasn't her name. Maybe it wasn't. It didn't matter, but it left me wondering why she was talking to me and what we were supposed to talk about. But I didn't want her to leave me stranded either, so I took a shot in the dark.

"It must be exciting working here."

"There are ups and downs. The money is the upside, obviously."

"And the downside?"

"The downside is always having walls up, so you aren't forced into anything, um, emotionally uncomfortable, you know. Yeah, that would be the downside. What about you?"

"There's nothing to tell, really. I just go to school, um, college, you know. Hang out with my friends. Shoot pool. The usual stuff."

"Yeah? That must be nice, going to school and hanging out with friends. I never got to do anything like that. I had to find my own way and, well, I found it here."

"Here?" I looked around the room, holding up my hands.

She laughed. "No, Las Vegas. I'm from Los Angeles, Hollywood, but Vegas is like the big league for dancers."

"A dream come true?"

Her smile faded — not on her lips, but the one in her eyes. It was the wrong thing to say.

"No," she said, reflecting on my question. "I wouldn't say that, Brady, Brady. It's just a job, not easy money but fast money, if you know what I mean. I always have to remind myself of that, you know, because I'm a good person. It's easy to forget that when you live in a fantasy world."

I knew what she meant. The job was different, but it was the same grind. I wasn't a drug dealer; I pretended to be one when the sun went down. Sandy understood what Cheryl could never understand. Some of us couldn't be a success being lifted up by someone. We had to find our own way in spite of everyone.

"So how does this work, this fantasyland," I said. "Guys just throw money at you? And then what?"

She looked as uncomfortable as I felt, a dark secret resting on her lips that she didn't want to tell. She took a minute to choose her words.

"Sometimes," she said. "Sometimes we just talk. Sometimes I give them a private dance. And sometimes they take private dances in a VIP room. It just depends, you know."

"I should probably tell you then, I don't have any money on me."

She frowned. "You think that's why I came over here?"

"I thought..."

"Look," she said, putting a finger to my chest. "I only came over because you're a cute kid and looked uneasy — a naive schoolboy averting his eyes, so he didn't tent up and embarrass himself before his big meeting."

"I'm sorry."

She stood up, wanting to show me she was angry. I wasn't fooled. I was just a fool.

"I thought, I don't know, maybe we could be friends. I don't have many in Vegas. Everybody in the Naked City wants something, but you don't look like you're from around here."

"I'm not from around here," I said, standing up and reaching for her arm. "And I said I was sorry. I mean it. And I get it. I know what it's like to be surrounded by people and all alone at the same time. I know what it's like to grind away trying to get ahead but dig the hole deeper. I know what it's like to ..."

"... to need a friend."

"Yeah, and that's why I'm here. I'm trying to save myself and my friends."

"I'm the one who's sorry then," she said. "You came to the wrong place."

She turned away and headed toward the bar. I thought about chasing after her. I thought about Cheryl. I thought about where I was and how I had gotten here. And then there was Sonny waving me over toward a back hallway. It was an effort to walk straight.

He led me into a dark office with low ambient lighting from a stained-glass Tiffany lamp. The furniture looked rich, all cherrywood and leather, and worn out. It said money, but not the clean kind you could pull from an ATM machine. This was dirty money, crinkled bills stuffed into g-strings and damp with spilt liquor.

Moe Dentz sat in a high-backed office chair, looking out onto the room through a one-way glass mirror. It wasn't the only one. Behind him, there was another one-way mirror, but with impenetrable reflective glass on our side. It was anybody's guess if someone or no one was behind it.

He wasn't alone. There were two chairs in front of the desk, and Tommy sat in one of them. Another man with a round face and a dirty brown comb-over stood up from the other as I entered, making room for me on the other chair by moving to the small sofa that framed the wall opposite the mirror Dentz was looking through.

"Mr. Wilks," Dentz said. "Have a seat."

Sonny led me to the empty chair, holding it for me like we were on a date. He whispered good luck to me, patting me on my shoulder again. I didn't know what he meant, but the tone was sarcastic.

"This is another associate of mine, Dion," he said, gesturing to the new guy, who gave me a casual salute. "And Tommy, you already know him."

"Hey, kid," Tommy said. "Good to see you."

"Hello." My voice cracked the one word I could muster.

Dentz turned toward Dion. "Mr. Wilks, here, or Brady, if he doesn't mind since we're all friends here, made quite the impression on Mr. Bigelow after he did an unsolicited favor. We are in his debt."

"Bravo, Mr. Brady Wilks." Dion patted his hands in a slow clap and shifted in his seat.

I bowed my head, more in unease than an acknowledgment of any compliment because I didn't know if it was one. He was amused. They were all amused except Dentz.

"Yesterday, Brady gave me a call and said he had a special kind of favor to ask. It seems he and his friends got themselves in a little trouble."

Tommy whistled. Dion sat up.

"What kind of trouble?" Dion asked.

"It comes in two parts, and Brady, feel free to correct me on any of the details as I move through it," Dentz said. "The first part is our young friend was part of a grab-and-dash cartel drug heist, guns blazing."

"Way to go, kid," Tommy smiled and punched me in the shoulder. "I didn't figure you for the type."

"And the second part is that he believes, with good cause, that one of his partners is plotting to keep the proceeds," Dentz said. "No honor among friends with this younger generation, it seems."

"He killed one of my friends," I muttered. "No reason."

"You're sure?" Dion leaned forward. "How did he do it?"

"The official report says he died of sepsis in the hospital," I said. "But Alex was there when Brett died, and the police found a hex bag in his bed."

"A hex bag? Is this kid for real?"

"He's the one with a favor, Dion. Hear him out," Dentz said. "What else, Brady?"

At that moment, I wished I had brought my drink in, but I left it on the table. My mouth felt dry.

"Alex believed Brett was going to tell the cops about the bad deal," I said.

"So he was going to snitch," Tommy said. "Some friends you got."

"This Alex kid might be behind the Haringer heist, too," said Dentz. "But I don't know. The robbery has cartel written all over it, which I don't like. It hits too close to home. All of it hits too close to home, really. Cartel heroin doesn't belong in the suburbs like that."

"What do the feds say?" Dion asked.

"Yeah, I checked with them," Dentz said. "This is an ATF thing right now, but the DEA wants in on it too if it turns out the cartel is arming up. And the more the DEA presses, the more the feds want to swoop in and take it all over. I mean, Haringer's shop is supposed to be off limits for everyone. The last thing the feds want is some of those guns turning up."

"Can you imagine?" Tommy whistled again. "That Giuliani guy would get a real hard-on if he knew."

"What a putz," Dion said. "But I still don't get it. What am I missing? Why would Alex be part of the robbery?"

"It's Will," I said. "The guns we used came from Mr. Haringer's shop. His son, Will, set it up and was our third driver."

Dentz produced a toothpick from a small box on the desk. I had forgotten his thing for toothpicks until he tucked one between his teeth. An unexpected craving for nicotine must have crawled up from Mr. Dentz' stomach.

"So what do we got, then?" Tommy drummed on the desk. "The Alex kid double-crosses the cartel and then starts double-crossing his friends to what end? Make good with the cartel?"

"I don't like it," said Dion.

"You're all overthinking this," Dentz said. "This isn't about all that yet. This is about our friend here. He's owed a favor. So what do you want us to do, kid?"

"I don't want Alex coming after Mick or Will or even Jamie," I said. "Maybe he needs to be scared or disappear until things calm down."

"Eighty-six," said Dion.

"You know what that means, Brady?" Tommy asked me. I shook my head. "Eight miles out and six feet deep."

"It doesn't have to be so literal anymore," Dion said. "I stuffed some guy into a barrel last week and sent him swimming with the fishes in the lake."

Eighty-six. Was that what I meant? Erase Alex from the equation? I was the one who wanted a toothpick or a cigarette now. Anything might have helped keep the acid in my stomach down.

"Hold on," said Dentz, turning to me. "That's a big favor, and I know you have the marker to do it. I know because I gave it to you. So what? Why waste it? I have a better idea, and it gives you double for nothing."

I stiffened, not sure if I followed. The other two men leaned in closer as if Dentz was about to drop a bomb of a secret onto the desk.

"Here's the play," he said, shifting his eyes from me to Tommy and back to Dion. "Brady is going tell us where Alex stashes the skag, and we lift it. Alex loses any incentive to double cross his friends and surrenders this make-good alliance with the cartel if he has one. When the cartel calls us on it, we tell them tough luck because they have no business selling smack in neighborhoods where our kids go to school. That business belongs in the hood. We put these kids under our protection for good measure because they did the right thing coming to us."

"I don't know," I said. "What about the money we were going to make?"

"What's money when you got friends?" Dion asked.

Tommy laughed. "That's a good one."

"Brady, I hear you, I do," Dentz said. "Here's the thing. Think it over. We can take your marker and scare this Alex kid or help him exit stage left. Or you can seize the moment and deliver justice upon your enemy, and we'll reward you for it with another marker, payable at the time and place of your choosing."

"Hex bag." Dion shook his head. "The last thing I want to see is us in league with the Black House again."

The three men looked at each other. They were solemn in a way I hadn't seen before, as if Dion had uttered the unutterable. I couldn't connect the dots, so I ignored it. Whatever code they were talking in wasn't my business.

"All right," I said, crossing my arms. "All right."

"All right, what?" Dentz asked.

"All right, I'll think about it," I said.

"Good boy," said Dentz before turning to Tommy. "Tommy, show our good friend out and ask Sonny to take him home. He's one of the good ones."

Except I didn't feel like one of the good ones. I was just one of the bad ones, and the bad ones were all taking sides. But what did I expect? I lived in the most sinful city in the world. Nobody ever knows if they are climbing out of a hole or digging one deeper. The casinos and clubs all counted on it.

The best you could hope for was to escape with your dignity somewhat intact. If that meant giving up the drug money, then so be it. You throw your lot in with people who honor you because the ones who despise you will destroy your self-esteem. Most people will never understand that, but maybe the girl I met there did.

Sandy approached me as I was leaving with Sonny and palmed me a piece of paper. It was a phone number without a name. Under the number, she had scrawled "a friend."

CHAPTER 20

BAD MAN

When I got home, I studied the paper Sandy had given me, taking in the soft curves of her handwriting. I was tempted to call her but felt guilty because I still owed Cheryl two calls. She had called again, telling my sister she was looking for a sweet time.

I knew what that meant. She wanted to see me, sure. But she also wanted another taste. That's what made the drug so desirable to push. It pushed itself. Sometimes it only took a one-time use to turn a casual user into a zombie.

There was no way Cheryl and I took enough to risk addiction. It was a bump on top of a few beers with the right company. I remembered being fuzzy when Cal woke me from a sound sleep, but not junk sick or anything — we didn't do enough of it for that kind of trouble.

But it still bothered me that Cheryl mentioned it. I expected other girls my friends knew to put the drug before the pusher, but not her. She was supposed to be different. The butterflies we felt in our stomachs at the drive-in were supposed to be about the chemistry between us, not the euphoria brought on by a few grains of heaven.

At least, that is what I thought, but maybe she felt different. So I slipped Sandy's paper into a sock drawer and called Cheryl instead.

We had two phones in our house. One was a wall-mounted rotary phone hung between the kitchen and the dining room. The other was a new alabaster cordless phone, already yellowing from its station on a coffee table next to an ashtray. I wasn't allowed to use that one because my mother was paranoid that the battery would run out. I didn't care because I never used it. The wall-mounted phone wasn't in the living room, so it offered slightly more privacy than the cordless one.

I let the phone ring ten times before hanging up. Like most people I knew, Cheryl didn't have an answering machine yet. But if she did, I don't think I could have left a message. I wouldn't know what to say. What would anybody say? "Hey, I called. This is the evidence."

"Who are you calling?"

It was my mother. I hung up the phone.

"Nobody." I didn't mean it as a lie. I didn't want to be bothered.

"That's rich," she said. "Do you want to try again?"

"It's none of your business."

"How about I put you on phone restriction for a month?"

"Cheryl. Okay?" I shrugged.

She laughed. "I don't know what that girl sees in you. I mean, you look like your father in some ways, but he had some meat on his bones. You, you're just a skinny Minnie. What does George like to say? 'If Brady were standing sideways with his tongue sticking out, people would think he's a zipper.'"

"You so skinny, you could hula hoop with a Cheerio. You so skinny, you could use floss as a towel. You so skinny, your underwear needs a belt. Yeah, I've heard them all."

"Oh, you can't take a joke now," she said. "Or is it that you can't take a joke if I make it? Only George can make the jokes around here."

"He's trying to be funny, even when he isn't."

"And I suppose I'm not."

"You don't say it to be funny."

"Then why do I say it?"

There are some questions you want to avoid answering because it will get you in trouble. And then there are questions you want to answer because you know they will get you into trouble.

"You say it to be mean."

She glared at me, thinking of what to say. It was as if she was writing a monologue in her head or thumbing through file folders for one she had pre-written and saved for this occasion. Then she found it and leaned into me.

"Do you think I enjoy being mean to you? I've had to be mean. I've had to be tough. It's the only way you'll respond with any emotion. You were so spoiled by your grandmother, and it's my job to undo all the damage or you won't make it in this world," she said. "You don't know. But I know. When I was thirteen, I was shipped off to different family members for a month at a time, and I can tell you what, none of them, not one of them, would put up with your crap. Precious little Brady. The sun rises and sets on Brady. Everything for Brady. Do you know why I took you when your grandmother couldn't raise you anymore? It wasn't because I was your mother. It was because nobody else wanted you. Everybody was sick and tired of your grandmother going on and on about how special Brady is ... she might have been right about a lot of things, but she sure got that wrong. You aren't special. You're nobody."

"Stop it. Stop It. STOP IT." I was crying. Her words hit me like punches.

"Oh, poor Brady," she said. "Did I hurt your feelings?"

"Screw you! What do you know about me? Nothing."

"I know there's something you aren't telling me," she said. "So what is it? What have you gotten yourself into?"

She was the one lying this time. She was trolling, laying a line, and hoping I might take the bait. Recognizing her play helped me regain control, and I started to calm down, breathing heavy but no longer crying. I pushed my initial panic away with anger.

"Nothing is going on," I said. "And you wouldn't understand it if there was."

"Try me. What did the police talk to you about? You never even told me. You just stormed off to see Mick. So I want to know what is going on."

So that's what this was about? Business as usual. Why is it the only time parents talk to their kids is when they want something?

"I didn't storm over to Mick's house," I lied. "We had just lost the friend we were closest to, outside of each other, and I didn't think he wanted to be alone. I didn't want to be alone, either. There. Happy?"

"You weren't alone," she said. "I was right there for you, but you never gave me a chance."

I huffed. Here it comes again. She was the victim. And now she was going to go on a rant about all the sacrifices she and George made to make sure I had a roof over my head and food in my stomach as if that was all kids ever need to trust their parents. Never mind that, in her case, she was pocketing a few hundred dollars a month from social security — the perks of having a kid with a dead dad. My rent and food were paid in full.

"What? Stay home and be lectured about how not to be Brett? No thanks."

"Okay, if not the police, then how about you start with what happened between you and Brett that night I dropped you at the hospital," she said. "You told me he was sleeping when you saw him, but that wasn't true. Was it?"

Sometimes I wondered if she knew all her conversations were instructions, threats, or interrogations. Other times I didn't have to wonder. She knew what buttons to push.

"What? Now you're saying I had something to do with it?"

"That's not what I'm saying," she said. "I thought it would be a good idea for me to know."

Her hand gestures were getting bigger. She wasn't going to let any of this go. She wanted a confession from me, and she would talk in circles to get it, trying to charm me, punish me, promise me, love me, hate me. It was all make-believe.

"Isn't it?" I countered, squinting at her. "Here's an idea. Why don't you ask me how I'm holding up after losing one of my friends instead of grilling me for answers. I'll tell you why, because you can't stand not knowing every little thing!"

"Maybe that's because you don't give me a choice!" she shouted back but then added in a calmer, quieter voice. "Maybe it's because I'm scared for you. Maybe because I don't want you to turn out like Matt Marquez."

I was stunned. Matt Marquez was a 17-year-old kid who shot one of his teachers just before the summer break. It was a different high school than mine, but we all knew the story. He walked into school with a small caliber handgun before classes started.

I always imagined that everybody at the school was too busy looking for their friends, copying homework assignments, and comparing wardrobe accessories to notice anything was different about him. Or maybe, just maybe, there wasn't anything different about him until he put his book on his desk, pulled out the handgun, walked up to the front of the room, and fired a single round into the teacher's chest.

Students who were there couldn't believe it. One of them asked if it was a joke.

It wasn't a joke. Then Matt walked out of the classroom and didn't shoot anyone else until, for no apparent reason, he decided to shoot two more kids. And later, as he headed home, he threatened to kill another kid's dog but ultimately didn't hurt anything or anybody else.

The news was all over the valley. Most news stories called him a loner, but he wasn't all that different from plenty of kids I knew. He played fantasy games. He read *Soldier of Fortune* magazines. He did his chores. He turned in assignments. He read his books.

The only thing that made him different from me before he snapped was his social life. He didn't like going to people's houses, drinking, doing drugs, or listening to loud music.

"So you do think I had something to do with Brett."

"You have it in you," she said. "You have your father's..."

She didn't finish her sentence. She didn't have to. She motioned to the bandage on my leg.

"Unbelievable." I wanted to spit at her feet.

I couldn't look at her anymore. She tried to call my name as I turned around and stomped to my room. I slammed the door. I flipped The Who's *Who's Next* into my cassette player and turned it up. Daltrey was wailing for empathy, unhinged and unheard. Me too.

As one song drifted into the next, I kept trying to puzzle out the problem with people. Maybe it's how everybody is portrayed in books and movies — defined others in one-dimensional terms. Good guys. Bad guys. Nice girls. Naughty boys. None of it's true.

While living in Ohio, I checked out library books about Geronimo because it seemed like he was the most famous Indian ever. I first learned about him by watching westerns on Sunday afternoons with my grandparents. His name came up during old World War II movies, usually yelled out by paratroopers jumping out of airplanes. It was something me and my friends had done when we jumped into ponds and lakes before we knew who he was or why we yelled his name.

When I did learn about him, I was surprised to find out Geronimo wasn't an Apache chief at all but a spiritual leader who used to travel with three different bands of Apache. And that's how I was introduced to another Indian named Cochise. Cochise wasn't as famous as any movie Indians like Lone Wolf or Crazy Horse or Sitting Bull, but he fascinated me because he was as compassionate as he was brutal.

He was a family man, had a sense of humor, and liked to tell great stories. Yet, he was feared by Mexican settlers and known for slowly torturing his enemies or anyone who tried to cross Apache Pass in the Dragoon Mountains. All those stories about covering cowboys with honey and leaving them for ants or hanging them upside down over a small fire to cook their brains or skinning them alive from their ankles to their earlobes — they were stories about Cochise.

But there were other stories too. There was one where he saved the life of a U.S. Calvary trooper who ran out of water while tracking Cochise. Another was how he allowed the railroad to build a stop in Apache Pass. And there was another about how he didn't want to fight Americans. He was forced into it after being falsely accused of kidnapping the son of a rancher.

I used to think about this a lot. Was Cochise a bad Indian or a good Indian? Was Moe Dentz a good guy or a bad one? Was Matt Marquez a good kid or a bad kid? Was I?

I once had a Sunday school teacher who would have said bad on all counts. She used to talk about how sin was like adding a little piece of raw liver to a milkshake. She would bring in a blender to illustrate her point.

"How much liver can we put in this milkshake before it's ruined?" she used to ask us while stirring it up excitedly until the white shake turned a murky reddish brown.

The answer was none. Nobody wants a milkshake with raw liver in it, even a little bit. Her point, of course, was that Jesus gives us the gift of a brand new milkshake through confession. But I always wondered, what about that milkshake in the meantime?

If someone asked me, I would always define myself as a bad kid. But I wasn't without honor. I was loyal to my friends. I didn't hurt people who didn't deserve it. So that meant I wasn't all bad, maybe, no matter what my mother said.

Maybe that's where my father got it wrong in his story about the finches. He may have been a white finch and my mother a black finch, but that didn't make me black too. I was gray, just like the whole world.

That's what happens when you mix black and white. Once mixed, you can never make it black or white again, only different shades of gray. It's the same thing when you're talking about milkshakes. None of it is any good. We're all bad men. We're all sad men. And it doesn't change when we get a new milkshake because the sin is still there. We merely heap it upon the pile that Jesus is asked to bear.

George knocked on my door and told me to turn it down. I turned it up another notch and let side one play out. Then I flipped the cassette over. The next time he knocked, it was because they were going out to dinner. I turned the volume up louder.

The third time he knocked, it was sometime around eleven. He wanted to know if I knew where Mick might be. So I opened the door.

"His mom is worried about him," George said. "Do you know where he is or when he's coming home?"

"He's gone." I shook my head. "He left without me."

CHAPTER 21

SILENT ANGEL

Over the next three days, George drove me around on the back of his motorcycle so I could hang up missing person fliers. The picture wasn't the best, but the rest of the description made up for it. How do you miss a six foot three kid with wavy red hair?

We put up the posters around all the haunts I could think of — even a few places that surprised George, like the small tavern on the southwest side that sometimes let us slip in as long as we kept to the back, where an unused pool table with torn green felt was stored. George wouldn't say anything to my mother. Sometimes he was a prisoner, just like me.

It was rare, but he reminded me of this unfortunate truth from time to time. Most often, I could see the parallel when my mother loaded up Tab and all her Girl Scout friends for a camping trip. He would wear a sly smile for days before their departure, telling me there was a no-tell policy in place anytime she was gone. The deal went for me or him as he spent those free nights at the bar.

Most of the time it ended in disaster. Sometimes it was something innocent and dumb, like when I fell through the ceiling in the garage while helping George move boxes into storage. Other times it was something not so innocent and stupid, like when I flew off the hood of a car because my friends had taken to doing movie stunts after Mick got his Buick.

My mother always said George would leave messages for her at the campsites, figuring she would have a few hours to cool off before pulling into the driveway upon her return. I appreciated him for it, just like I appreciated that he called in sick so I could hang these posters. It was a big deal because he never called in sick.

We finished around seven as the shadows grew long over the desert. When George let me out on the street before parking his bike in the garage, I noticed a large number of cars parked in front of Denise's home. I didn't recognize most of them, but two were familiar.

Alex hadn't dumped his car after all. More importantly, Cheryl's orange Pinto stood out. I smacked myself in the head. The messages she had left for me had stacked up, and I hadn't been able to reach her for days while looking for Mick.

"Hey, George," I said. "Cheryl is over at Denise's house. Can I head over?"

"Sure," he said. "But if your mother asks, it didn't come from me."

"Thanks," I said, handing him the helmet and running fingers through my matted hair.

I set off across the street with a chip on my shoulder, perturbed by how quickly our neighborhood could replace Mick's home for another party house. Nobody seemed to care that his parents were getting a divorce or that he had taken off for parts unknown.

Of course, this was Las Vegas. People fly in and out of a scene all the time. It wasn't like Ohio, where friendships forged in the first grade were lifelong. Everybody is transient in this town. Most people jumped jobs and homes every two to five years, and their kids went with them. Some of it had to do with the growth. Some of it had to do with people discovering that they weren't compatible with a 24-hour town.

The casinos kept the booze, drugs, gambling, and nightlife flowing nonstop, and the town had taken to making that rule of thumb for everyone. Grocery stores, gas stations, smoke shops, and taverns kept to the same schedule, catering to the never-ending cycle of shift workers who gave their children a house key when they were enrolled in the first grade. What else can you do in a city with no last call?

So there it was. I was naive to think Mick would somehow be treated differently. He wasn't the nucleus of our neighborhood after all. He was as disposable as the rolls of quarters people feed slot machines in the vain attempt to hear the incessant clinking of a payout. Except there was no payout. People didn't build this place on winners.

I knocked on the front door, and some kid opened it immediately. He had a red cup in his hand and a stupid grin on his face. I had never seen him before in my life. I know because if I had seen him before, I would have kicked his dopey head in.

"Denise around?"

"Check the kitchen, man," he said, perm bobbing on a small head with a long neck.

The scene was decidedly different from Mick's place, with more jocks and preps than we ever catered to. These were the cliques Tom and Denise gravitated toward, with stoners welcomed as a symbol of empathy for Mick's disappearance. Otherwise, it was just another house party that emulated the steady stream of teen party movies that Hollywood had started pumping out. The cops would shut it down by ten.

The house was crowded, with small clusters of kids having loud, drunken conversations. I saw Jamie was part of one cluster. He spotted me too, pausing just long enough to flip me the bird. I rolled my eyes at him and pushed past a guy trying to convince his girlfriend to go upstairs.

These were the kinds of parties I hated. Amateurs with big hair, combs sticking out of their back pockets. Sleeves rolled up to make up for the lack of muscle. Wasted drinkers chugging down the contents of their red cups on command as if they needed an excuse to get any drunker faster.

It was clear the keg was in the kitchen because I had to weave in and out of tighter groups as I made my way inside, some of the partygoers pausing long enough to chant something like "smoke bomb," "teenage delinquency," or "rock on, man."

I grinned at them all but was unable to appreciate any of it without a buzz. No wonder Alex made money. If there was a sucker born every minute, two of them must have relocated to Vegas with their sucker kids in tow every thirty seconds.

"Hey, Brady," said Trish Two, brushing up against me as I tried to move past. "Any word on Mick?"

I shook my head and accepted a drink from her cup. It was cheap beer from the tap, already going flat. I kissed her between her blond bangs as a thank you. She squeezed my arm.

Denise was hanging with Tom in the kitchen, just off from the pony keg they had set up in the sink. She was folded into Tom's arms and swaying back and forth to the music in between, taking drags off a shared cigarette.

"Hey, Denise," I said. "Tom."

"Brady, bud," Tom said.

"Hey, Brady, glad you could make it," Denise said, tilting her head and raising an eyebrow in concern.

"No, nothing yet," I said. "Hey, you seen Cheryl around?"

"Um, let me think." She frowned, eyes closed. "Last time I saw her, she was with Alex."

I wrinkled my face. "Alex?"

"Yeah, that's the last I saw of her."

"I didn't see them coming through," I said. "Any ideas?"

"Check outside," said Tom. "Then come back around for a shot of Jäger."

"Right on." I moved toward the back door, but some girl was standing in front of it. She had locked eyes with some guy across the room and started unbuttoning her pants.

"Do it, baby!" he called out to her. His friends hooted in agreement.

"I'm on fire for you, buddy," she cried out to him, showing off boxers with little flames all over them. "I'm on fire. I'm on fire."

I laughed and placed my hands on her shoulders to get by so she wouldn't fall over. She leaned into me anyway, tongue out and laughing.

"You're a cutie too," she said.

I squeezed past, and the other guy came to her rescue as her jeans bunched around her ankles. She didn't fall down, but beer slopped out of her cup and onto the carpet.

Outside, the crowd was thinner. I spotted Alex right away, exchanging little baggies for cash on the far side of the yard behind the pool. I walked right up to him when the last customer took off with his cronies.

"Hey, Brady, I got something for you," he said, all grins as he reached behind his back.

I'm not sure what I expected, but his movement made my heart jump. I instinctively paused and ducked, wondering if I could tackle him before he got the drop on me.

"What?" He looked at me like I was crazy, and then laughed with recognition. "Oh, don't be an idiot. I left the Beretta in the car. This party is the minor leagues."

He thrust his gun hand out at me. It was a roll of cash.

"What's that?"

"Your cut," he said. "Don't look so surprised or happy."

I wasn't smiling. I was numb and wanted to punch him. I didn't reach for it, but clenched my fists and cocked my arms.

"Go on, take it," he said. "Take it and get out of here. With Mick out of here, I'm not carrying you anymore. You're out."

I wanted to tell him I didn't want his money. I wanted to take it and throw it in the pool, making the offer as insignificant as he was to me. I wanted to punch him in the face and stomp on his head. I didn't do any of those things. I took the money.

"This doesn't make up for what you did to Brett," I said, shoving it into my jeans.

"Don't pin that on me, punk," he said. "I had nothing to do with it."

"I don't believe it."

"Believe what you want. The Lord works in mysterious ways." He looked up at the sky and then bowed his head, bringing his hands together in prayer. Then he inverted them and laughed.

"But you're the one who left the hex bag. Admit it."

"What? You think everybody is Jayne Mansfield? No, Brady. Most people do it to themselves."

"You're saying Brett gave himself sepsis?"

"I'm saying your girlfriend is upstairs doing it to herself right now."

"What?"

"You weren't around, so I set her up," he said.

"What did you do?" I took a step toward him.

"Easy, pal," he said. "You gave her the hunger. I only fed it."

I wanted to grab him by the shirt and yell in his face, but his words stuck in my head. She was in the house, upstairs. So I turned around and ran, almost knocking a football player into the pool. He called after me, but I didn't look back.

I ran into the house, pushing past people without any of the earlier niceties, and sprinted upstairs. They were all talking about me in my wake, wondering what had gotten into me. I didn't even know what had gotten into me. Somehow I knew, I just knew, that Cheryl was in trouble.

She was lying on the king-sized bed in the parents' room like a silent angel. Her arms were outstretched over her head, legs splayed. A rubber tube hung loosely around her left arm. A syringe lay abandoned with a spoon and a spent cigarette filter on a nightstand under the only light left on in the room.

"Cheryl," I said more forcefully as I rushed over to the bed. "Cheryl!"

"Hey baby," she said, slurring. "Where have you been?"

I was relieved by her voice at first. But then I knelt on the bed and my heart sunk. Even in the low light, I could see she was pale, and her lips tinged blue. He had given her too much. I had to get her moving.

"Hey, I'm right here," I said gently. "Let's get you up."

"Noooo," she said, whispering in protest. "Lay down with me. Float away with me."

"Come on, Cheryl," I was a little more forceful now, pulling on her arms into a sitting position. "'Up and at 'em."

"I called, Brady," she mumbled. "No, Brady. Not home."

"Hey, never mind that. I'm here now. How much did he give you?"

"Fly away."

She was drifting off again, her head lolling from side to side. I circled my arms under her armpits and tried to stand her up. She didn't resist, but I couldn't pull her up.

I almost had her, but I couldn't get her feet under her. They were limp, like her arms, and I had to sit her down again. Her breathing was shallow, while mine was elevated. I had to get help, so I laid her back down on the bed, her shirt lifting up as I did.

She mumbled something I couldn't understand, nonsense words that came across as guttural syllables.

"Help! I need some help in here!" I ran to the sink to wet a washcloth with cold water. Two kids looked in, but then ducked out again. They didn't want any part of it.

I placed the washcloth on her head and raced back to the medicine cabinet, sweeping everything inside onto the counter. I grabbed a bottle of Tylenol and popped the top off. My hands were shaking, tablets spilling off the counter and onto the floor.

I grabbed a couple of the pills and a cup of water from the bathroom, whispering how sorry I was as I knelt beside her. She wouldn't sit up, so I held her nose until her mouth opened, forcing the pills inside and pouring water into it.

She was coughing, but I held her nose closed anyway. She was pushing against me, arms flailing and slapping my face.

"I need you to swallow, Cheryl," I said. "Just swallow them and get up!"

"Hey buddy, what are you doing to her!" A new voice called in from the doorway.

He wasn't alone, but he was the only one rushing into the room. He grabbed my shoulder and pulled me back. I reacted, shrugging him off, but then he hit me. A couple more of his friends came into the room, trying to wrestle me off her.

"Overdose! It's an overdose!" I shouted, a blow glancing off my head. "Call 9-1-1!"

It wasn't until I was knocked to the floor, taking a few kicks to my ribs, that one of them finally saw what was happening. I wasn't trying to hurt Cheryl but save her.

"Oh, man, call 9-1-1!" hollered one of the kids who had struck me. "We need an ambulance!"

As the hands let me go, I crawled back up onto the bed and pulled her shirt down, rolling her over onto her side so she wouldn't choke. She was coughing, water running out of her mouth.

"Hey, man," said the first guy who had entered the room. "I didn't know. It looked like, it looked like you were, you know."

I didn't even look at him. "Yeah, I get it. I know." I was rocking her back and forth on her side, trying to keep her conscious until help could arrive.

The party was breaking up, kids dumping their cups and bottles onto any open counter space or table they could find. A few took flight down the street or jumped in cars before the medics and Metro arrived. Even the guys who had jumped me took off eventually, muttering apologies before disappearing into the death throes of a busted party.

Denise poked her head in once but didn't say anything. I looked back at her; she was just standing there, looking through me and playing with the cross she sometimes wore around her neck. Maybe she was saying a prayer. I couldn't think of any. The only ones that ever came to me anymore were those we recited, almost without meaning, for communion practice. Even that felt like ancient history.

I didn't leave her side until the medics arrived. They asked me a few questions, most of which I couldn't answer. I only knew a few of the answers. I knew it was heroin but didn't know with what it was cut. I knew she injected it. I said it was her first time. I told them I had force fed her some Tylenol, and they gave me funny looks. I couldn't tell if they were surprised that I knew to try it or if it was a stupid thing to do.

One of the medics wanted to look at the contusions on my face, but I brushed him off. They didn't have time to help. They had stabilized Cheryl, but she still needed to be taken to the hospital. I'd been hurt worse.

The house downstairs looked like a teenage war zone, but Tom and Donny were already trying to pick it up. I told Donny I had Cheryl's car keys if anybody asked. I had slipped them out of her pocket so they wouldn't get lost. Denise was talking to one of two police officers who were standing by the front door.

"What happened to you?" one of them asked.

"He's the kid who found her," Denise said. "He saved her life."

"Hey kid, you all right?" He tried to engage me again.

"I just need to get home," I said, pointing across the street. George and my mother were standing outside, looking my way. They weren't alone. All of the neighbors were meandering outside for a better look. How strange, they must have thought, not to see Big Al responding to a disturbance on our block.

"Okay," he said, giving me enough room to pass. "But don't go anywhere. We might have a few more questions to ask you."

"Yeah, it's cool," I said. "Anytime."

Once I was past the entryway, I didn't look back. I didn't look ahead either. I kept my head down, eyes averted from anyone.

It didn't stop my mother from asking. "Brady, what's going on now?" Nails on a chalkboard. I didn't answer. I pushed by them, walked into the house, and over to the phone in the kitchen. I dialed.

"Hello?" The voice was familiar, but it wasn't Dentz.

"Yeah, I have an address for you."

"Go ahead."

I gave him Alex's address. I told him how the house was laid out and where his bedroom was located. I said there was a section of drywall behind his bed where Alex kept his stash. When I finished, there was a long pause on the other end.

"Not good enough, kid."

"No?"

"We want you to call us when you know he's not home."

"How am I going to know that?"

"That's not our problem." The line went dead.

I let out a long breath. If Alex had cursed me like he had cursed Brett, it was working. If the devil can't make you bad, he'll make you busy. I couldn't tell which was more true anymore.

CHAPTER 22

FEELINGS RESTRAINED

Mick made it as far as St. George, Utah, before he turned himself in to the police. He had run out of bottled water by the time he reached the Moapa River Paiute Reservation and was rolled for his cash in Mesquite.

He had three thousand dollars on him but made the mistake of flashing too much of it at a casino buffet. Three men followed him back to his hotel room and took the money. Mick didn't put up a fight. He gave it all up, except for a hundred dollar bill he had tucked in his shoe.

He tried to press on anyway, catching a ride with a trucker to St. George the next day. Then he had lunch and lost his resolve, looking at his dwindling resources. He asked for directions to the local police department and turned himself in as a runaway.

Those were the facts, but not the details, most of which came from his parents. He wouldn't talk about it, not even to me. We talked about other things instead, mostly superficial stuff about fantasy books, music, and games. But sometimes Mick would open up and talk to me about other things, like how much he missed Brett and how much he was going to miss me if he moved in with his grandparents like his sister.

We had plenty of time. We had to drive around and pull all those missing person posters down.

"Remember when we had a wake for John Belushi?" I asked him.

"How could I forget?"

"What if we did that again? Nothing out of control. Just a few friends."

"My place is no good for any of that, Brady. After running away, I think they would flip out and ship me off someplace."

"Welcome to the fishbowl, man." I laughed, but it was uncomfortable.

"Yeah, I get it. Sucks."

"You spend as much time on the outside as you can," I said. "Anyway, it doesn't have to be your place."

"Denise won't be hosting a party either, from what you said. Not for a while, anyway."

"Nah, not there," I said. "We'll host the party at my house."

"Yeah, right."

"My mom is heading out with the Girl Scouts this weekend," I said. "George won't care as long as we keep the guest list light."

Mick considered. Three days on the road had changed him.

"He won't even be around," I continued. "He'll spend most of the night at the bar, and we'll pick up everything before he comes home. Heck, he won't even know there was a wake, not that he'll care."

"I don't know," he said. "If we do, can I crash at your place that night?"

"Do you think they'll let you?"

"Yeah, I think so. Maybe it will help them feel like everything is normal."

It felt odd to hear it from him. It felt strange for him to say it, too, both of us cringing almost as soon as he said it. Things would never be normal again. We both knew it — him for the first time in his life. The confusion, shame, and numbness could be overwhelming. It became the motivator to make bad choices because those were the only ones you felt like you could control.

"Maybe we'll keep it clean. Just beer."

"Yeah, maybe."

"Well, the weed has to stay outside at my place anyway. George won't go for that."

"I get it," he said, mulling something over in his head. "I talked to Alex earlier."

"What did he want?" I didn't care.

"He wants to make amends," Mick said. I bit the inside of my cheek. "I know he said you're out. He told me. You're not out."

"I don't know if I want to be in," I said. "He almost killed Cheryl."

"Heroin almost killed Cheryl."

"Come on," I said. "She had help. Cheryl didn't know anything about shooting up. Why are you always defending him? First with Brett and now with Cheryl."

"Sepsis killed Brett." His voice was flat. He didn't want to go down this road. I pressed anyway.

"Sepsis killed Brett. Sepsis killed Brett. You keep saying that. Alex keeps saying that. Even the cops are saying that. But we both know it isn't true," I said. "A bullet killed Brett. It was a bullet from a scoped gun fired by a cartel shooter from a hill we didn't think to recon before setting up our insurance policy. And we needed to because Alex knew he was going to blow it all up. He knew, Mick."

"Shhhh, man. Someone might hear you."

"So what?"

Mick turned his back and walked to the next pole. He tore down another poster. I brushed by him to the next. He made an effort to catch up to me.

"Did you have to put up so many?" He forced a laugh, trying to change the subject. I wasn't having it.

"You know, before you ran away, you acted as if nobody cared about you. I was standing there the whole time, right in front of you. You're like a brother."

"I know. That's part of the problem. We're more like brothers than friends sometimes. Maybe that's why I treat you differently. Ever thought of that? I do. We're brothers."

I didn't say anything. I didn't think of it that way and didn't want him to think of it that way either. It always came back to my age, as if two to three years changes everything. I wasn't his little brother. I was supposed to be his best friend.

He tried to change the subject again. "How's Cheryl anyway? You never told me."

"You never asked."

"I'm asking now."

"She'll be fine. They're keeping her in the hospital for a few days. Observation. My mother won't let me go see her. She thinks Cheryl is the root of all my problems. It's the other way around. Anyway, I'll see her when she picks up the keys to the Pinto."

"Right on," he said, considering. "Want to go see her now?"

More than anything in the world, I thought. I pulled down another poster.

"Let's get this block first."

"Your call."

He started walking to the next pole, and I tried to catch up. Some kids were riding toward us as we did. They had wads of paper in their hands.

"Hey, mister ... found you!" One of the kids shouted and unloaded the handful at Mick. The other two kids followed their friend's lead, showering him with more posters. They were laughing. We were laughing.

"Come on," he said, kicking the fliers scattered around his feet. "I can't do any more today. Let's go see your girl."

"You mean it?"

"You're impossible, Brady," he said, shoving me and then breaking into a run toward his car. I started running too. The kids picked up speed ahead of us, thinking we were chasing them. Seeing this, Mick yelled after them, playing along.

For a minute, it was like old times. The two of us just being us, acting our age.

Before heading to the hospital, we stopped by Farm Basket. Will wasn't working, so we didn't get his employee discount, but we ordered up anyway. I was flush with the money Alex had given me.

Farm Basket served up stuff you won't find anywhere else. Sure, they had meals similar to Kentucky Fried Chicken, but they also served a deep-fried chicken breast on a toasted hoagie and rolled chicken tacos. Some of the menu names were ridiculous, things like a Gobbler and Clucketo. That's what we ordered.

This local hot spot was second only to Naugles, a fast-food transplant from California that served tacos, burritos, and burgers. Naugles was open twenty-four hours, which is why it edged out the Basket among stoners and teens with cars. We had made plenty of memories at both locations — trying to order food through the drive-thru before Mick had a car or one time, shortly after selling a big bag of pot, ordering one of everything on the menu.

Part of the appeal was the smell. As dumb as it sounds, you can always tell fast food quality by the smell of its oil. If they don't clean the fryers daily, the entire place can take on an acrid smell. All we could smell here was the food.

"We should do this more often," Mick said, shoving a Clucketo into his mouth. "They don't have anything like this in Utah."

"Nobody has anything like this," I added. "The tourists don't even know about it."

"Heck, half of them think we live in hotels." He laughed, nearly choking.

I handed him his soda. This was the Mick I thought I had lost, and it was good to see him back. I felt guilty, wondering how long this would last. Clean Mick wasn't anything like the one who did drugs. But then again, I suppose I wasn't the same Brady either.

After lunch, he drove me to the supermarket so I could pick up flowers and then on to Lake Mead Hospital, where Cheryl had been under observation. No matter how often she tried to tell them that she never intended to commit suicide, they persisted in treating her like a high-risk patient.

I asked Mick if he wanted to come in with me, but he preferred waiting in the car. He made some joke about Cheryl being my girlfriend, although he wouldn't rule out making a play for her one day. It was easy to laugh off because he wasn't her type.

Once inside, I had to stop by the information booth to get her room number. Cheryl never told me because it seemed impossible that I would ever get the chance to see her.

I was grateful she was here and not where I had last seen Brett. It would be too soon if I never stepped inside that hospital again. This one was starting to wear on me. My hatred for them stemmed from my youth, visiting my grandmother every time she was admitted for tests, surgeries, or sicknesses that her body was too worn out to fight off.

I never thought of it as a place to get patched up as much as a place to die. If I tried to push that thought from my head, the smell of antiseptic attempting to cover up sickness and secretions always brought me back to it. In a way, they weren't much different from a casino, except you checked in and gambled with your life.

Cheryl was on the far end of the second floor. So I kept my head forward, avoiding eye contact with other patients looking out of their rooms desperate for a visitor — family member or friend — to help break up the monotony of pinpricks and needles.

The door was open, so I took a hard right turn into the room, hands up with the flowers over my face to hide my smile. It was corny, but who couldn't use some corny in a hospital?

"Delivery for Ms. Cheryl," I said, drawing it out like a nasally New Yorker. "Flowergram and a little dance."

She giggled, and I lowered the flowers. My excitement turned to embarrassment. She wasn't alone. A twenty-something guy sat next to her, with long hair and scruff. He was smiling too.

"Oh," he said, reaching out for the flowers. "Want me to see who they're from?"

My smile turned into a scowl, with my lips quivering. I pulled the flowers away and let my hands drop to my sides. I shook my head.

"Sorry," I said. "Wrong room."

"Brady, wait," she said. But it was already too late.

I ran out of the room, dropping the flowers into the first trash can I could find. I could hear the guy calling after me as I waited for the elevator, but I never looked back. I slipped inside as soon as the doors opened. It was headed up, but I didn't care.

I was trying hard not to cry in the one place nobody thinks twice about seeing someone cry. They always assume the worst. Your family member or friend lost the ultimate wager. But what they didn't know was I had only lost my heart.

It took a few minutes to find Mick's car in the parking lot, which gave me enough time to transform my heartache into an unspoken rage. When I popped inside and slammed the door, Mick immediately knew something was wrong.

"What's wrong? Didn't you see her?"

"No," I said. "She had already checked out."

"What happened to the flowers?"

"I gave them away," I said. "Somebody's grandma needed them more than she did."

I wished I had thought of it while I was in the hospital. Somebody's grandmother would have loved them. I know my grandmother would have. But I didn't think of it until it was too late.

Mick and I didn't say anything to each other the rest of the way home. I wasn't talking, and he knew not to press. There wasn't anything to talk about anyway. I was just a dumb, pathetic kid.

CHAPTER 23

BLOWN AWAY

Mick was resistant to the idea of a wake until I pointed out the obvious. He needed closure. We all did. But since Brett's family had decided to hold funeral services in West Virginia, none of us would benefit from it.

Instead, we were left with an emptiness deeper and darker than anything we had experienced when Brett moved away. It wasn't just the grief but the guilt.

I started by inviting everybody on the block, even those who didn't know Brett well. The more, the merrier, Mick had said. So, for his sake, I asked Jamie. It was easier than I thought it would be. Jamie agreed to a temporary truce for one night.

The harder ask was Alex. He was the last person I wanted at Brett's wake, but I didn't have a choice. Mick wanted me to give him another chance. I protested at first, but I always knew I would invite Alex. There would never be a better opportunity to know exactly where he was going to be. And if he left early, I would be the first to know.

The ask was easier than I expected. Alex knew about the wake by the time I called him in the late afternoon. He was already running the numbers in his head. Twenty or thirty kids would add up to a dozen new customers.

He didn't even care when I asked him to leave the heroin at home. All he wanted was the chance to press some flesh and make some connections.

"You're not still sore about what happened to your girlfriend, are you?" he asked.

"She's not my girlfriend," I said. "It's over."

"She dump you?"

"Something like that."

"I always knew she would," he said. "I tried to tell you, man. She was nobody."

I bit my tongue. As soon as he agreed to come, I made my follow-up call. Moe Dentz answered his own phone this time. He said he was expecting me. He called me a natural-born wise guy, and said he had another surprise for me.

The surprise came a few hours later. Instead of sending one of his associates, he sent Sandy, the underage stripper I had met at his club. When she first came to the door, I didn't recognize her. She was wearing jeans and a white V-neck blouse. Her hair was a mass of loose curls framing her face, and she downplayed her makeup for a more natural look.

She looked just like any sixteen-year-old girls who went to my high school, and so did her car. She didn't drive a big car like most of the Dentz crew, but a baby blue Ford Escort.

"Hey, Brady," she had said at the door, waiting a full minute before laughing at me. "Are you going to invite a girl in?"

"Um, hey," I said, pushing the door open and stepping outside. "Let's talk out here, on the porch."

"Oh, it's like that," she said. "I thought you liked me."

"No, it's not you. It's my mother."

"Your mother?"

"Yeah, she's in there cooking dinner."

"Oh, what are you having?" She teased me. "I haven't had a home-cooked meal in a month of Sundays. You like that expression? My momma used to say it."

"Yeah, sure." It was all I could manage while stuffing my hands in my pockets. "What are you doing here?"

"I'm doing a favor." She held out an envelope. "Everybody was busy, so he asked me."

I took it. I didn't have to open it to know what was inside. I could feel it through the paper. It was a coin, a twin to the one he gave me when we first met.

"What about work?" Sometimes my stupidity amazes me.

"Even working girls get a night off, Brady." She took a long look around. "So, this is Mr. VIP's natural habitat. It's very *Leave It to Beaver* around here."

"Hardly," I said. "Not this house anyway."

"No? You'd think so if you spent any time where I live."

"So, is that it?" I asked, holding up the envelope. "Nothing else?"

She looked at me, her eyes searching for something. Her tongue moved behind her lips, tracing the front of her teeth as if she was trying to work something out. Then she took a step toward me, invading my space, and batted her eyes like a dramatic gag.

"I like you, Brady," she whispered. "I want to do things with you. Let's do things."

I swallowed and took a step back. "I could call you."

She looked inside my house through the front window. "Right, your mother."

I followed her eyes and looked inside. My mother had been setting the dining room table and saw us. She stopped what she was doing and turned our way, hands on her hips. She was staring right at us. I didn't have long.

"See, there's this girl."

"There's always a girl," Sandy rolled her eyes.

"No, it's not that." I was stammering. "My mother doesn't trust her and, well, I don't think she's ready to meet another, um, girl while I'm trying to sort things out. If you know what I mean."

"I can see why Mr. Dentz likes you." She laughed. "You're not making any sense right now, but you're so cute that I'll give you a pass and get out of your hair."

"Thanks." I managed.

"But do me one favor." She kissed the tip of her finger. "You have my number, so call me. If you need to. If you want to. I mean it."

Then she pressed her finger to my lips. It was electric.

"All right," I said. "I will, Sandy."

"Good night, big shot," she said, flashing another smile over her shoulder before walking to her car.

I stood there for a minute and watched her drive away. I was still processing it all when I went back inside. My mother was waiting to hit me with twenty questions. She wanted to know who the girl was, how I knew her, and what she had given me.

"Oh, nothing," I said, holding it up. "It's just an old coin."

She considered. "Well, at least you're talking with someone your own age."

She didn't say anything else about it, and I was relieved she didn't. I had too much on my mind to keep everything straight. What she knew. What she didn't know. What she thought she knew. If she hadn't been finalizing the camping trip, who knows what would have happened while I was still reeling from seeing Cheryl with another guy, a guy her age.

I still felt the sting of it all over again when Cheryl called me later that night. We didn't talk long. She said she wanted to explain it to me in person when she picked up her car keys. It wouldn't sound right on the phone, she insisted.

But I already knew what that meant. She would give me some story about gratitude and how I was a great friend, but a friend nonetheless. The odds were ten to one, but somehow I was still holding out for the one. It took hours before I finally fell asleep.

I felt better about things the next day, upbeat even. It was too hard not to. The summer sky was bright blue and cloudless and my mother was pulling out of the driveway.

Tabitha and a car full of Girl Scouts were packed up and frantic for a summer camping trip. Everyone was all smiles, girls waving out the back window. Stuffed animals were hoisted up and down in jubilance.

George and I were all smiles too. We were cheering them on — a two-man crowd on a concrete dock, watching a cruise ship sail away and wishing its passengers well. We would have thrown confetti and streamers if we had them.

As soon as they turned the corner, George didn't waste any time. He held up one flat hand, arm bent.

"Bye, bye," he said, grinning. "Don't wait up."

"Free at last," I said, waving my hands in the air. "Free at last."

He brushed his hair back with a free hand and slipped on his helmet. Then he mounted his motorcycle and drove away, leaving the house in my care. I didn't waste time heading inside and clearing breakables from my mother's many bookshelves.

I gave the place a quick dusting and vacuumed the floor. If everything went as planned, Mick would make it over around six with a case of Miller Genuine Draft plus a backup six-pack stash of dark beer. It was a bring-your-own-booze party for everybody else, and while someone might poach one or two of our beers, nobody ever touched the dark stuff.

I was still setting out extra ashtrays for the party when an old Mustang pulled up in front of the house. The party wouldn't start for another couple hours. Cheryl was in the passenger seat. The guy driving was the same one I saw at the hospital.

I met her halfway between the front door and the street, hesitant with each step. She didn't share my awkwardness. She rushed up to meet me, throwing her arms around my neck.

"My hero!" she screamed.

For a moment, everything was right with the world again. We were hugging and laughing and spinning in circles. It felt like one of those dumb movies when two star-crossed lovers are reunited. They run toward each other and embrace, a wave of emotion that leaves them breathless, laughing and crying at the same time.

It was just like that, until I tried to kiss her. As soon as my mouth moved toward hers, she stiffened, put her hands to my chest and gave me a gentle push. She was still smiling, except for her eyes. They revealed a sadness I had never seen in her before.

"Something wrong?"

"No, I mean, yeah," she said. "Oh, Brady, I mean, you saved my life."

"Yeah," I said. "I guess I did."

"How can I not love you for it?"

It was the tone of her voice that tipped me. I bit my lip.

"There's a 'but' in there somewhere, isn't there?"

I was in love with her but too cowardly to tell her. All of it welled up inside, without reason and despite our age difference. She had been the life preserver keeping me from drowning all these days, and when it was my turn to save her, it came at a cost I could have never imagined. I almost wanted to take it back, saving her. Because if I did, she would have died as my lover. But now, instead, I was the one dying.

"It's my fault, Brady," she said. "It was never going to work, but I let myself get swept away with you. This stupid, indulgent romanticism of mine."

"What's wrong with that?"

"It was never supposed to go so far, Brady. You've got your whole high school experience ahead of you. And for me, this summer was the end of mine."

300

"So I was just some boy crush ... so you could hold onto high school for a little longer?" I wanted to send her away with this revelation, but I couldn't part with the agony I felt.

"It wasn't like that," she said. "I love you, Brady. I really do, but this relationship is impossible for you and me. Don't you see that?"

I knew what she was saying, but I wasn't ready to admit it. She wasn't in love with me. She was addicted to my childish invincibility and could no longer play the game.

"I may be a boy," I whispered, trying to remember the words. "'But when I loved ... with the love of a man, I loved her simply because I found her irresistible.'"

"Oh, you silly boy. You actually read the book," she said, choking out a laugh. "Just don't quote Dickens to me again. You're going to make me cry."

The guy she had come with got out of his car. He walked around the front of the Mustang and looked at us, arms folded. "Hey, is anything wrong?"

Everything was wrong. We were just standing there, holding hands, hearts breaking, but not wanting the pain of it to end. She leaned over and kissed my forehead.

"You never know when it's going to be the last of something until it's too late," she said. "I want us to know it."

She moved her lips down from my forehead and kissed me. It was deep and passionate, but she took her keys out of my hand while we kissed. Then she spun around, lifting them in the air to show the stranger in front of my house a victory. Except, we both knew it was a tragedy. We had everything, and we had nothing.

"Goodbye, Cheryl," I said.

"Goodbye, Brady."

It was over. Another ending added to all the other endings of my life, each new one woven into the previous. Somehow the freshness of this one hurt the most. And yet I knew, deep down, it wasn't the worst. There were many more to come.

CHAPTER 24

WITCH HUNT

It started like all teenage house parties, with the host pacing the house, wondering if there were enough seats, making sure the first mixtape fit the mood, and turning on and off lights to find the right amount of lighting. Then the host starts second-guessing himself as the sun sets, wondering whether anybody will show.

I had another problem, too. I was still reeling from Cheryl. The last thing I wanted to do was host a party. And now I didn't know if it would happen. I tried to lose my feelings in the details.

Mick never had these problems. His home had been the hot spot, so it was never a matter of when people showed up but who among the never-ending procession of regulars and drop-ins came, like any bar or club in town.

It was people like me who were more hit and miss. Any one-time party was contingent on what other parties might be the rage and who said they were going to what.

All my worries were idiotic, of course. This wasn't a typical teenage rage looking for warm bodies, but a wake for a friend that Mick and I knew but most people only knew of. Brett was one of the original Three Musketeers before his family stole him away from Las Vegas, and then Las Vegas stole him away from his family.

The core attendees were already known: Mick, me, and anybody associated with his death. It blossomed out from there, mixing in people from around the block like Trish One and Two, Denise, Tom, Donny, and any ancillary friends who might be in tow. If Alex was packing heroin, his pretend friends would fly in and out, cash in hand.

Everybody came late, after dark. I didn't know the first arrival. He knocked on the front door and cast a worried glance around the house until I invited him in. He almost left, but two more came after him. Then Mick came after that, alleviating any concerns it would be a bust by sacrificing a few of our beers.

It was a shaky start until Trish Two came with two girlfriends. That changed everything. Guys will stick around any party when the ratio between the sexes tilts in their favor. More than the drinks or drugs, girls were the reason house parties existed. You get really drunk. You convince the girls to get really drunk right along with you.

After that, it was all about getting lucky. Break away from the main scene and find a quiet corner or empty room. If you wanted any rooms to be off limits as a host, you locked the door. The downside of making my parents' room off limits was cutting our two-bathroom home down to one.

Nobody cared unless the lines to the bathroom got long. If that happened, there was always a risk some joker would use the sink in the adjoining bathroom or find a corner in the backyard. Nobody cared, and given our limited experiences and questionable role models, all of it was considered normal.

After an hour, our wake for Brett looked like any other party, except for the quick drawing I had made of him on poster board. I had set it up on an easel in front of the bookshelves. The picture wasn't my best work because I had limited source material. Few kids owned cameras and film was too expensive.

I had two photos of Brett. Mick's mom had taken one of them at a pool party a few years ago of the three of us. Brett and I were in the pool looking up at Mick, suspended in midair, tucking himself into a cannonball.

The other was one I had taken with George's old Canon 50mm. Mick and Brett were standing in one of the undeveloped desert lots with BB guns and a pump action pellet rifle. They tried to pose like Bonnie and Clyde, pretending to be gangsters. I had forgotten all about it until digging through a shoebox of photos I had taken last summer with the one roll of film my parents had allotted me.

It unsettled me as an eerie foreshadow, not unlike those spooky photos in *The Omen*, a horror movie about the birth of the antichrist. In the movie, unexplained shadows appearing in photographs predict someone's death. There were no shadows in the one I took of Mick and Brett, but it creeped me out anyway.

Nobody was creeped out by my drawing, a composite of the two. Most of the kids in my house didn't notice it. Those that did would pause in front of it and raise their glass in a quiet toast. Even if they didn't know him, word had spread that this was a party for a lost friend, a last hurrah before he ascended into Valhalla.

The rest of the party was starting to take on its own life. Someone had turned on MTV but muted it in favor of the heavy metal mixtape I had put on earlier. Geddy Lee was singing about "Tom Sawyer" as if dubbed over the top of the band Survivor on television. They were decked out in leather, walking down North Beach and Broadway. A small group of kids I didn't know were relaxed on the couch, watching it, feet up on the coffee table and ashtrays in their laps.

In the dining room, a game of quarters had already found some players, every chair taken, and some people were standing, crowding in to take their turn.

Most of the ones I knew were camped out in the kitchen, guarding whatever beer and booze they brought with them. Another cluster had formed on the back patio, a bunch of guys flipping bottle caps at a target I couldn't see from inside the house. I wasn't worried. Mick and Jamie were with that group. I kept my distance.

The only thing missing was Alex, which made me nervous. If he decided to blow off the party and stay home, I didn't know what would happen when Dentz's crew rolled up on what was supposed to be an empty house; his mom was visiting her sister and her boyfriend was working graveyard. Anything could happen. Knowing Alex, he would probably confront them with the Beretta and go out in a blaze of glory.

"Great party, Brady," someone said behind me, covering my eyes. She let go and laughed as I turned around. It was Denise.

"Thanks, Denise," I said. "Glad you could make it. Tom here too?"

"He'll be by later. He had something to do."

"Cool."

"Hey, I'm sorry about Cheryl and all. I know you liked her."

I was trying not to think about it. The scab was too fresh to pick.

"It's all right," I lied. "I knew it was never going to work out. Let's face it. I'm too young for her."

"Yeah, I guess. She wanted to come tonight, you know."

"Really?" My heart leapt at the thought.

"She has it in her head that you two can still be friends. I set her straight and told her not to come."

"Oh." I didn't know what to say. Her words crushed me, so I played it off. "Thanks."

"You know, she's a good friend and all, but you could do better, Brady."

"How's that?"

"You're a cute guy."

"Yeah, right," I said. "I'm sure Tom would appreciate you saying so."

"No, really," she said, reaching for my glasses and taking them off. "If you put these away and do something more with your hair, you're a cute guy."

"Cute skinny guy, you mean."

She put the glasses in my shirt pocket and tried combing my hair with her fingers. She looked at me in a way she never had before, like a big sister taking pride in a little brother.

"I wouldn't worry about that," she said. "You've filled out a bit more this summer."

"You think?"

"Come on, Brady," she said. "Give yourself a break. Cheryl wasn't hanging out with you as a charity case. And what you did for her? You saved her life, kid."

"I just did what anybody would have done," I said.

"Give yourself a chance, Brady," she said before seeing a couple of her friends in the kitchen. "Hey, it's your party. Find yourself a rebound."

We both laughed, and she gave my hands a squeeze before making a beeline for two other girls she had seen join the throng in the kitchen. I went back to pacing the rooms, looking for people I knew and figuring out who the others might be. It almost felt normal. Better than normal.

The party was shaping up to be a success. People were having fun, but not out of control like *Animal House*, Brett's favorite movie, or the drug-fueled gatherings Mick hosted. If there were any drugs, they were kept out of the house or dropped before they ever came through the front door.

"Brady, helluva party."

"Thanks, man," I said. "Good to see you."

In truth, a house party success like this was a low bar. As long as the drinks held up, the girls stuck around, and nothing catastrophic happened like the cops showing up or someone overdosing in a back room, everything would be fine. I started to believe it because the buzz coming on had convinced me. I was the hero of my own teenage party movie, and some of the girls were taking an interest.

"Hey, Brady. Sorry about Cheryl."

I shrugged and lifted a bottle. "Drink the pain away."

After another hour, the hurt had dissipated. I had started talking to a new girl, Melissa. She was a blonde from a different high school who knew nothing about me or my crowd. It was refreshing to disassociate from the stigma of being a part-time dealer.

She was a sophomore with an interest in English and theater. We talked about some of the small parts I had taken and how I planned to enroll in theater next year as an elective. She had more talent than I did, having stolen away a lead role from a senior as a freshman. Her favorite movie last year was *On Golden Pond.*

I hadn't seen it, given my parents hated going to the movies. They didn't want to go anywhere they couldn't smoke. I had managed to see *The Road Warrior* with Mick and Brett, but I didn't think that would impress her. It didn't matter. Despite being shook by Cheryl, Denise had given me a boost of self-confidence to enjoy Melissa, which lasted right up until Alex arrived.

He came in with a new kid I had never seen before. The new kid was older, flanking him like a hanger-on or bodyguard. It was hard to say which one. He came right up to me and interrupted the conversation.

"Hey, Thumper," he said, hissing a laugh and winking at Melissa. "She looks like a good time."

"Thumper?" Melissa asked.

"Yeah," Alex said, laughing at his joke. "He's like a rabbit, and any minute now, he's going to start humping your leg. Just look at him."

Melissa made a face like she had just gotten a whiff of bad air. She stood up, making room for Alex, who was trying to crowd in on us.

"It was nice to meet you, Brady, Thumper, whatever your name is," she said. "I think I'll leave you two to it."

She headed straight to the friend she came with and whispered something, looking back at Alex and me. Then they left out the front door. I hadn't gotten her number.

"Brady, this is Bricks. Bricks, Brady," Alex said. "Bricks is taking your spot."

"I thought Mick said I was back in," I said despite being on the fence.

"Things change," Alex said. "Where is Mick, anyway?"

"Out back, last time I saw him."

"Good boy." He patted my cheek as he got up.

"You know, you didn't have to scare her off like that," I said, standing up with him.

"Scare her off? No man, that was all you, Thumper."

He moved his hips back and forth like he was going at it. Bricks laughed.

It didn't take a minute, and he was already under my skin. I wasn't alone either. As soon as some new kids saw him, they peeled off toward the front door. Alex had a reputation for trouble, which was fine for the stoner crowd. It wasn't fine for a mix like this one, so I took a shot at my replacement.

"Don't bend over, or he'll be right behind you doing that," I said.

Bricks stopped laughing, but Alex didn't care. He smiled, shook his head, and flipped me off. Then he headed out back toward Mick, flipping off the drawing of Brett as he went. Maybe I should have cashed in the first favor when I had the chance.

The party continued, but the mood changed along with mine. Fewer people stopped by, and some took off, as it felt like it was winding down. It was as if someone had sprayed the place with sulfur, and everybody could smell it. The few that didn't care weren't the ones I wanted to keep. I caught two of them lighting up a black widow they found on the front porch with lighter fluid.

I confiscated the lighter fluid and put it back where it belonged. The dopes didn't take the hint. They were right back inside, looking for the next stupid stunt. Somehow, I had to rein the party back in before the devil took over.

"Everybody. Everybody!" I tried to get their attention, turning off the television and the stereo. "Can I get you all in the dining room?"

"What's going on? Are the cops here?"

There were other mutters and questions, but some people started to get it. Tom and Denise were whispering to their group in the kitchen. They seemed to have a second sense of what I was about to do. Trish One stuck her head out the sliding glass door, calling everyone inside.

There were fewer than two dozen kids left, a few more exiting after I called everybody together. They weren't here for anything other than the beer. It was fine with me. I never anticipated having so many people here anyway.

"Hey, we'll all get back to having a great time, but I wanted to mention why I had this party in the first place," I said. "It's a wake for our friend, Brett. By friends, I mostly mean me, Mick, Alex, Jamie, and Will, who couldn't be here. But a few more of you knew him too. Tom, Denise, Donny, Trish One, and Trish Two, who had to go. I dunno, maybe a few more of you."

Mick moved closer to me, taking up a position to the right of the poster board. A couple kids were already raising drinks in a silent toast. I'd like to think so, at least.

"As most of you know, Brett died in the hospital a few days ago, his life cut short, the victim of a stupid accident." I looked at Alex, who was smiling at me, his eyes wide with interest. "He didn't have a funeral here, so it just seems right to say a few words about him. Brett was one of the good ones."

I looked over at Mick. He was nodding, head down. I'd guess he was getting choked up. I thought he had cried out days ago.

"Brett was a junior at Bonanza High School last year before his family relocated to West Virginia. He was born there, you know. And his family decided to move back. Las Vegas wasn't his home, but he made a home here. He was Mick's best friend, and I counted him among mine too. In his short life, Brett was a good kid. Yeah, I mean, he drank just like us — one liter at a time. But he was a good kid."

There were a few hoots and laughter. A couple of the crowd took it as a cue to take a swig.

"But what you might not know is Brett enjoyed playing Dungeons & Dragons, always a dwarf with an attitude ten times bigger than his size. But that didn't make him a nerd. He also had a passion for woodworking and hunting. He loved the outdoors. We took hikes at Red Rock together and sometimes Mt. Charleston. He had a big heart, too, always being the first of us to plan Halloween at his house, just to pass out candy and entertain kids. Sure, that didn't make him popular at school, but it did demonstrate how this kid, our own John Belushi, with his animated eyebrows and gift for comedy, touched us in ways we'll never forget. You know, this one time..."

I had to stop talking because Alex had started clapping. It was a slow, drawn-out clap meant to interrupt me.

"Good lord, man," he said. "Don't deify the kid."

"What the heck are you doing, Alex?" Mick asked.

He put a hand out, motioning to Mick to give him a minute. Mick wasn't the only one horrified by the interruption. Those who knew Alex sensed he would take it in the wrong direction.

"I didn't know him long, this Brett kid, like Mick and Brady here or Thumper as I like to call him," he laughed at his own joke, stepping into the space between the poster and everybody else. "But what I knew of him, I didn't like much. He could talk the talk, but not walk the walk. He was a snitch, a rat, a poser. He did a dirty deed and was going to take us all down. His friends Mick and Thumper included. He sucked."

I stepped up. "That's enough, Alex."

"Enough? It's not enough. He didn't even like you, Brady. He thought of you just like I think of you — a little pinhead tagalong third wheel who doesn't have any friends." He was enjoying himself. "I know because that's what he told me about you."

"You're lying!"

"I'm not lying. You wish I was lying."

"Mick, tell him he's lying."

Mick didn't say a word. I looked back at him for support, but he didn't move. The giant who had always had my back in every real and imagined adventure wasn't moving.

"I was there the night before he died." I don't know why, but I was pleading with the audience as if I were on trial. "He said I was a true friend. You're the snake who screwed us."

"Right," Alex said. "Now, who's lying? You're lying to yourself, just like you lied to yourself about that girl, Cheryl.'

"Don't talk about Cheryl. You almost killed her."

"So what? She didn't love you. Nobody loves you, Brady. Not even your mommy."

The world was spinning away from me, and the words were failing me. "Shut up."

"What? Who's going to make me? You?"

I don't know where it came from, but I shoved him. As soon as I did, he squared up on me.

"You don't want to do this," Alex said, waving Bricks off. "I'll take your head off."

"This is my house. You're not going to tell me what to do in my house. Get out."

"Bang off, Thumper."

I took a swing. It was unplanned and wild, and I nearly fell over taking it. I was out in front, all my weight on my front foot. Alex sidestepped me and punched down on the side of my head. I collapsed on the floor and lay there, hurt and humiliated.

"He's not going to heaven, you know," Alex said, gesturing to the poster. "No, I sent that soul straight to Satan."

The entire room was quiet, every kid shocked by the spectacle. I started to get up, ignoring Mick's quiet plea for me to stay down. This was my house.

I stood up and faced him again. Alex grinned, the spit pooling in the corners of his mouth.

"You want some more?"

"No," I said. "I'm done. I want you to leave."

"It's a party!" he said. "Let them party."

Alex faced me, waiting for me to make a move. So, I didn't make one.

"Yeah, it's a party," I said, rubbing my head and shrugging. "The fight's over. Everybody have a good time."

Without missing a beat, somebody turned the music up. A few people headed toward the door, including Tom and Denise, but some tried to restart the party. I looked for Mick, but he brushed by me to say something to Alex. This was my opportunity.

I turned around and headed to my parents' room, opening the door with a small rod I had kept in my back pocket. That's how our inside locks worked. There was a small hole in the doorknob, which could be jimmied if someone locked themselves in a room.

The buzz I felt earlier was gone, replaced by a throbbing headache and a sense of desperation. I wanted Alex out of my house and out of my life. So I reached under my parents' bed and came up with a small .22 caliber handgun. I was going to end the pain. I was going to kill him.

This is how it happens. Forget all those books you've read or movies you've seen. There isn't some big dramatic moment that makes you find your resolve to take a life. All it takes is one small insult on a mountain of previous hurts and insults.

That's how it happened for Matt Marquez before he shot his teacher. That's how it happened to my father before he killed himself. And that's how it was happening to me. Something random tips the scales in one direction or the other. You kill yourself. You kill someone else.

Everything slowed as I turned the corner of the hallway from the bedroom. The party — the kids playing quarters, the ones already deciding to duck out, the few fishing for beers in the refrigerator — had dialed down. The music, another Rush song, droned on in the background.

Then someone screamed, "He's got a gun!"

When Marquez testified about shooting his teacher in the classroom, he said it was as if he was disconnected from his entire body, looking down a tunnel and not in control. He didn't feel anything. He just pulled the trigger. None of it was real.

Everybody started screaming. A couple of kids ran out the front door. Several piled out back, pushing each other out of the way. Those who couldn't get to a door fast enough ducked under the table or behind furniture. Everybody was running or ducking or hiding. Everybody except Alex.

He turned toward me, reaching behind his back for the Beretta. But then his eyes grew wide behind his aviators. His gun wasn't there. This party was the minor leagues.

He tried to regain his composure, acting like the mistake didn't phase him. He held up one hand instead, making this odd contorted gesture, two fingers pointed at me with the first knuckles bent down like the fangs of a snake.

"You ain't going to shoot me," he said. "I'll curse you to hell if you do."

"Get out of my house. Get out."

"Brady, man," Mick said, reaching out a hand. "Put it away."

I wanted to listen to him, put the gun down, and take his hand. But I couldn't do it. This was it. I had come too far. All the pressures building up for weeks had come to a head.

"He killed Brett, Mick. You heard him. He killed Brett."

My finger tightened around the trigger. It was swollen like the rest of me, ready to burst.

Alex laughed, his face like a devil. "Tell him, Mick. Go on and tell him."

"Tell me what?" I was looking at Mick but kept the gun on Alex.

"I know, Brady. Brett was going to rat us out."

"You knew?"

"I always knew. We all knew, except you and Will."

I wanted to pull the trigger, but I wasn't sure where to point it anymore. They say it's worse to be betrayed by a friend than an enemy and they're right.

Mick had sucked all the air out of the room. The anger I felt toward Alex decompressed like someone letting the air out of a balloon. My entire world was turned upside down. I lowered the gun and stood there unmoving, hands shaking.

"You're such a loser. See you around, Thumper," Alex said, turning his snake gesture into a finger gun and pulling the trigger. Then he headed out the front door as if nothing happened. Bricks and Jamie followed him, both of them flipping me off as they left.

All I could do was stare at the door as a couple more kids left. They all kept as far away from me as possible, shielding themselves with their hands, fearing I still might do something. I didn't blame them. I considered it.

"Brady," Mick said. "I'm sorry."

"Go on, man," I said. "You can get out too."

"Brady?"

"I don't want to see you again," I said. "You chose your friends."

"Suit yourself." It was the last thing he said to me.

I stood there for a few more minutes in my empty house. The music still played, but nobody was left to hear it. In the emptiness, I felt like a shadow of my former self. The Brady Wilks I had been a minute ago was dead. And I didn't know who I was anymore.

I put the gun back under the bed and turned off the stereo. I shut the front door and turned off some of the lights. There was a lot to clean up, and I would be cleaning it up on my own. All the cups, glasses, bottles, and dirty ashtrays. Someone had puked in the bathroom, the adjoining one with a bathtub.

Before starting to clean up, I went to the wall phone in the kitchen and dialed a phone number I had never called before but spent an afternoon memorizing. I let it ring.

"Hello."

"Hey," I said.

"Brady?"

"Yeah, it's me."

"I'm glad you called. Did you want to, or did you need to?"

"I needed to," I said and started to cry. "I really needed to."

I spoke to Sandy for a couple of hours. She listened for a long time and shared a few stories she thought might help. She offered to come over and help me clean up the next day. I told her it was all right, and then we kept talking until I fell asleep sitting on the floor, the receiver tucked under my chin.

That's where George found me the next day. He didn't say anything. There was nothing to say.

EPILOGUE

The last time I saw Mick was a week after the party. He was moving out of his home. We exchanged a look but didn't say anything. After that, I didn't see him anymore. His grandparents were zoned for Clark High School, an older school closer to the Las Vegas Strip.

I didn't see Alex around when the summer ended and school started either. The smoking area in the quad, an open area in the center of the school, was banished to a back parking lot. He skipped most days anyway, and one day he never came back.

The Dentz crew did visit his house the night of Brett's wake, leaving an empty hole in Alex's bedroom wall. Nobody told me how much was found. Sandy just mentioned it in passing one day.

"Mr. Dentz said you done good, and to stay out of trouble," she told me.

It didn't matter what Dentz had said to me that night. I was never going to be a wise guy or anything like that. I was just a kid with a couple of favors owed, and I didn't even know what that meant.

Sandy didn't know either. She said she just worked there. And when she wasn't working there, she spent some of her free time with me, right up until school started. Then we saw less and less of each other but kept in touch on the phone.

Sandy was two years younger than Cheryl, but still older than me. So, despite the chemistry between us, I never pretended it would go anywhere. As she called it, we were mutual lifelines. I was lucky to have one. I didn't have anyone else.

It took a few months before it started to change at school. I still felt like an outsider but becoming more involved in school activities opened up some doors to different friend groups, mainly through theater and wrestling. Other kids stopped seeing me as on the fringe of the stoner crowd, but on the periphery of their crowds — theater geeks on one side, jocks on the other.

What I learned in those first few months back is that high school is more malleable than most kids think. Sure, a few act self-assured and are full of themselves, but most are wandering around looking for someplace to fit just like the rest of us. When I met them halfway — getting involved in their clubs and sports or whatever — I made new friends.

It took some effort, more effort than sitting around and smoking a bowl or snorting a line anyway, but at least their clubs and sports gave me something to carry along. Drugs only took things from me. And they took everything from Brett.

Sometimes I lay awake and think about it, asking myself how much of what happened was my fault. It was easy to blame Alex and Mick, but I was right there along for the ride, hoping that one payday would provide me a way out.

There are plenty of kids out there like that, I imagine. They don't know they can stand up for what's right. They haven't found a place where they feel like they belong. They don't have anyone they can tell that they're being bullied at school or, for some of them, that they're being bullied at home. They don't know that getting out never comes as a windfall as much as one step in a different direction.

At least, I hope it does. I have a long, long way to go. My home life hasn't changed. I still look over my shoulder, even at school. I'm filled with self-doubt like I don't deserve any of the little wins that come my way. I still have the scars, some that can be seen and some that can't. And sometimes, I wonder if Alex really did curse me that night, compounding whatever sins were passed down to me by my father.

But life is like that. I don't know what's going to happen. I just keep trying different things, hoping that everybody who says I won't amount to anything is wrong. I don't want to give them the satisfaction.

ABOUT THE AUTHOR

Richard R. Becker is the author of the best-selling short story collection *50 States*, which won first place in the Spring 2022 BookFest Awards for short stories, the 2023 Book Excellence Awards for short stories, and the ABR Book Excellence Awards for literary fiction, psychological thrillers, and short stories. It was also named a finalist in the IAN Book of the Year Awards.

The following year, he released a brisk ten-story companion piece called *Ten Threads* as a Kindle exclusive. *Third Wheel* is his first novel.

To learn more about Richard R. Becker, visit him at richardrbecker.com or copywriteink.com

Milton Keynes UK
Ingram Content Group UK Ltd.
UKHW021826131023
430526UK00015B/636